Intent to Hold

Meredith Ryan Mystery
Book 2

Thonie Hevron

ROUGH
EDGES
PRESS

Rough Edges Press
An Imprint of Wolfpack Publishing
9850 S. Maryland Parkway, Suite A-5 #323
Las Vegas, Nevada 89183

roughedgespress.com

Paperback ISBN 978-1-68549-261-8
eBook ISBN 978-1-68549-260-1

To my husband, partner, coach, and business associate, Danny: thank you for working hard so I didn't have to. You gave me some of my best ideas and freed me up so I could write them down. Most importantly, you inspired me and kept me honest. I couldn't do this without you.

Intent to Hold

California Penal Code 209 Kidnapping

(a) Any person who seizes, confines, inveigles, entices, decoys, abducts, conceals, kidnaps or carries away another person by any means whatsoever with intent to hold or detain, or who holds or detains, that person for ransom, reward or to commit extortion or to exact from another person any money or valuable thing, or any person who aids or abets any such act, is guilty of a felony, and upon conviction thereof, shall be punished by imprisonment in the state prison for life without possibility of parole in cases in which any person subjected to any such act suffers death or bodily harm, or is intentionally confined in a manner which exposes that person to a substantial likelihood of death, or shall be punished by imprisonment in the state prison for life with the possibility of parole in cases where no such person suffers death or bodily harm.

Chapter One

"DAVID TWO, ON SCENE." NICK REYES SLAMMED THE MIC INTO ITS holder and flung open the door of the tired Taurus. Parked in an abandoned gas station, today's mission was to serve an arrest warrant on Wilbur Franklin Storey. The warrant for 245(a) (2) of the California Penal Code, Assault with a Firearm, necessitated a strategic and well-planned execution. The potential for a violent confrontation dictated the need for SWAT personnel.

At the open trunk stood Nick's partner, Meredith Ryan. Nick shrugged into his Kevlar vest. Snugging the Velcro straps, he glanced over at Meredith. "You okay?" He slipped on his olive-green windbreaker with yellow block letters stamped on the back, SHERIFF.

Meredith lifted a too-casual shoulder. "Sure," she said. Nine months ago, an arrest warrant would have ignited her adrenaline. This was the stuff she had once thrived on—the way a case was built slowly and methodically, then leapt forward with a jolt. She'd never known anything more thrilling. As the excitement of the job faded, she chalked it up to her rookie phase wearing off. She'd been on patrol for seven years but, for the past ten months, was assigned to Violent Crimes Investigations—VCI—at Sonoma County Sheriff's Office. Arrests and door-busting weren't daily occurrences, but they were a chance to jumpstart her enthusiasm after a long week of reports, phone calls, and interviews.

But she'd killed a man. Even though he was inches away from stabbing a deputy, it instigated a worse series of incidents that had almost killed her. The last months had drained her in ways she never knew existed and allowed the insidious contamination of betrayal to gain a hold of her. Faith in the system she'd worked for and defended had ground away. When things went south, the department hadn't protected her. They'd abandoned her to a space that made her feel like an outsider.

"Hey!" Nick handed her a shotgun from a box in the trunk. He searched her face—easy when she was a mere three inches shorter than his six-foot-three height. She claimed six feet even, but only in heels. "You sure you're okay?" His deep coffee-colored eyes probed hers. She met his gaze. It was easy to see how women melted under that expression. The way his eyes narrowed when he smiled; his lean, muscular frame stood tall and solid. All the records clerks thought he was a hottie. He was her partner and best friend—Nick, who usually knew so much about her. Now the thoughts churning inside her went far beyond what partners share with each other. This was a burden she didn't want to make him carry.

She nodded, suppressing a silly impulse to cry at his concern. "I'm fine. Let's do this." She slipped on an earpiece and clipped a phone-sized radio to her shirt.

He lifted an eyebrow, then cupped his hand on her shoulder. "Okay, it's showtime."

THE MORNING FOG chilled the faded home in an unincorporated quadrant of northwest Santa Rosa. From the aerial photos, Nick knew the target was the end house. It was bordered by a vacant weed-strewn gas station and, on the other side, a home similar to the target's one. The house sat in the middle of the lot, a typical Northern California post-World War II tract home built for returning GIs. A chain-link fence encircled the front yard while weathered pine slats rimmed the back and sides. Missing fence boards allowed an easy way for the suspect to escape. In the backyard, a large redwood tree covered an entire corner of the yard. Behind was a neglected hay field. Securing the back of the yard was Nick's objective.

On the radio, one by one, a half-dozen deputies reported from their posts. Nick and Meredith moved into place. They positioned themselves west of the building, ready to enter the yard through a sagging wooden gate. The sergeant barked a radio command, and they moved up. With Nick in front, shotguns at the ready, they crept over scruffy Bermuda grass. Stopping at the outside halfway point to observe, they leaned on oxidized Masonite siding behind a shrub.

From there, they saw a run-down shed hidden below the broad redwood boughs. From the overhead photos, it had been invisible. Just large enough to hide a man, it was a new threat. Nick imagined the possibilities of ambush and crossfire situations. He studied the building, then leaned back to Meredith to whisper. "I'm going to circle the gas station and come in from the field. We've gotta cover both sides of that shed."

After whispering his intentions into his mic, Nick sprinted through the front yard to the gas station. He followed a beaten path on the field side of the fence line, stopping at the target house and quickly updating his position. From where he stood outside the fence, the shed was an arm's length away.

The structure sat lopsided, weathered slats tacked together with rusty nails. It had been carelessly built with scrap plywood; the obvious intention was to store garden tools. The closed-door faced the back of the house.

A sharp order crackled in his earpiece. The plan was for the primary detectives, Jerry Peters and Emil Anderson, to follow the entry team. It was their case; they knew who and what they were after. Nick heard the announcement, then the crash of the battering ram shattering the front door. The thump of heavy boots and men's shouts thundered through the house. Deputies shouted directions amid squawking radio reports that clogged the channel.

The racket from the entry team amped Nick's own adrenaline. He waited for the signal—the final "clear" from the house—before he and his partner would enter the shed. Radio traffic dwindled. Get ready.

A squeak from a rusty hinge interrupted his thought. The shed door opened an inch.

He had time to whisper his partner's name on the radio before the door swung open. A skinny man with spiked blonde hair poked his head outside and glanced around. He stepped out into the shadows of the redwood. Nick didn't see a gun on him, but a knife sheath was strapped to the belt that held up his jeans. Even in the gloom, Wilbur Franklin Storey looked just like the photo Peters had shown at the briefing.

Storey broke into a run, heading toward the hole in the fence.

Nick rose, poised to trip him when he came through.

The suspect stopped and whirled around. He must have seen Nick.

Backtracking, Storey flew past the shed and headed straight to the side yard—towards Meredith. Nick hissed into his radio. "Mere, he's coming your way."

She was already in motion. As the suspect passed the bush, Meredith leaped out and tackled him like a linebacker. Her shoulder clipped his knee, bringing him down. He sprawled head-first on the sun-bleached lawn. She planted a knee on his back while grabbing a tattooed arm and slipped a handcuff on his wrist. Then, she twisted the other arm, snapping the cuff around. Panting, she leaned over the proned figure. "Gotcha."

Then, the rest of the team swamped her. Peters took custody of Storey and, with two other deputies, pulled him to his feet. Storey's pinpointed pupils settled on Meredith. His jaw dropped, then his mouth twisted into a howl. "A bitch. A goddam bitch cop."

Beside Meredith, Nick smiled at the prisoner. "Bitch or not, she took your ass down, dog."

Chapter Two

"COME ON."

Nick shrugged into his tan corduroy sport coat. He felt for his holster, then pulled the badge off his belt and shoved it in his pants pocket. Reaching for the bulging briefcase under his desk, he huffed. "Meredith, get moving. I have to be home by six." He stomped toward the door.

"All right. All right." Meredith answered absently, clicking her computer down. She pulled her wool jacket off a coat hook and headed to the detective's chalkboard to log them out for the evening. They were on call tonight, so she picked up keys for the least hideous of the undercover cars—a faded blue Monte Carlo seized in an asset forfeiture after a drug conviction. She checked the board to make sure her cell phone number was up-to-date. The boss, Sergeant Don Leahy, was resolute in his resistance to using a computer to find phone numbers. The board was a hallmark of Violent Crimes Investigation—a chalkboard to keep track of detectives, instead of the computer the rest of the department used. Meredith saw it as a metaphor for working for Leahy.

"I'm coming," she shouted at Nick. Reyes was ten yards in front, hustling through the back door to the parking lot, his broad shoulders rolling with momentum. "We're taking the Monte Carlo." He waved an arm in acknowledgment.

When she caught up with him, she noticed a deep crease on his forehead. Nick's lips pressed into a small frown. He'd been unusually quiet today. He wasn't a moody guy, so this must be serious.

"Nick, is there something wrong?"

With a lazy grunt, he got into the passenger seat of the sedan.

Head-slap moment: she should have put it together sooner—and she called herself a detective? He must have heard from his wife, Angela.

Meredith started the ignition. "Did you get another letter from Angela's attorney?"

"Worse than that." He stared out the side window, avoiding Meredith's gaze. "She left a message on my voicemail. She's going to call tonight."

Meredith stifled her surprise, but a budding sense of alarm took hold. Since Angela left Nick a year ago, she'd moved back to Mexico with her family. The mail had become their sole form of communication. Nick figured since Angela's brother was a divorce attorney, he'd convinced her to distance herself from her husband.

A phone call implied a sense of urgency that was not lost on either detective.

NICK'S HOUSE sat on a sycamore-shaded street in north Santa Rosa, a redwood-shingled bungalow with a detached garage. His small mowed and clipped yard was a model of tidiness.

Meredith pulled up in front of Nick's house. He was half out of the car before she said, "Hey, how about a pizza and some Pacifico?"

Nick hesitated. Have his partner around while he had what promised to be an emotionally trying phone conversation? He leaned in the door and nodded to Meredith, unable to reconcile his confusion of 'I wanna be alone' and 'I don't wanna be alone'.

As the Monte Carlo sped off to the store, Nick slid the key into the lock of his back door. He paused as it swung open, and then he sighed at the silence. He missed Angela.

Most days, he managed it—package up his feelings and stuff them so deep no one saw them—especially himself. Today, knowing she was going to call, it all sat right in front of him. He missed all the blessings she brought to their marriage. He missed the way their house looked with the lights on and her bustling around inside. He missed having someone to talk to.

Angela had been gone eleven months, two weeks, and five days. She'd given in to the paralyzing pain that came with the accidental death of their infant daughter two years ago. Nick and Angela knew nothing could have prevented the baby's death, but they each carried an inconsolable guilt in their souls. Nick saw it every day in Angela's face, the sag of her shoulders, and the absence of a simple smile. While he also suffered, he was unable to find a word or a caress to comfort her. In unguarded moments, he saw a ghostly illusion of his wife drifting away from him. The toll of the tragedy mounted, along with the guilt he felt for not being able to give her something to live for. They couldn't talk without tears, anger, and words soon regretted.

Still, it was a shock to come home from work two months after the funeral and find his wife gone. A scrap of paper on the coffee table told him what he already knew. She had left him. The note said, "I can't live here anymore."

Days later, when she knew he'd be at work, Angela left a message on the house phone. "I'll be fine. I'm in Bucerias with my family for a while. I'll call next week." She had made the call. When he pleaded for her to come home, it was so painful to both that she hadn't called since. Her next correspondence came from her attorney.

An attorney. It still shocked him a little.

Tonight, he would hear her voice. Waiting for Angela's call opened all the portals he'd shuttered the past year. Memories of their life together lingered through the house—he remembered the smell of sautéed garlic coming from the stove, a promise of another adventure in culinary disasters, and her unselfconscious voice singing bits of Latin hip-hop that blared from her iPod earbuds. He still navigated through a bathroom counter filled with the debris of her beauty regimen. Even though he hated the untidiness of it, he couldn't take the step to box her things up.

Sometimes he thought he heard little Mia crying. He pushed away his confused feelings. He wanted Angela back, but after almost a year, he was settling into his solitary life with something just short of acceptance.

Swinging open the refrigerator, he reached for his last beer. He twisted the top off and tipped the bottle to his lips.

At first, after the baby died, he felt like a huge part of his life had been mislaid. How does one cope with this loss? It was against nature. Even this place he called home felt foreign. He wandered from room to room, revisiting a place in his past before all this pain. He remembered his surprise when he met Angela at school. How could a girl this beautiful be as warm and kind as Angela? He saw the devotion in her face when they exchanged their marriage vows, their dreams of forging a future that included a large, rambunctious family.

In the corners of the rooms, shadows filled with the sorrows of unfulfilled promises, of lives cut short and damaged hearts. He wasn't sure he would ever recover from the loss of his little angel, Mia. The ache saturated everything he did—waking and in his dreams. He hadn't slept more than four hours a night since Angie's shrieks tore through his sleep that horrible night.

Angela wouldn't recover any time soon. Her family wasn't strong on working through tough times; rather, they made everything a drama until the original issue was eclipsed by the sheer force of their emotion. He wasn't sure how being in that atmosphere would help Angela heal.

Then again, maybe it wasn't healing she was after. Maybe she just wanted out.

The telephone rang, making him jump and spill the beer. He jabbed at the phone while trying to keep the foam off the earpiece.

"Hello? Angela?" My God, he sounded so anxious.

"Nick?" Her voice rose as she said his name. "I'm here, baby."
Silence.

"I asked you not to call me that."

"Oh yeah, I forgot." Like hell, he thought.

"Just skip it, okay."

"Is everything all right down there?" News reports placed the
Mexican state of Nayarit on the fringes of a drug war, cartel hostili-
ties between a local gang and the militia. "That's why I called."

"Are you okay?" Nick's stomach muscles clenched as if waiting
for a punch.

"Yes, I'm fine."

The silence drew out as Nick wondered what she wanted
from him.

"It's a delicate problem," Angela said, "and I think you're the
only one who can help."

She needed him. Why? What problem could he help with?
Serving civil papers? Kicking out some relative's good-for-nothing
boyfriend? He couldn't help his skepticism. "I haven't heard from
you in months, and now you need me?"

The picture was so familiar, he saw her frown when she sighed.
He'd pissed her off and hadn't meant to. His voice softened. "What
is it, Angela?"

He heard her breath suck in between her teeth. "It's Rigo."

"Rigoberto, your brother?"

"Um hm. He's in trouble."

Nick's deepening voice matched his growing dread. "What kind
of trouble?"

"He's been kidnapped. They're holding him for ransom."

"Who kidnapped him?" Nick asked, but he knew the answer. A
gang who had spotted Rigo's ostentatious lifestyle. An easy mark.

"Miguel Vega, I think. The caller didn't say, but Vega's a local
gangster who does this kind of thing."

Something in her voice triggered his suspicion. "Why Rigo? I
didn't know he had enough money to be worth taking. Last I heard,
he was spending every peso he made."

"Nick, please. He's an important lawyer in this community. He has many influential friends."

"Angela, he's a divorce attorney, who specializes in gutting the estates of rich men for gold-digging women. No one wants to admit knowing him."

"Don't be so crude. Besides, it's called Family Law."

Nick sighed. The argument was familiar. Next question. "Who did the kidnappers talk to when they called?"

"Mama. She's been terribly upset. She can hardly talk about it."

Predictable. It was an understatement to say Angela's mother was high-strung. "What did they ask for?"

"They want twenty million pesos." Her breath exploded with pent-up tension. "We can't find that kind of money. What do they think—that we are rich?"

"Hold on, calm down. How much is that in dollars?"

"About 1.5 million."

He whistled his surprise. Did the kidnappers know something Angela's family didn't? "You don't have it? What about Rigo's house? Can you mortgage it?"

"No. It's his name on the title. Even though we all live here, the bank won't work with us."

They'd already tried to raise the ransom. "Is he insured?"

Her laugh was a joyless sound. "For kidnapping? Nobody can afford that."

Nick could sell his house; raise half the ransom, which would take time they didn't have. Would he do that for his brother-in-law? The guy who was arranging his divorce? Rigo was family even though he was trying to sever the connection. He hesitated. "So, what do you want me for?"

"Negotiation. If they won't negotiate, I want you to find him."

Nick considered all the things that made this a bad idea. "It's dangerous. I can negotiate, but what if it goes south? Go find him? I can't do both. If I'm gonna find him, I need to start right away. When was he taken?"

"Two days ago. They called mama that morning."

"Too many things can go wrong. People could get hurt. Your brother could get killed. I could get killed."

Silence from the other end. He pictured her biting the corner of her lower lip. Then her voice, thin and plaintive. "Please, Nick. The family needs you. I need you."

His sigh came from his toes. For months, he'd wanted her to say that. But not like this. He felt like a marionette in the hands of a puppeteer with strings pulled so taut that it might break them both. Nevertheless, there was never any question in his mind. Angela knew that.

"I'll find a flight down tomorrow."

Chapter Three

"THAT'S HOW IT WENT." NICK'S VOICE SOUNDED SO TIRED. Meredith wanted to reach over and touch his hand, to lessen his pain. Knowing her partner, a simple touch wouldn't do it. Instead, she balled up a greasy paper towel and tossed it at the empty pizza box. She pushed herself away from the heavy oak table, went to the refrigerator, and pulled out two more beers.

Twisting off the cap, she asked, "How do you see this playing out?" There were no happy endings to this story. She set the bottle down.

"I don't know yet." His eyes lost focus. She imagined the scenarios running through his mind. The possibility of getting shot during the exchange, the Mexican police doing any number of stupid things, along with the threat of losing their jobs for doing mercenary work out of the country.

"Do you think she'll come home if you do this?"

Nick leaned on the table and used the heels of his hands to rub his eyes. "I haven't figured that out yet," he answered. "At this point, I can't even hope for it."

"So you're just going to march down to Mexico and save your

brother-in-law—who is, by the way, your wife's divorce attorney— from a gang of professional criminals. Does that about cover it?"

Nick leaned back in his chair with a small chuckle. "It doesn't sound so doable when you say it that way." His eyes narrowed. "You have any better ideas?"

"Yeah, let him get out of this mess by himself. You're only going because Angela asked you." She shrugged. "You think maybe, if you go down there, you'll have a chance to get back together. She's playing on your sense of loyalty. I just don't know what you can do for her." Of course, this was the simple answer. Nick was Nick. He had to do something.

She tipped her Pacifico to her lips. Her eyes opened wide as she choked on the beer. "She wants you to rescue him without paying the ransom! Doesn't she?" What a cheap shot.

"I think so," he nodded.

"That's crazy, Nick. Mexico is not the US. If, by some miracle, you and Rigo don't wind up getting killed by gangsters or caught by the police, they can lock you up for any reason and lose the key. They don't like Americans coming in and doing their job for them. You don't know your way around, and they've got snakes and spiders that can kill a person in seconds." She shivered at the thought.

"You're afraid of spiders. I forgot." His brown face split into a smile. "On the other hand, I do speak the language."

Meredith lifted her palms in frustration. "You're going to go anyway."

In assent, his head moved up and down just once.

"Damn it! Angela knew you'd do this because you're so damned loyal." She leaned toward him, frustration threatening to get the better of her. "Think about what you're doing." Her hand found his forearm, and she grasped it.

He smiled broadly. "Loyalty is one of my most appealing qualities." His even teeth formed an irresistible smile.

Meredith sighed. What could she do? Nick's damn loyalty had saved her ass more than once. She treasured that in him. Angela was willing to use him or endanger him. Who acted like that with someone they loved?

She heard herself ask, "You want some help?"

"WHEW! Leahy shit kittens, no doubt about it." Meredith stowed her backpack behind the passenger seat of Nick's truck. "You sure you don't want to take my car? I mean, leaving your precious truck in an airport parking lot is a risky thing."

"I wouldn't be seen in your ugly-ass Subaru." It was a familiar battle.

As the door closed, she said, "Car snob."

"How'd you convince Leahy to let you go?"

"It was easy. Our caseload is down to almost nothing, and I got a nasty-gram from personnel last month about going over my limit of vacation time. I need to burn some, or I lose it. With you gone, he was more willing to let me go, since you wouldn't be around to 'handle' me. He made a bunch of noise, but I could tell he was glad to see me out of his sight for a couple of weeks."

He nodded. "You're right. You could use the break anyway. It's been what—eight months since…"

"Nine months next week."

THEY RODE IN SILENCE. Almost a year ago, Meredith nearly lost her life to an obsessed man. The stalker cloaked himself in the security of his position as a Superior Court Judge while arranging the murder of several people—including Meredith's husband. The judge had caught a bullet as he threw her off her deck. She'd held on to the railing while she dangled over a steep canyon. Nick arrived just in time to rescue her from a surely fatal fall.

The DA's investigation, and Internal Affairs investigation that followed, became a secondary nightmare. Thankfully, Nick's steadfast support lessened the trauma. Through those five tumultuous months, Meredith never took a day off that wasn't ordered. She'd been proud of that. During the investigation into the shooting, she'd been placed on paid administrative leave, then interviewed by detectives from Santa Rosa PD, the DA's office, and her own agency—the Sonoma County Sheriff's Office. She was required to meet with psychologists and a psychiatrist who insisted on regurgitating the shooting, in addition to her estrangement with her father and the precarious state of her marriage before her husband's murder. These things filled her days—her nights were occupied with nightmares, doubt, and regret. When she awakened, she rarely felt like she'd gotten any rest.

All this weighed on her, along with the frustration over her boss's lack of action when Judge Stephen Giroud threatened her. She'd felt betrayed when they forced her—and Nick—to handle the Judge on their own. Bureaucracy was one thing, but this was much more serious. A small kernel of bitterness had taken root in her heart, decaying her loyalty to the Sheriff's Office.

"NOT TO CHANGE THE SUBJECT, but how's the house deal going?"

Meredith thought about what to say. As if the judge wasn't enough trouble, after her husband Richard's death, she'd found out he had used the house like an ATM. It was mortgaged, second mortgaged, and he'd even taken a third mortgage. To pay off the loans, she'd put the house on the market and was surprised at how soon it sold. The price was right—low enough to attract a buyer—because there had been a violent death in the home, something her realtor insisted must be disclosed to buyers.

There had been a time when Meredith felt like it was her home, but not anymore. She hadn't stayed in it since that night. She wasn't upset about having to sell. The house was a showplace anyway—more Richard's style. If all went well with the sale, she'd clear enough to put a down payment on a small condo in Petaluma.

"Escrow closes at the end of the month, I hope. I should be packing." She stared out the window at the lush green vineyards that stitched across the Sonoma countryside. The sun heaved itself over the hills, promising another warm August day. She'd rather be bobbing down the Russian River on her kayak than going to the wilds of Mexico on a dangerous and likely futile mission. No back up, no built-in infrastructure for support. Lord, what were they doing? They couldn't even bring their guns.

"When does Christy get back?" Nick pulled into the airport parking lot, making sure to park in a corner where his precious truck wouldn't get a ding. Christy was Meredith's best friend and sister-in-law. She'd been caring for a relative in Illinois for the past year, letting Meredith stay at her apartment after the incident with the judge.

"She's been back for a few days." Thinking of Christy made Meredith smile. "I'm sorry her aunt died, but I'm glad my bud is home. I missed her."

"She's a good friend. Even with her own troubles with David and all, she stuck by you." Christy had been married to Meredith's brother, David, who was another victim of her stalker's raging jealousy. The judge staged Meredith's brother's suicide attempt. The resulting fall eventually killed him. By the time Judge Stephen Giroud was killed, he was found to be responsible for at least four deaths. Several other lives lay shattered, Meredith's included, although work provided the glue to fit the shards of her life back together.

"Enough of that crap," Meredith thought, fighting the weight of her past. She asked Nick, "What do you know about where we're going?"

Nick thought for a moment. "Rigoberto's house is in Bucerias, Nayarit, just north of Puerto Vallarta. Angela and her parents live with him—good thing it's a big house. Bucerias is a tourist town, but his place is in an expensive area." He paused. "First, I want to talk to Angela and her family. They may be able to give me something helpful. We have to move fast. We'll find him and get him out as soon as we can. I figure someone will negotiate with them—buy us some time—while we break him loose from wherever they're holding him. They won't be expecting that."

"What do you know about Rigoberto?"

Nick shrugged. "He's an okay guy. Kind of self-centered, if you ask me. At least he didn't get married and make some poor woman miserable. He loves the ladies, and even though he's pushing thirty-five, he is a playboy. Shows no signs of settling down. Fast cars and faster women." Nick glanced out the window at vineyards and pastureland to the west as he flipped on the signal to take the Airport Drive offramp. "Of course, I haven't seen him since before Angela left."

"Meaning, he could've changed?"

Nick smiled. "Nah."

"You said he's an attorney. Anything there that could help us? Like, is he defending a drug lord or something?"

"He's a blood-sucking divorce attorney. Not controversial, just predatory."

"Being on the receiving end, you'd think that, for sure." Meredith completed his thought. "She hasn't asked for anything yet, has she?"

"No." Unblinking, he studied the road before him. "She hasn't made up her mind. Rigo just sent those letters so she didn't have to hear my voice on the phone and be reminded of Mia." His lips twisted in a grimace of resigned frustration.

She changed the subject. Mia was "off limits," even to Meredith. Knowing Nick so well, she saw it was still all too painful. "What are we going to do when we get there?"

"I'll see how the situation looks. Then I'll make a plan. I'm thinking this gang might be from around Ixtapa. There's a prison close by called Santo Domingo. Where there's a prison, there are prisoner families and friends on the outside. I'll look at that."

Meredith sighed. "This isn't going to be pretty—no matter how you look at it."

"You're probably right."

Chapter Four

THE ALASKA AIRLINES BOMBARDIER Q400 TURBOPROP TAXIED TO A terminal and eased to a stop. Two flight attendants opened the door. From the back of the plane, the glaring reflection from the tarmac rebounded onto the white walls of the galley. As the second engine powered down, passengers got to their feet and lined up in the aisle. The air conditioner shut off, and in minutes, oppressive heat punched through Meredith's seat to the rear of the cabin.

Meredith watched Nick rise and reach into the overhead compartment for his duffel. He looked tired already. They had both dozed on the plane, but 30,000 feet up with someone else driving was never quality sleep. He looked like he could use another eight hours. She knew him so well, she saw behind his stoic exterior. Even exhaustion couldn't keep the excitement out of his eyes while his clenched jaw foreshadowed the tenuous circumstances.

Meredith slipped on her backpack and followed the last of the passengers. She and Nick descended the steps to the tarmac, where an airport employee directed them to the correct entry door. Inside, they met with another staff member who inspected their Tourist Permit forms. The stop at Customs was uneventful, then it was on to the security scanning station. Meredith resigned herself to this as a necessary evil in today's need for safety precautions.

Meredith slipped on her Keen water sandals after a security search that included scrutinizing her shoes. She glanced toward a long line at a currency exchange broker. Nodding toward the sign, she asked Nick, "Do we need to exchange our money?"

"No, we wait until we get into town." Nick slung his duffle over his shoulder by a strap. "The exchange rates are lousy here. I'm going to get more cash anyway."

People crowded around the exit. Once outside, hawkers bombarded them—for tours and timeshares. They were aggressive enough that Meredith's anger stirred. She tried to remember that these were people trying to make a living, but they still irritated her. In the end, she followed Nick's example and ignored them, plowing through the crowd.

"Nick, Nick!" Meredith heard Angela's shouts before he did. Meredith elbowed him and pointed toward his wife, standing just inside the dark glass exit doors. Nick searched the mob, and his eyes widened when he found Angela.

Meredith turned away to give her partner a moment without scrutiny, but not without seeing his face relax into an unusual softness. He was still in love with her. She dreaded this. It could be a real mess for her friend and partner. She scanned the crowd, but didn't see anything that caught her interest—no one watching, no one that she saw was armed.

Her attention fell on Angela. Meredith watched her pull away from Nick's embrace, looking away from his eyes, fidgeting with her purse strap. She was shorter than Nick by almost a foot—she probably topped out at five foot three. Petite but not thin, her curves filled out smoothly. She was dressed in a demure yellow sundress. Meredith squelched a stab of envy over Angela's flawless bronze skin. The woman was named well—her face was that of an angel—cherubic with a classic beauty. However, her almond-shaped eyes had shadows beneath them, and her small mouth closed tight, her jaw twitching with tension.

Nick read her reaction, and his arm fell away from her shoulders.

Angela put a hand on his arm and said something that Meredith couldn't hear over the noise. His glance summoned Meredith, who moved to stand in front of Angela. Meredith had thought a lot about this moment and how they both would act. She'd decided to keep herself as pleasant as possible. The situation wouldn't be helped by rudeness.

She took the lead. "It's good to see you again, Angela. Sorry it's under these circumstances."

"I'm glad you're here with Nick." Angela's smile revealed a vulnerability Meredith had never noticed. Angela was as keyed up as Nick. Did she still love him? Before she could say anything more, Angela's expression shifted to resolute determination. "We should go," she turned toward the exit.

Nick hitched up his duffel, stepping next to his wife. Meredith fell in behind them.

The automatic doors slid open, and Meredith caught her breath at the heat and humidity. She felt like she'd fallen into a sauna. She'd worn jeans and a T-shirt for comfort on the flight and in anticipation of the sun. Nick didn't react to the weather, even though he was wearing jeans and a cotton shirt. His attention was on his wife.

A white SUV sat parked and running at the curb. Angela motioned to a man waiting behind the wheel. The driver popped the hatchback, got out, and met them at the back. He was dark, with powerful, weightlifter shoulders and a sullen, pockmarked face. Meredith's shitbird radar alerted. She watched the big man move when he stepped aside as Nick stowed their luggage in the trunk. His shoulders definitely told her that he lifted weights, and maybe even juiced.

Angela spoke without smiling. "Nick, Meredith. This is Oswaldo Enrique Santos. He is an associate of Rigo's from his office." Nick reached toward him for a handshake. Oswaldo hesitated, then stretched his hand out. When Meredith did the same, Oswaldo glanced at her and, with no expression on his face, turned and got back in the car.

Meredith shrugged off his rudeness. After almost a year with Sergeant Leahy, a little bit of Hispanic chauvinism was nothing. She had developed a thick skin to survive at work. Even so, cultural differences didn't excuse the man's bad manners, and Oswaldo's behavior reinforced her initial feeling.

Nick tapped Angela on her shoulder. "We need to stop at a bank to get some cash." Oswaldo nodded, as if he'd expected the request.

With Angela in the front passenger seat and Meredith and Nick in the back, Oswaldo pulled into traffic. Angela turned to Nick. "I'll explain everything when we are at home. Mama and Papa want to be included in this, so I promised that I'd wait."

Nick leaned forward so she could hear him over the blasting air conditioner. "Really, Angela? Every minute counts. The sooner we're up to speed, the sooner we can get Rigo back."

She glared over her shoulder. "We wait."

Chapter Five

A WARM BREEZE FROM THE BAY OF BANDERAS DRIFTED THROUGH the open windows, doing little to cool the six people in the living room. After introductions, Meredith stepped back to watch the interaction between Angela's parents and Nick. He seemed to hold back, unsure how he would be received. Angela's mother, Liliana, was a fine-boned beauty with straight, shoulder-length, salt-and-pepper hair. Her face glowed with pleasure at the sight of her son-in-law. As with her daughter, Nick almost bent double to embrace her. She clutched him tightly, and Meredith saw the woman's shoulders shake. Soon her wailing filled the room. With his lips pressed tight in dismay, her husband, Emilio, pried her away from Nick and led her to the kitchen. Angela followed, shoulders slumped, looking at a loss.

"Mama and Papa," Meredith said, as if this explained who they were.

Nick nodded. His lips spread in a reluctant grin.

Oswaldo slipped out through a glass slider onto the patio. Meredith watched him cup his hands against the breeze as he lit a cigarette.

She hadn't seen much of the upstairs, beyond dumping her backpack in a guest bedroom. Now, she took the time to survey the beach house's first floor. The exterior was an odd blend of red granite rock, brick, and stucco in an angular modern form. With its unconventional flat roof, the house sat like a gravestone in the middle of a concrete lot, surrounded by an iron fence and large gates at the front.

In the living room, a gray cat slept on a sun-soaked window ledge. Native Mexican rugs hung on the white stucco walls, along with bright oil paintings and colorful textiles. Yellow chintz accent chairs and mahogany tables surrounded an indigo cotton couch in the center of the room. A rustic monastery table and benches sat in the dining room near a hutch that displayed colorful enamelware. Whoever decorated this place had a love for nice things and a reverence for Mexican art.

At the moment, it was obvious that all thoughts of impressing guests had been forgotten. The empty glasses, dirty dishes, and overflowing ashtrays told any observer that the occupants of this room were doing some serious waiting. The thought brought her back to the task before them. Nick leaned a hip on the back of the sofa and his face clouded. Meredith saw resolve conquering his emotions. She had to do something. She glanced into the kitchen and then moved on instinct.

"Mr. and Mrs. Borrego, let's get started," Meredith shouted. "Time is critical. If the kidnappers call and Nick doesn't have a plan, well, it could be dangerous. Let's work on this together." Yuck, she sounded like a cheerleader, but hell, whatever was necessary to motivate. She'd learned that on the street. People were more willing to do something if they believed it was in their best interest. Her eyes moved past Liliana and Emilio, and settled on their daughter. Angela flashed a relieved smile and herded the parents back to the living room. "If we all speak English, then I can follow along." Meredith smiled politely, hoping not to mess with any rules of culture.

Nick didn't wait for them to settle in, nor did he wait for Oswaldo. He stood, pulled out a small spiral notebook, and addressed Angela's father. "Emilio, can you tell me the last time you saw Rigo? Friday, no?"

After the old man nodded, Nick continued. "What time? Where were you, and what was he doing?"

"We had just come back from daily Mass, Rigo was getting in his car, leaving for work." Emilio handed his wife a tissue, then sat down heavily beside her. He dropped his gnarled hands to his lap. His English was precise but slow and sad, as if Rigo was already dead. "He looked as he always looks—like he was a lion getting ready to feast on a deer. He loved his work, but more—he loved the money and the power it gave him." Emilio's graying head bowed. "Divorce is a sacrilege, I told him…"

The slider screen rumbled open. Oswaldo stepped inside, an acrid cloud of cigarette smoke clinging to him. His gaze found Angela and lingered. When his attention switched to Nick, his jawline tightened. He looked at Meredith, leaned against the wall, glancing away with a sour smile.

Nick eased the old man back on topic. "Did he say anything to you?"

"No. He just got into his car and drove off, too fast."

"What time was that?"

"A little before nine A.M."

Meredith asked the next question. "Did you see anyone around the neighborhood who didn't belong here?"

"No," Emilio shrugged. "It's hard to say. This is a tourist area; the beach is less than a block away. There are always strange cars and people coming and going. That's why Rigo put the fence and gates around the property." His wiry arm swung around, indicating the whole area.

Liliana choked back a sob. "It didn't help at all."

Nick focused on her. "Liliana, you took the phone call?"

Her eyes widened. "Yes, it was so frightening. The caller ID said it was Rigo's cell phone" She crumpled the shredded tissue in her hand.

"What time did you get the call?"

She answered without hesitation. She'd been asked this before. "It was eleven in the morning, just before lunch."

Nick scratched the time in his notebook. "So it was about two hours after you last saw him, right?"

Liliana nodded, slipping her hands between her knees. She looked like she wanted to crawl under a rock. "Emilio called Rigo's office, but he wasn't there. His cell went to voicemail. Then we knew."

Nick sat on the coffee table facing the couple. "Liliana, I know this will be difficult, but I need you to tell me every word they said."

She choked again and Emilio put his hand on her knee. She seemed to gather courage from his touch. "He said, 'We have your son, Rigoberto. Give us twenty million pesos and he will go free. If you don't, we will kill him.'" She rocked back and forth, her arms now across her chest. "My son, my son. What will happen to him, Nick?"

Emilio looked away as Liliana began to sob. Angela swept across to her mother, kneeling before her and whispering earnest, reassuring words in Spanish.

Meredith stood. "I'm new around here. Can someone tell me precisely what a negotiator does?"

Oswaldo stepped up. "What kind of question is that from a policía?"

Meredith stared hard at him before answering. "Humor me."

Oswaldo jutted his square chin at her. "The same as the US. Talk to the kidnappers. Try to lower the ransom; then arrange for the money-drop and pick up the victim."

Angela looked up at Meredith. "I'm afraid it's become an industry here in the past few years."

"Have you ever negotiated before?" Meredith asked Oswaldo.

"No." The color of his brown face deepened.

"Now is not the time for lies, Oswaldo." Liliana's eyes flashed with fury. She stood and faced the huge man. "It's time for hard truths." She looked at her son-in-law, her complexion reddened as she told outsiders the truth. "He tried to negotiate when his cousin, Ishmael, was taken. He offered them so little that they were offended and killed him." She turned to be sure everyone in the room had heard. They had.

"Guess that answers my question about why they called you for help," Meredith mumbled to Nick as she slid into a chair.

Nick studied his in-laws. "I have to ask: why me? I mean, with the history between Angela and me, are you sure there isn't someone else who could be of more help?"

"And who would we call? The police? It is very likely that they had a hand in this," Liliana answered. "It is precisely because of your history that we need you. We know and trust you." After stating her simple truth, she rose, stacked empty glasses and coffee cups, then strode into the kitchen. Emilio followed her.

"Who do you think is behind this, and why?" With his pen over his notepad, Nick looked at Angela.

Oswaldo answered, his voice deep and confident. "We think they are part of a new gang who just moved here. We have had more kidnappings in the past six months than ever before. My contacts told me that these guys moved into an abandoned farm in the hills between Bucerias and Sayulita. I think they must be using kidnapping to finance a dope farm."

His studied self-assurance irritated the hell out of Meredith. This clown shouldn't even be here. "Your contacts? What are you, a PI?" Meredith tried to keep the snark out of her voice, but she heard it, clearly.

So did Oswaldo. His eyes hardened. "Yes. I work for Rigo's firm." "Oh, I get it. Angela introduced you as Rigo's 'associate.' Silly me. I assumed you were an attorney. Not some lame-ass gumshoe who follows cheating husbands around."

He stood tall, his knees locked. He looked like he might launch himself across the room and punch her out. "You would be surprised at the info I can turn."

Nick cut across their squabble. "Angela, is there any chance you can raise the money?"

"Maybe we could make a few thousand." Angela's brown eyes looked even sadder. "But this is Rigo's house. It's in his name, and the bank won't even talk to us about a loan." Angela glanced into the kitchen. "Papa said he can cash in his pension, but then they both would have to go back to work. I have a little money put aside..."

"What about Rigo's firm? There should be money in his business."

"His partner said no. Apparently, Rigo spends everything he makes. He just keeps the bills paid." She waved a hand at the house. "This place is expensive. His mortgage is over two thousand a month."

"Dollars?" Nick's astonishment got the better of him.

Angela's voice dropped just above a whisper. "He supports all of us." She reached out and grabbed Nick's arm, preempting his protest. "I get your money every month, don't worry. I use it to live on, but I try to help the folks, too."

"Wait." Nick squared off with her. "Your father said he has a pension. Why does Rigo need to support him?" Something wasn't sitting right.

She cast a "shhh" glance at the kitchen, where Emilio was helping his wife with the dishes. "He lost a huge chunk of his pension when the stock market fell. He doesn't know how much— Rigo handles all the finances, so he supplements what little Papa gets, as do I." She looked away self-consciously, refusing to meet Nick's gaze.

"We don't need to negotiate," Meredith spoke before giving it thorough consideration. "We have to stall so Nick and I can find your brother."

Wide-eyed, Angela dropped to the ottoman. "What do you mean?"

"It means someone stays here to take the call from the kidnappers," Nick answered. "That person delays negotiations however he or she can, until we find Rigo and rescue him." He said it calmly, like he was explaining something to a child. Meredith smiled inwardly, pleased that Nick had understood her logic—and agreed to it.

"Won't they kill him?" Angela's voice trembled.

Nick folded his notepad and slipped it into his back pocket. "I don't see we have any choice. We can't get the money, but the kidnappers don't know that. You'll have to string them along to give us a chance to do our job."

Angela's brown eyes latched onto Nick's. "Me? Why me?"

"You're the only one who can do this." Nick knelt and took her hands in his. "Your mother is hysterical half the time. Your father is too worried about her to function, and Oswaldo—well, let's just say I don't like his track record. Besides, I want him with us."

Meredith's gaze met Oswaldo's across the room. Nick didn't trust him any more than she did. A slow smile spread across Oswaldo's generous lips, but there was no hint of humor.

Crap, she thought.

Chapter Six

OSWALDO'S CELL PHONE CHIMED A SALSA TUNE FROM PUBLIC Enemy. He pulled it from his pocket, checked the caller ID, and turned away. Meredith watched his massive back as he slipped outside to the patio. He hunched over the phone, his arm moving briskly as if the caller could see him.

Angela's gaze shifted to Nick, then Meredith. Her focus moved to her trembling hands. Self-consciously, she pulled them away from Nick's and tucked them under her knees. "There's something you should know about Rigo."

Oh, no. Here it comes, Meredith thought. Victims were rarely the single dimension originally presented—especially by the family. From experience, Meredith knew that some people put themselves in jeopardy, kept themselves there, or were targets of retribution. Of course, there were innocents. For example, her first homicide case, Violet McMurray was an elderly woman raped and beaten to death by her housekeeper's grandson. Rigo's kidnapping sounded like nothing more than a poorly planned abduction—so far.

"Rigo was seeing someone."

Nick wanted to be sure he understood. "As in dating? Regularly?"

Angela bowed her head. "I know we've talked about this before, how he's phobic about commitment, but recently he's been secretive, spending money like it was water. Yet, he seems—seemed—happier than he'd been for years."

"Sounds like love to me, or at least, lust." This woman might be a good starting point for their inquiries. "Do you know her name? We'll need to talk to her."

"No. Papa was after him all the time to get married, settle down, and have kids. I think she wasn't the family type, so he kept her under wraps. I thought she might be married." She paused, taking a deep breath. "Yes, he was hiding something. I figured it out one night when he came home smelling like a perfume factory. I didn't tell Papa, and Rigo doesn't know I found out. I'll say one thing, though," she met Nick's eyes. "He used to hang out with cheap women, but this one was different. It was an expensive perfume, not a knock-off."

Nick pulled his notebook out of his pocket and jotted something down. "Sounds like one woman, then. Any idea where they met?"

"Sayulita. I saw a book of matches from a hotel there."

Meredith was on it. "Is the matchbook here? Do you remember the name of the hotel?"

"Oh, yes. Los Arcos Iris. There's a club there that Rigo has gone to in the past called Sueños."

"Can you get us a photo of Rigo, something recent?"

Chapter Seven

RIGOBERTO BORREGO FELT NEEDLE-LIKE STICKS ON HIS RIGHT THIGH piercing his tropical-weight wool slacks. Under the blindfold, his eyelids shot open. He couldn't see, but he knew what had touched him—a rat! With a seizure-like jolt of his pelvis, he shook the rodent loose. He heard it thump to the floor and skitter away with what Rigo thought was a promise to return after dark. He didn't know if he could stay awake all night to protect himself against the rat's return. He was so tired and hungry. And he had to piss again.

He tried yelling through the filthy handkerchief tied around his mouth. What came out was a muffled yelp. He kept it up for almost ten minutes, until he heard the door swing open with such force that it bounced closed again. Someone yanked the blindfold off. He paused to allow his vision to adjust to the light.

The guard was short, stocky, and built like God had mashed him together in a hurry. He flipped open a pocketknife. A grim smile spread on his chapped lips as thick fingers waved the blade side to side.

Rigo wasn't afraid. He was well known in Bucerias. It would be too risky to kill him. Kidnappers who killed normally did it right away because there's less upkeep ransoming a body. These gangsters were after a simple payoff. If they were the kind of thugs who cut off an ear or finger, they would have done it by now. He was a little worried, though, that he didn't know the man guarding him. He'd always prided himself on knowing all the families in the Bucerias area, where he lived and worked. This guy wasn't from around here.

The guard leaned close to Rigo's head. A cloud of sour beer breath hung in the air. The guard pressed the knife blade to his captive's cheek. He traced a line with the point along the top of the rough cotton gag—hard but not quite breaking the skin. Then, with a deft turn of the wrist, he slid the knife under the knot, yanked, and cut it through.

Rigo jumped, shoving away his alarm. A blur of fine dust rose from the sod floor. "Hey, untie me, will you?"

The man stood silent. His dark eyes held his hostage while his thumb ran along the edge of the knife.

"Come on. I gotta take a piss."

When the guard looked at him like he was an idiot, Rigo lost his temper. "Look, there's one door and no windows—where am I gonna go? I've gotta go to the bathroom sometime." He took a deep breath to calm himself. "Let me have my hands or there's going to be a mess."

It was silent in this place of shadows, the light from outside reluctant to spend itself in the dingy room. In a sudden movement, the guard stepped backwards to a bookcase that blended into the dark wall. Rigo heard a scrape of metal and braced himself. An empty three-pound coffee can hit him in the chest, bounced off, and rolled onto the floor.

In a swift movement, the guard pushed Rigo's head to his knees and cut the jute bindings from his wrists. Rigo released a breath as the guard walked out the door. He'd be back, no doubt. Just like the rat. Rigo wobbled to his feet, rubbing his wrists to get the circulation flowing. He'd been sitting too long. His legs were unsteady but they held. His bare feet balanced on the warm dirt. He missed his shoes, socks, and tie—they were taken from him soon after his abduction. He must look like a bum.

After moving the urine-filled coffee can next to the door, Rigo wandered around the dim room, looking at the humble furnishings. What a mess he was in. There was no money for ransom. Angela didn't have enough to make a difference. He was in debt up to his ass, and his parents were in worse shape, although they didn't know it. He'd pilfered from their pensions to finance his high-life. More recently, he had been introduced to the seductions of gambling. Silvia nudged him to it. The glamour of the nightclubs, bars, and discos was wearing thin, so she'd taken him to a closed club where she'd gone once. With Oswaldo acting as their chauffeur, he'd been so proud to arrive with her. Like a couple on the Hollywood red carpet.

He sighed as he thought of her—her long chestnut curls bouncing around her shoulders, pale skin, and eyes so clear and blue that he swore he saw the ocean in them. And her laugh, so full of promise and mystery. The wagering was almost as exciting as being seen with her. For a minute, he lost himself in the memory of Silvia, the smell of her skin, her moist kisses, and his fingers caressing her breasts.

He had to talk to the leader of this gang and reason with him. Rigo was too important in the community of Bucerias to be kidnapped. Sure, he'd pissed off some of his colleagues by making their wives happy in bed. It was unfair that he should be punished for making women happy...

He'd insist on talking to whoever masterminded this stupidity and make him see the sense in releasing him. Escape wasn't an option, even though he knew the hills were riddled with tunnels and abandoned mines. He felt sure that he was in the mountains above his home. The air was thinner yet oppressive with the sweet smells of the jungle. He thought he recognized the rutted, dirt road the kidnappers drove on, and the trip had lasted long enough to put him in the hills of Los Lobos.

There hadn't been any official silver mining up here for decades, but he and Angela played in these hills when they were children. They'd explored while their parents searched the ground for artifacts and interesting rocks. Emilio was an engineer by trade, but his hobby had been archaeology and geology. Rigo had fond memories of those days. It was a huge area. Because he didn't know his exact location, he couldn't trust himself to find the caves. Getting lost in this jungle could cost him his life.

Still, he had one more ace in the hole.

Chapter Eight

"Angela." Nick caught her attention as she hustled her parents up the stairs. She told them she'd follow them in a minute, then turned to Nick. His voice was almost a whisper. "Where do I sleep?"

Angela tipped her head as she studied her husband, her face a blank canvas. "On the couch. Put your pack in Rigo's office next to the bathroom."

Disappointment settled into Nick's chest, even as he tried for control. Losing the battle, he didn't trust himself to speak. His mind whirled with things he wanted her to know. He just couldn't figure out what to say.

Her chin jutted toward him in a challenge. "That is, unless you plan on sleeping with Meredith."

Nick was stunned. Everything he'd wanted to say for a year—all the words he had carefully threaded together, flew out the door. "No." It hurt that she thought he would be unfaithful to her. "I'm still married to you." He wasn't made that way, and she knew it—at least, she used to.

Angela sighed and turned her head, so he couldn't see her reaction. He'd wanted to say something powerful, filled with his enduring love and commitment. He'd wanted her to understand how he felt— married, yet not. He wanted her to know she wasn't alone in this life.

She turned back, her eyes rimmed with tears. "Our marriage is just a formality, Nick. You know that." He hated when she cried.

"No, I don't." He reached toward her, and she dipped a shoulder to evade his grasp. She stepped past him and down the stairs, taking refuge behind the breakfast bar.

Following her, he dropped his hands to his sides and set his jaw. "No. We took a vow—in front of God—to live together, to love each other forever. No matter what. I take that seriously."

She brushed a tear away with her knuckle, then turned her back to him. "We can't talk about this now, Nick. We have other more important things to deal with."

"Why not now? We can't do anything to find Rigo until morning. Your parents and Meredith are upstairs. Oswaldo took off. This is as good a time as any."

He saw her set her shoulders and he knew what she was going to say. "No, I can't deal with this while Rigo's kidnapping is hanging over our heads."

His voice softened. "I know you've been through a lot in the past year..."

A spark of anger burned in her dark eyes. "You don't know anything. I needed you after...but you were never around. I've managed alone because I had to. You're always working."

He whispered. "I was with you as much as I could be, Ange. I had to work. We had bills to pay." He studied her face as if he could find a reason for her feelings. Somehow, this felt all wrong. She'd never said she'd resented him for going back to work.

Wrath still in her gaze, she straightened. "Oh yeah? I thought it was for you to be around your partner."

"Meredith? We weren't even partners when—"

"You were friends, then. I know you saw her."

He'd never seen any kind of suspicion or jealousy from his wife before. They'd been married six years and he'd never seen this side of her. In the silence that hung between them, he chose his words with care. "There is nothing romantic or sexual between Meredith and me. I'm disappointed that you think so little of my character." He dropped his focus to his hands. "You know I'd never get involved with another cop, and especially my own partner."

She whirled around the bar and ran to the stairs. For the first time, it dawned on him that she might not want to come back.

MEREDITH WOKE to the smell of coffee. She searched the room for something familiar to orient herself. Faint daylight seeped through the large window facing the Pacific. She had left it open overnight, trying to catch a cool breeze. It had failed—the room was already warm. Tossing all night, she got little sleep. She missed Sonoma County evenings, when the fog from the Pacific cooled summer nights to a comfortable temperature.

The gray cat kneaded her backpack, circling, ready to settle in. Throwing back the cotton sheet, she hopped off the bed. "Oh, no, you don't, kitty."

The cat eased sideways while Meredith yanked her pack to the bed. Then it hopped onto the rattan seat, circling and kneading, more or less as originally planned.

Meredith wondered at her alarm. Gus, her own beloved feline, had often slept on her clothes. A little cat hair never bothered her.

Meredith distracted herself with the prospects that lay before them. This was Nick's show. She was here for help and support. She expected they would hammer out a plan today. Tugging on jeans and a T-shirt, she gave in to the idea that she was here for her partner—for both Rigo's rescue and how he resolved his problem with Angela.

She pulled her auburn hair into a ponytail and then washed her face. She grimaced at her image in the mirror, thinking, that's as good as it gets without makeup. Her warm brown eyes took in the nose she thought was too long, lips too thin, and jaw too square. She shrugged her observations away, grabbed her backpack, and made her way downstairs.

Taking the steps two at a time, Meredith dumped her bag in a corner at the landing and let her nose guide her to the coffee. Angela sat at the table in a short robe, hair twisted up in a clip, sipping from a mug. After an insincere exchange of "good mornings," Angela's eyes followed Meredith around the kitchen as she poured herself a cup.

Meredith slid onto the bench opposite Angela and cautiously tasted her coffee. Feeling the other woman's focus, she met Angela's gaze with a smile.

Angela started, surprised by the smile, and then sighed as the quiet stretched between them. Angela cleared her throat. She put her hand on the table near the mug. "It's good that you're here with Nick." Her fingers traced the grain of the wood. She studied them with a fierceness that put Meredith on edge. "He needs you for this... mess." Angela's hand flew above her head to indicate what Meredith thought was the kidnapping. "I'm too emotional to be of any help."

"You are helping. Coffee is a good start."

Angela smiled at the humor. "I'm glad we have some time together."

Hoping she sounded more sincere than she felt, Meredith mumbled, "Me, too."

Angela laced her fingers around the mug. "When Mia died, I thought I wanted to die, too. Nick just didn't get it."

Meredith felt like she was transparent, like Angela didn't even see her. Holy crap! How did she get herself into this? Her partner's wife confiding in her about the failure of their marriage? How awkward could this get? How could she not believe that Nick was just as shattered as she? "I know it was tough on both of you."

"He stayed with me until the funeral. Then he went back to work. I wanted to die to be with my baby, but God wouldn't take me. When Nick was home, it was like he was on another planet. It felt like we didn't even speak the same language."

Meredith was not good at this kind of thing. What could she say? "You seem to be doing better here with your family. Of course, now you have your brother to think about."

Angela's eyes still had a dreamy quality. "Nick will find him."

"If anyone can, it's Nick." Meredith buried her face in her mug.

God, why wasn't anyone else in this house awake? It's almost seven. Don't leave me alone with this woman!

"You know," Angela focused on Meredith. "In some ways, I think you know Nick better than I do."

"Not better, just different. I see him at work, and your perspective is from home. Behaviors for everyone vary between settings."

"No, there's more to it than that. I think you two sometimes speak without words. You know what he is thinking."

"Yes, sometimes." Meredith nodded. "But not always. That's the common denominator of a good partnership. That and trust."

Angela smiled. "He trusts you. You wouldn't be here if he didn't."

"I know." Meredith worked hard for that trust. "It's a two-way street. I know he's got my back. He's proven it." Meredith didn't think Angela knew about the mess with the judge. She wasn't going to fill her in.

Angela's eyes met Meredith's. "Nick will do what I want. He always has." Her face held a serene self-assurance, like when someone says, "The sun will rise."

Meredith held her irritation in check but didn't want to let Angela get away with this. It sounded like she thought he was a fool to lead around by the nose. Nick was his own man, even if he loved Angela. He would do the right thing.

Meredith pushed her empty mug toward the center of the table.

"He'll do what he thinks is right." Angela sat back. "You are very loyal."

"He deserves that."

The kitchen door flew open. Buried in grocery bags, Nick ambled in. He dropped his burden on the counter, glancing from Angela to Meredith. "What? What?"

Chapter Nine

BREAKFAST WAS A HURRIED AFFAIR. LILIANA RE-HEATED THE PORK and chicken tamales Nick had bought at the neighborhood market. Angela laid out papaya and bananas on the kitchen counter, along with hot chocolate and coffee. By the time Emilio returned from Mass, the two women were already cleaning up. In the living room, Nick and Meredith hunched over maps.

Angela had put aside tamales for her father.

"I'm not hungry." He waved off the food. Before she could encourage him to eat, a light tapping at the front door caught Emilio's attention. He hopped off the stool, his voice carrying across the entire first floor. "Someone is at the door. Someone is at the door." As he looked for Nick's approval to answer it, an electric tension sparked in him.

Meredith went up the stairs two at a time, stopping at the landing. She peered out a small, porthole-sized window. Her voice was all business. "It's Oswaldo and another male."

Angela swung open the heavy door. "Javier. I knew you would come."

Meredith had a clear view of Angela's face. The lines of worry softened from the anxiety she had worn the past day. The warmth of her smile surprised Meredith. That was a smile reserved for someone special. Very special.

She wondered at the significance. Angela was lying to Nick, maybe everyone in Bucerias. Lying gets easier as you do it. What else was she dishonest about? Nick should know about this. Right away.

Angela led Javier to the living room. Javier had a few inches on Angela—he was 5'8", and every inch was arrow straight. His white linen suit and sky-blue shirt set him apart from the rest of the room. A cloud of department store cologne drifted in with him. Meredith thought he looked like a strutting rooster.

Oswaldo followed, sullen as yesterday—an oil slick behind Javier's yacht.

"Nick, this is Javier Davalos Aguilera, Rigo's partner." Angela's introduction held a hint of familiarity.

Nick turned to Davalos and the men shook hands. The attorney had a smooth voice, with perfectly executed English syllables. "A pleasure to meet you, Nicholas. I am here to offer my services, humble as they may be."

Nick crossed his arms. To anyone but Meredith, it appeared he had taken an instant dislike to Davalos. However, she knew that he was taking his measure of the other man. He would have noticed the manicured nails and the eyes that darted around the room.

Nick hadn't seen the welcome expression on his wife's face at the front door. How would she tell Nick about that? If this guy evoked that response in Angela, what did it mean for Nick? Had she been acting at the breakfast table? What did it have to do with why Angela remained down here? Should Meredith just butt out?

"I have news." Oswaldo walked between the men, glancing at the maps on the coffee table.

Emilio rushed to his side and put his hand on Oswaldo's arm. "What news? What have you heard?"

Oswaldo shook off the old man. He pulled a pack of cigarettes from his breast pocket, a study in control. He lit a smoke while his gaze challenged Nick to ask him about his information. Liliana and Angela crept toward Oswaldo, both with painfully hopeful expressions. Javier waited with the detachment of a man not directly involved in this family tragedy.

Meredith was not so patient. "What's your news?" Nor was she going to play into this man's plan for self-importance.

Oswaldo glanced toward her, then Nick. "It is as I thought. There is an abandoned rancho in the hills of Mexico 200 between Bucerias and Sayulita. A bunch of gangsters moved in six months ago, and the policía believe that is where the kidnapping ring operates."

Emilio's eyes widened. "I know that place. The Old Sotelo Mine is on that road below El Rancho. That's what the owners' place was always called. They lived there until the silver diggings played out." Then, his face drawn in anxiety, Emilio pawed Oswaldo's muscular arm. "Surely you did not tell the policía about Rigo."

Oswaldo sucked on his cigarette, then blew smoke through his nose. He shook his head.

"How reliable is this information?" Nick asked.

Oswaldo cocked his head in a shrug.

"How many at El Rancho?" Meredith pressed him.

"They said no less than two." Oswaldo kept his attention on Nick.

"What kind of weapons do they have?" Nick asked.

"What don't they have?" Oswaldo shrugged.

Fed up with Oswaldo's flip answers, Meredith wondered if Angela's brother was still alive. "Has anyone seen Rigo?"

Oswaldo shifted to acknowledge Meredith. His full lips curled in distaste. "I couldn't ask the policía that, could I, Miss Detective? Otherwise, they would know he's been kidnapped."

A sob exploded from Liliana as she dropped to the sofa. "They know. Emilio, the policía must know. If they stick their fingers into this mess, Rigo might be killed."

Emilio and Angela flanked her, trying to calm her down.

Oswaldo crushed out his smoke on a plate, his eyes roving in a challenge from person to person.

Nick twirled a pencil in his fingers. "Liliana has a point, you know." When he was sure he had their attention, he continued. "If the locals know about Rigo, it opens up two potential problems.

First, someone in the kidnappers' back pocket may pass the info on to them, and it might end up badly. Second, if the policía raid El Rancho to rescue Rigo, it could also turn to crap. There is the possibility that they would be successful in returning him safely, but I wouldn't bet on it."

"The police here, are they honest?" Meredith knew it was too simple a question.

"They are people like anywhere else," Javier spoke up at last. "Most are honest, hard-working people, with families to keep safe. Others are bought every now and then. Then you have the eyes of the matónes—the ones who spy on everyone and report to the head man."

"Any way you look at it, we can't take a chance with them." Nick echoed Meredith's thoughts. He looked at Javier. "How safe is the family here?"

"They should be fine." Javier glanced around the room.

"Safe? Us?" Liliana grew wide-eyed. "Why would we be in danger?"

Emilio's chest puffed out, "We are safe here. This is our home." He curled his sinewy arm around his wife's shoulders, as if it was enough to keep her out of danger.

"What if the policía come here to ask you about Rigo? What will you tell them?" Nick leaned toward his mother-in-law, his voice softening. "Will you lie and tell them he is traveling?"

She sat up, her shoulders stiff with resolve. "Yes. I would lie."

Nick stood. He nodded his approval. "Okay. You'll all stay here for now. Angela, I need you to take over the phone. Whenever it rings, you must answer it. I don't want anyone else to touch it. Understand?" He glanced from Liliana to Emilio to Angela, waiting for their nods of agreement. "Oswaldo, do you have guns or know where we can find some? We'll need semi-auto handguns and full-auto rifles. And we'll need a car, preferably something that's dependable but doesn't stand out."

Oswaldo fished keys from his pants and threw them to Nick. "It's the gold Toyota outside—my cousin's car. It's a little beat up, but it'll get you around. I put some firepower in the trunk."

"Can you get a few things together and stay here with the family?" Nick's chin jutted toward the occupants of the sofa. "Javier, it would be best if you kept to your routine. You should go back to work."

Javier made no secret of his irritation. "Thank you for your permission, sir." He bent over in a mock bow.

Nick said nothing. Cocky little asshole.

"I'll go get a toothbrush from the store on the corner." Oswaldo sauntered out, followed by Javier.

The door closed, and Nick sat down. "Let's get some things straight here." All eyes were on him. "First, Angela. When you get a phone call from the kidnappers, do everything you can to stall. Tell them the money is delayed or whatever—just buy us some time. I'm going with Meredith to El Rancho to get the layout. We'll be back this afternoon. But here's the thing: you cannot trust anyone outside this room."

Nick hushed Angela's protest. "I don't trust Oswaldo, and I don't know Javier. Got it?"

Angela's lips thinned. "I know Javier. I worked in the law office with him and Rigo. He has the highest integrity."

"I can't take the chance." Anger flickered in Nick's voice. "Let me run this gig." He collected himself. "He can come and go, as long as this house is secure. If there is any trouble, I'm moving your mom and dad out, call forwarding the phone, and stashing you someplace safe."

"Oswaldo may have some loyalty to the family, but we need him out of our way," Meredith spoke up. "That's why he has to stay here. You can keep an eye on him, too. Let us know if he does something unusual. And update us instantly if you get a call from the kidnappers."

The three on the sofa nodded in unison, their eyes wide.

Nick and Meredith stood. "We're going now, before they get back. Angela, do you have Meredith's cell number? Good. We'll see you later this afternoon."

Chapter Ten

THEY CLIMBED THE NARROW, RUTTED ROAD FOR AN HOUR, CLOUDS of gray dust swirling around their feet. It was so hot even the insects had stopped buzzing. Brush encroached onto the dirt-packed road, brittle stalks reaching out to pull against Meredith's jeans. Lethal-looking weeds scratched through the openings of her sandals. She'd pulled off her shirt and was down to a tank top. Using the shirt-sleeves, she mopped sweat off her temples and neck. Even with her hair in a ponytail, the heat pressed on her shoulders beneath the backpack. Tree cover was sporadic, and she knew her iridescent Irish skin would sunburn, even through the SPF 50 she'd applied before they left.

Oswaldo told them to leave their car at the bottom of the hill because it could be heard coming miles away. Meredith was sure he knew the hike up to El Rancho was a bitch and wondered how much fun he was having picturing their trek.

Nick walked beside her, his eyes constantly scanning the hillside. They spoke little. Until they saw the layout of the place, there was nothing to discuss. Both watched for anything that moved.

A few times, they noticed small fields of vegetables set back from the roadway. Someone tended them, but in each case, they saw no one around. Tire tracks on the dirt indicated the road had been traveled by car sometime today. Sheds—shacks really—dotted the periphery of the fields, and Meredith wondered if they were living quarters. She doubted any of them had plumbing.

Nick turned off the road and made his way to a lanky scrub oak. Leaning against it, he pulled his water bottle out. He offered it to Meredith first, but when she waved it away, he took a swig. She found her water and took a drink. "How much farther, do you think?"

His eyes narrowed against the sun. "I'm not sure this is right. Oswaldo said keep going until the road switches back. El Rancho is supposed to be just above that. He said the road is about ten kilometers to the end."

"I can't tell how far we've walked, but we've been climbing long enough. I hope we find it soon."

"Me, too. C'mon." He twisted the plastic cap back on his water bottle, stuffed it away, and slung the pack over his shoulders. Before they left, he'd rigged his duffel to carry like a backpack. Meredith slipped hers on, then patted the Sig Sauer P220 in her pocket. She'd picked it from Oswaldo's stash in the car.

They were gaining elevation. A switchback lay just ahead. Nick moved to the chest-high brush, motioning Meredith to follow. Pulling out a pair of lightweight Nikon binoculars he'd borrowed from Liliana, he steadied his footing and scanned the road. Meredith waited, forcing herself to calm her breathing. He must be looking up the hill.

Nick whispered. "Nothing. We have to get closer." He dropped the binoculars to his chest and pointed east. "Move around that way. We'll be below the road, but should be able to see better."

"There's no vantage point from above?"

"This will have to do for now. It's just a recon. I want to take it slow and easy, so we don't get caught."

Meredith agreed. That would be a disaster.

Rustling eastward through the brush, Meredith found a small game trail, something deer would use. They followed the path down to a tree-studded ravine, a gentle slope dropping to a creek-bed at its base. It was dry now, but would carry rain down the mountain from afternoon thunderstorms. The opposite incline was almost flat. It reminded Meredith of picnics at Samuel P. Taylor Park in Marin when she was a kid. The ground was covered with generations of oak and bay leaves, trees fallen years ago decaying on their sides, and the heady smell of humus. All that was missing was a picnic table.

The trail faded under the trees. Nick hopped the rocky creek and veered toward the road above. Glancing back at her, his brows drew into a deep 'V' as he processed new information. With his hand, he motioned for her to find cover.

Meredith pulled out the Sig and eased toward the trunk of an ancient oak. Her elbow touched the rough bark.

Something cool and smooth jabbed her shoulder blade. "¡Alto!"

Her spine twisted in a slithering motion. She jabbed the muzzle of the Sig in the ear of a fat, sweaty Mexican policeman. His automatic rifle slid to the ground while Meredith twisted his huge arm behind his back. It was tough to bend the man around—he was stiff, and his bulk got in the way. Meredith's fingers were slippery on his damp skin.

The faintest breath of wind danced in the leafy canopy. Errant rays of sun shot through then were blocked. The effect was like an old silent movie; flashes of light, then dark. A sense of disorientation slipped over Meredith. The image of Rusty Webber's face came into her mind. She replayed the horrible moment when her bullet slammed into his chest. Her heart lurched. She made that decision in a split second, and it had changed her life. Now she faced a similar situation. What would she do?

She stole a quick glance toward Nick.

The cop who held a meaty arm around Nick's neck was almost invisible in his navy blue fatigues. The murky shadows obscured the expression on Nick's face, but the set of his shoulders said it all. She watched the pistol slide from his hand and fall to the forest floor. Why drop his gun? Because these guys are cops, that's why. Her mental fog cleared to an astonishing lucidity.

Another cop emerged from the gloom, spitting orders in rapid-fire Spanish. A half dozen others materialized from behind trees. The men double-timed behind the officer in a crescent formation.

Sunlight dappled the officer's face as he marched up to Meredith. Stopping three feet away, his long face pulled into an angry grimace. Pale stitch marks left over from an old wound tracked down one side of his cheek. His dark eyes challenged her.

"¡Suéltala! ¡Suéltala la arma!" Spit flew from his mouth.

Never give up your gun. The lesson had been hammered into her as early as her training at the academy. However, that example presumed the opponent was a bad guy. These were cops, probably crooked but cops, nevertheless.

A drop of sweat coursed down her back. Her T-shirt stuck to her skin. Rusty Webber's rheumy eyes bolted again through her memory. The blossom of blood as her bullet exploded his chest. Her legs felt like spaghetti.

With one arm, she shoved Fat-boy, her captive, at the officer. She held out the Sig Sauer with the other so she didn't get shot. The two cops did an awkward tango, trying to disentangle themselves as the backup officers tensed, waiting for a command. Scarface, the officer, snatched the pistol away from her fingers. He pushed the other cop away and stretched for Meredith's arm. Sinewy fingers dug into her skin as he forced her to turn around. He shoved her against the rough tree bark. Twisting her arm behind her back, just as she had to Fat-boy, he leaned into her, sharp metal pressing against her bare skin. He hissed into her ear, saying something in Spanish that she couldn't make out.

Maybe she should've kept her gun.

Chapter Eleven

A SWEET FEMALE VOICE ON THE OVERHEAD SPEAKER ANNOUNCED THE next flight to Los Angeles, departing in ten minutes. Meredith pulled out her passport and the boarding pass the officer had given her. Officer Muñoz—Scarface, who turned out to be a lieutenant in the local policía—stood behind her, his posture ramrod straight. His gun remained holstered, but the threat was as obvious as a dark cloud hovering over Nick and Meredith.

Muñoz grabbed Nick's forearm when he turned away from the ticket agent. His voice was low, and he spoke in earnest Spanish. "We don't need your kind here to show us how to do our job. Don't come back, or you will face more serious consequences." Meredith didn't understand all the words but used context to complete the message.

Muñoz pulled their cell phones from a pocket, then handed them over.

Nick yanked his arm away from Muñoz. He snatched the phones from the policeman's hand. Nick shifted his backpack to his other shoulder, stuffed the phones in his pants pocket, and stomped to the gangway.

Muñoz watched as they boarded the plane.

NICK STAYED silent for the first two hours of the flight. Meredith left him alone, even when an afternoon thunderstorm buffeted the plane after take-off. She kept her white knuckles to herself and let him stew. When the flight attendant came around for drink orders, she asked for two coffees. It had crossed her mind to get beer, but something about Nick's bearing made her think that he didn't need alcohol. Caffeine was in order.

When the captain announced their descent to LAX, Meredith sensed her partner shifting in the seat.

With a question in her eyes, she twisted her body to block out the passenger nearby. A wiry, middle-aged Mexican man in a Western shirt with mother-of-pearl buttons napped fitfully beside her.

Nick pressed his lips together. When he spoke, his voice was just above a whisper. "No one pushes me away from my family. No one." He reached for the coffee and drank it down.

"Ah, but Rigo's not even your family." That was irrelevant, but playing the devil's advocate was something Nick often did. Now, it was her turn.

"I'm not talking about Rigo. I'm talking about Angela." He slapped the cardboard cup down.

"I knew that."

Nick squinted at her. "I can't believe you're okay with this."

"Are you kidding? I'm plenty pissed off about what happened. But this is your rodeo, dude. Not mine. You're the one calling the shots." Nick huffed in approval, looking out the window.

The flight attendant came by, picking up trash. Meredith dropped their cups into the plastic bag and then twisted back to Nick. His eyes were darker than she had ever seen, his brown face flushed, and his arms across his chest. He spoke in a curt sentence. "What are you going to do about it?"

A saccharine smile crossed her lips. "Whatever you want, honey."

He ignored her tease. He leaned in, his mouth inches from her face. "We're going back. We're going to find Rigo and bring him home."

She'd expected this. What she didn't know was—how? She waited.

"I haven't gotten it all figured out, but that's what we're going to do. We need to get back across the border."

"They'll have us flagged by Immigration. Flying would be foolish."

"I know. Renting a car and driving would be chancy, too." He looked outside, watching the alternately arid and lush green Southern California landscape grow closer as the plane descended.

A slow smile spread across his tanned face. "I think I have an idea."

NICK WAS tired of talking on the phone. He was sure his ear was swollen. His mental acuity was fading—he was exhausted. The crowds in the airport Starbuck's created havoc with his calls. When people swelled into the coffee bar, the noise threatened his conversation. He struggled to remain civil while he cajoled help from the person on the other end.

Three hours into his phone marathon, Meredith slipped a tall Americano and a smashed ham and cheese Panini under his nose. He drank the coffee when he wasn't talking, peeled the bread off the sandwich, and picked at the ham. Breakfast had been eight hours back, and his stomach was growling. He didn't want to take the time to eat. The sandwich didn't look very appetizing, anyway.

Glancing at his watch, Nick did some mental calculations. Yes, it would work if they made it to Redondo Beach within the hour. "Okay, we'll be there. We're leaving the airport now. Tell him not to sail without us." He punched the "end" button to disconnect.

Nick rose, and Meredith followed. He mashed the sandwich together and stuck it in his mouth as he grabbed his backpack. The coffee went into a trash bin.

Meredith slung the straps of her pack over her shoulders. "Where are we going?"

He chewed as they walked down the wide airport hallway. "We've got to rent a car and get to Redondo Beach as soon as we can. There's a guy—Peters' brother—who's moving some rich guy's sailboat to Acapulco for him, and we're hitching a ride. He'll drop us off in PV."

"Wow—sailing into Mexico." Meredith hustled to keep up. "That's creative. How'd you ever think of that?"

"Last week, Peters told me about his brother's job. I guess you'd call him a contract captain—people pay him to move their sailboats and yachts around for them. Pretty sweet deal. He's got a gig sailing from San Francisco to Acapulco. He'll be at Redondo Beach tonight. We're going to catch him, and I'm going to talk him into taking us to PV." Even as he said it, the whole deal sounded crazy.

"Have you ever sailed, Nick? Are we crewing or paying passengers?" Meredith reached a hand out to slow him down. "Do you know what you're doing?" She'd sailed with her husband and their friends often enough to know there aren't truly any passengers on a sailboat.

"We'll pay him. Well, I will." Nick kept moving, ignoring the pressure of her hand. "I know it will take a long time to get back. There is no other way we can sneak into Mexico without the cops knowing."

Meredith had to skip a few steps to catch up. "How are we going to get to shore? The Mexican Navy patrols the harbors, you know. There'll be a Customs Officer we'll have to dodge in port."

Nick and Meredith had been on the move since sunrise—they were both exhausted. A lot had happened already; seeing Angela again, getting caught by the Mexican cops, then being thrown out of the country. In addition, there was the promise of much more to come—soon. They had a narrow time frame within which to work, and he felt every second of the pressure. "I'll get one of the crew to motor us to the shore. We're not going through Customs."

From the corner of his eye, he saw Meredith shake her head with resignation.

Nick picked up his pace. They didn't have time to waste.

Chapter Twelve

THE FIFTEEN-MINUTE DRIVE DOWN THE PACIFIC COAST HIGHWAY took ten, and was mostly driven with less than four tires on the pavement. By the time they arrived in Redondo Beach, Nick and Meredith were frazzled from relentless traffic and the cruel voice on the GPS. They were ready for a beer, but they were out of time. They left the rental car in the lot at the Redondo Beach Marina, got out, and stretched. While Meredith rubbed the circulation back into her neck, Nick called Captain Gary Peters' cell. He left a message on voicemail with his phone number and Meredith's as well.

Nick used his thumb to end the call. Slipping his cell into his jeans pocket, he crossed his arms and leaned against the car. A late afternoon breeze came in off the ocean, ruffling the collar on his shirt. He squinted against the sun's reflection off the water. Meredith couldn't figure out what he was looking at.

A 737 roared overhead, heading for LAX. Meredith had to wait for the airplane to pass before she spoke. "How long do we have to wait until he gets in?"

The waves lapped against the shallow shoreline. Nick ran his fingers through his hair. "He must be still out there," Nick said. "I left a message to call when he gets in." He rubbed his eyes with his thumb and index finger. "Let's find that deli we passed on the way in and get something to eat."

"Got my vote. Beer, too. A beer would be good. " Meredith's attention swept the scene before her. Redondo Beach was an energetic city. Here at the marina and along the beach, people jogged, walked, bicycled, and skated, even as the sun hovered above the ocean. Tidy buildings landscaped with florid tropical plant life made long shadows in the waning light of the day—an advertisement for Cali. And the weather was perfect. It was still in the mid-eighties, but the marine breeze freshened the air enough to keep her comfortable. She wished she were here on vacation.

"WE'RE NOT TELLING anyone we're coming back." Nick yelled into his phone. "Let the family think what they want. The more who know, the bigger the chances we get caught. The cops won't be so nice next time."

Angela was silent on the other end.

Nick's gut churned with the cardboard panini and a half-digested turkey sandwich. The bay breeze flitted across his brow. He took a swig from his Pacifico. Holding his phone, he saw the open ocean beyond the harbor. He wished by searching the waves he could bring Gary's sailboat in. They'd parked in a lot off Yacht Club Way, facing the ocean, the nose of the car up against the concrete of the breakwater. Still scanning the horizon, he waited for his wife's protest.

Angela said nothing.

Nick stood stiffly at the open car door, his back cramped from the drive and the tension of talking to Angela. "You want me to get Rigo back, don't you?" He pushed her for an answer.

"Yes, but I don't want to endanger anyone else." There was a whiney quality to her voice. When did she start that? It could get on his nerves.

Nick sighed into the cell phone. "Either you want our help or not. It's that simple."

"It isn't simple at all, Nicholas. The policía came to talk to Papa this afternoon. They said they would take him away. We're all worried to death."

"Papa hasn't done anything. There's nothing to worry about." Nick knew this was a lie. Mexico was the land of possibilities. Anything might happen. The local cops had shown their hand. They wouldn't need to show cause to hold Emilio. They could take him and keep him for as long as they liked. Rules aren't even guidelines down here. Angela wasn't stupid. "They're not like U.S. cops, Nicholas."

"Yeah, I know." Nick finished the beer as Meredith's cell phone rang. He watched his partner's face as she answered. With wide eyes, she nodded at Nick and mouthed Gary's name.

"Gotta go, honey. This is the call we've been waiting for."

Dang it.

He slipped and called her 'honey'. An old habit. She hung up before he could apologize.

"WHAT D'YOU mean this won't work? It should be easy." Meredith didn't like what Captain Gary had to say when she heard him. The connection was scratchy. "Look, how long will it take you to get to Redondo Beach? We're waiting for you."

Static all but obliterated his raspy voice. "I'll be…less than an hour."

Meredith snapped her phone shut. "Well, it sounds like he'll be here soon." She glanced toward the ocean as if he would appear ahead of schedule.

"What else did he say?" Nick's face showed strain. The lines under his eyes were deeper than before, his jaw set for the next brutal disappointment.

Meredith lifted her hands, palm up. "About this not working? I couldn't say. The line cut in and out. That's all I heard."

Nick slipped behind the wheel, leaving the car door open. A breeze wafted in, cool in the dusky glow. He dropped his head on the headrest and closed his eyes.

Meredith settled on the berm and passed some time on her phone, catching up on emails. Soon she stood to stretch and looked at her partner. He was asleep. How different he appeared here in this alien environment. His face was relaxed, free from worry. A warm glow seeped through her core. With a start, she realized how attractive he was. Oh crap, she thought. Don't go there.

As the sun shimmered low on the horizon, Meredith pushed Nick's shoulder. "Hey, wake up. I think that may be our man."

Nick shot up in the seat. "Where?"

Meredith pointed to a tanned, thirtyish man with sun-bleached hair in rumpled colorless cargo shorts and a faded University of Michigan T-shirt. He approached the Harbor Master's office. Aside from his rolling gait, there was nothing to suggest he was related to Peters.

"How do you know it's him?"

"I watched his boat cruise in. It seemed about the right type and length, so I hit redial on my phone and called him." She smiled. "He has to check in first. Then he'll be over. I told him where we are and what kind of car we're in. He won't be long."

Nick rubbed his eyes, then rolled out of the car. He propped himself against the sedan to wait, shoulders slumped.

It was ten minutes before Gary sauntered to the car. Pleasantries were exchanged, and Gary steered them to a taco truck parked on the street. "I need a beer, man. I ran out three days ago."

An overweight Hispanic woman stuffed into a silver spandex T-shirt and leggings handed Gary a Modelo as Nick brought the conversation around to business. "You told my partner this idea wouldn't work. Why? What's the problem?"

Gary settled on a concrete planter and took a deep pull on the beer. "First, tell me what you need. The phone connection wasn't so good, and I want to be sure I have all this right before I tell you what you should do."

Nick's lips pressed together as he battled his impatience. "We have to get into Mexico without the Mexican police knowing it. We've been '86'ed out of Puerto Vallarta but that's where I...we need to go."

Gary's chapped lips split with the self-assured smile of a man who had all the answers. "Then you better not go." He tipped the bottle back, drained it, then pitched it in a garbage can.

Nick fought the urge to grab Gary by the neck to make him listen. He formed his rebuttal. "The thing is, if we don't get back, it may cost my brother-in-law his life."

The boat captain sat up, shedding his arrogant slouch. "A cartel?"

"Probably, but we don't know for sure. He's been kidnapped."

White teeth flashed against Gary's tanned face. "Oh, that's a problem all right. But most folks just pay the ransom and get the guy back. See? It's simple."

Meredith spoke up. "No, it's not. It's complicated."

Nick's impatient hand interrupted Gary's retort. "It doesn't matter." His eyes met Gary's and held the gaze. "We're going back to Mexico."

Gary shrugged away his argument. "What's your time frame?"

"ASAP," Nick said while Meredith bought another Modelo and shoved it at Gary. The captain smiled at her foresight, then took a second look at her. The beginnings of his coy smile were shattered with Nick's shout, "Dude, the longer you take coming on to my partner, the less chance we have of getting this job done."

Gary rolled his eyes. He gave Meredith another long look. "All right. First, your time frame won't work. In this boat, it takes eight or nine days to get from Acapulco to PV."

"Damn, that's too long. Our time frame is two days or less." Those two days would be filled with activity. After they get ashore, no time to sleep or eat. After the initial blow, the plan he'd dreamed up would have to be executed quickly. Once the cops and the gangsters got wind they were back, the whole countryside would be crawling with hostiles. Rigo wouldn't stand a chance.

Gary kept talking. "Then, you have to figure out how you're going to get to shore in PV, without the authorities finding out."

"That's just one of our problems."

"We planned on taking a dinghy or raft in," Meredith offered.

"If you could get a crewmember to bring you in, the dinghy wouldn't be left behind. Of course, you'd have to figure your own way out, afterward." Gary cocked his head. "You can't fly into another city, why?"

"We assumed Mexico has a computer system logging passports coming into the country."

Gary raised his bottle in a toast. "You mean a master computer like the DMV or US Customs?" He took a sip, then belched with gusto. "Dunno. I could be wrong, but normally the left hand doesn't know what the right hand is doing."

Meredith looked at Nick. "What are you thinking?"

Nick shoved his fists into his pants pockets, trying to contain his excitement. "What if we fly to an airport closer to PV, then charter a boat to bring us up?" He looked at Gary. "What's the closest airport to PV? Mazatlán?"

Meredith answered, "I don't know how close..."

"I do," Gary interrupted. "Mazatlán will work, and I may have just what you're looking for. I have a buddy who's in Mazatlán right now picking up a boat; taking it to Acapulco for some Seattle dotcom millionaire. Maybe I can talk him into giving you a ride. You'd have to pay, though." Gary's watery eyes sparkled with the thought. "Depending on the water, you could make it from there to PV in 24 hours, if you traveled all night." A crooked smile revealed small, even teeth. "That's where the extra money comes in. He'll have to stay awake for the whole time."

Nick pushed himself up to Gary's sunburned nose. "Call him." Gary hesitated as he absorbed the force of Nick's reaction.

Nick's voice lowered. "I said, call him." It was as close to Nick losing his temper, that Meredith had ever seen. He was pushing too hard—himself and everyone around him.

Gary swallowed and murmured a "yeah, okay." He curled his beer into the crook of his elbow while he punched numbers into his phone.

Chapter Thirteen

MEREDITH STOWED HER PACK IN AN UPPER LOCKER AND TESTED THE mattress in the tiny cabin. Thin, but it will do, she thought. She was tired and keyed up at the same time. In unfamiliar waters, both metaphorically and in reality. She felt off balance, like the boat was already rocking. Her life had been spent following the rules. However, the past year had thrown her into a whirlpool of doubt and contradictions. She was tired of feeling that she was barely keeping her head above water. She wanted to move on. With a surge of resolve, she decided that when she got home, she needed to focus on re-building her life.

Now, she had to finish this. There was too much unsettled about this trip, and it was dragging her down. Wanting to have a plan in place, and knowing there wasn't, made her a little crazy. Just like at home, she was better with a schedule. Enough of that crap, she thought. She had to talk to Nick, get a plan hammered out.

Nick's voice floated down from the deck. She heard him summarize what Gary had told them. "He said, for some extra incentive, he'll take us to a beach close to Bucerias at night."

The captain's reply drifted away with the breeze. Meredith

couldn't decipher anything for a moment, but from Nick's next sentence, she assumed he had agreed. "A hundred?"

Meredith shrugged into shorts and a clean T-shirt, then mounted the steps to what she considered the living room. She leaned on a counter, waiting, while the two men stood on the back deck. A cigarette hung from the captain's lips.

Captain Morris, Gary had told them, had solid nautical skills. He sailed anything. Chartering was out of the question because he was an utter failure at schmoozing with the public. "Captain Mo is your man. You better call him Captain Morris." Gary continued, "Mo rents himself out as a contractor to move ships around up and down the coast. He makes good money, and most of the time, he solos. That suits him just fine. Not me, man. It'd drive me nuts to…" Gary had blathered on, filled with beer and self-absorption.

He'd passed on cell numbers for them to arrange to meet the next day. Nick drove them back to LAX, where they returned the rental car. After sleeping in terminal chairs for four hours, they caught an early flight to Phoenix, figuring only flights from LAX would be watched. They landed in Mazatlán shortly before 6 A.M.

Again, the humid air assailed Meredith when the plane door opened. She and Nick descended to the tarmac beneath a warming sun. She thought she smelled the ocean, but dismissed it when the odor of aeronautical fuel overwhelmed her.

She prayed that Gary was right about Mexican customs. The thought of being arrested by the Mexican Police again was more than humiliating. It could mean their jobs back home. She held her breath as the automatic doors to the terminal swung open. Air conditioning brought instant relief from the heat.

Nick kept moving but slowed to take in the airport's security arrangements. As before, Meredith and Nick were pushed through with little notice. At a podium-type desk, a chubby Customs officer glanced over Meredith's passport, then handed it back to her. No computer terminal close by, she noted. She moved on. Nick stood in front of the officer as he read the stamps on his document. His attention lingered for a moment, then he slapped the passport shut and pushed it back to Nick.

Meredith exhaled. Nick caught up with her, and they strode through the airport. They met with Captain Morris just after nine A.M. on board the Mary Elisabeth.

Morris, a lanky, square-shouldered sailor deep in his middle years, had an unruly patch of salt and pepper hair above a sun-bleached Hawaiian shirt and frayed Dockers shorts. A ring of cigarette smoke formed a contrary halo above his head.

The boat was an Offshore 48-cabin cruiser. To Meredith, it was just a means to an end. She had no appreciation for power boats. She had gotten a little excited when Nick first mentioned sailing, but this cruiser would be noisy and smelly. She forced herself to study it, anyway: A white fiberglass cabin sat in the middle of a well-maintained teak deck. Above the cabin, an open flying bridge was shaded by a nautical blue Bimini top with Eisenglass windows rolled up and secured. She guessed it was forty-eight feet long, with a deep "V" hull. Two staterooms sat at either end, separated by a salon (that's what Captain Morris called the living room). A lower helm sat in the corner. The more she studied the Mary Elisabeth, the more she liked her. The boat was trim and neat: a mature motor yacht, but a beauty. The brass was polished to a high shine, the teak and other wood was oiled or varathaned to be neatly sealed against the salt water.

There were plenty of places to hide if needed.

"Get us as close to Bucerias as possible. You drop us at a beach, then you're back to your boat, and you've never seen us."

Morris' dark eyes nestled in tanned creases in a permanent squint against the sun, watching Nick. He pulled the cigarette from his lips with a thumb and index finger while his other hand stuffed the cash in his pocket. "All right." He tugged on a ball cap, dipping the bill low over his eyes. "Sleep where you want, I'll be up. Any trouble, you both hide in the engine room. It should take us about twenty to twenty-two hours. That should put us there between sunrise and noon tomorrow. Unless you want to wait until dark, I'll take you in then."

"Okay, let's go." Nick smiled.

"Oh, and don't help me unless I ask for it." Morris hopped the four steps to the bridge and disappeared.

Nick's smile vanished.

Chapter Fourteen

WHILE MORRIS FIRED UP THE NOISY DUAL ENGINES, MEREDITH walked out to the deck. "Are you sure about this?" She whispered. "This guy looks like he would slit our throats without a second thought."

"He's all we have." Nick sat on the railing. "We'll take turns sleeping. We're going to need rest, and we won't get it once we make Bucerias. I want to do our planning with a few hours' sleep under our belts."

Meredith winced against the sun on the water. "You want to go first?"

"Nah, I'm too wired. You go."

Meredith rolled over on the thin mattress, sighing. Tired as she was, she couldn't calm her mind enough to find sleep.

The wave action in the bow rattled her teeth. She wondered if Morris angled the boat to hit the waves this way on purpose. Perfect, she thought as she swung her feet to the floor. A clock wedged into a railed shelf told her she had slept—almost three hours.

In the tiny bathroom, the pump throbbed and vibrated as water trickled from the spigot. Meredith splashed her face and rubbed her eyes. Time to check topside.

Morris was slumped in his cushy seat at the wheel in the flying bridge. All but the front windows had been unrolled and snapped closed to reduce the wind. He gripped a Pepsi in one hand, a cigarette in the other. One leg folded under him. He looked at the ocean and the breeze caught his cigarette smoke feathering it past her.

With a lazy glance, he eyed Meredith. He didn't say anything.

Neither did she. The man was dead cool. A good quality for a contract captain, or maybe a smuggler. She looked around for Nick until Morris pointed to the bow outside.

Backing away, she moved gingerly down the narrow side deck. She hadn't yet accustomed herself to walking with the pitch of the boat. She found Nick up front, sitting comfortably against a teak-paneled window frame, relaxing behind his sunglasses against the glare of the gleaming sun on the ocean. His hair was splayed back from the warm wind. Again, it struck her how attractive he was. In another world, she could've easily fallen for him.

Morris was hauling ass, but Nick didn't seem to care. For the first time since yesterday, Nick looked relaxed. Meredith reached out and touched his shoulder. He started, reflexes in motion before his brain engaged. He grabbed her forearm with one hand and lunged at her throat with the other. His fingers curled around her neck before her yelling got through to him. He'd been asleep.

Nick dropped back to the deck, pushing up his sunglasses to squint at Meredith. Exhaling in relief, he shook his head. Meredith gulped at her close call, she saw the pulse pounding in Nick's neck.

She slid down beside him.

"You fell asleep," she shouted over the wind.

He answered with a rueful half-smile.

"Let's talk about what we're going to do." She yelled again.

Nick pursed his lips, pushing himself off the deck. He jutted his chin toward the cabin.

INSIDE THE SALON, they settled next to each other on a brown leather sofa. The doors stood open, but Meredith was confident the breeze would snatch their words away. She still didn't trust Morris. "Tell me what you have planned for when we get onshore."

Nick's elbows rested on his knees. "I've been thinking we might see if we can find Rigo's girlfriend. She might know something about this."

"We don't even know her name." Meredith shook her head.

"We'll have to find it. She might be able to help. What if she's connected to the kidnapping? Rigo kept her under wraps, right? Why? Suppose she was married, with no plans to divorce, and he was hiding their affair."

Meredith considered this. "Angela could tell you whose divorce he was working on last. Doesn't she work in his office?"

"Yeah. That's a good idea. We'll try to find this woman, see if she can tell us anything. The general plan for now is to find him, stage a diversion, free him, then get away clean, all without guns."

An errant gust of wind whipped Meredith's long hair across her face. She studied her partner to see if he was joking. "No guns?"

"I don't want to take a chance on hooking up with any of the idiots who sell them. I don't trust Oswaldo or Javier, either. I'd bet a beer that one of them tipped off the policía."

"What about Emilio?"

"Emilio doesn't know anything about guns."

Meredith's chest churned with frustration. She wondered if it was time to tell him. She couldn't imagine doing all this for a person who didn't give a rat's ass about him. Yes, it was time.

"Nick, why are you so loyal?" She tried to ease into it. "I don't understand."

"It's what you do for your family." He shrugged, elbows still on his knees.

"What if Angela doesn't want to be your family anymore?" She held her breath.

Nick's dark eyes flashed anger, then confusion. Then, hurt. "Something on your mind?"

She leaned toward him until their knees touched. Her voice was just above a whisper. "What if she doesn't love you anymore?"

They were as far from their comfort zone—Santa Rosa, the VCI office, their badges—as they might ever be. The yacht bucked forward, impatient against the great power of the Pacific. The engine droned. Nick's voice was low, and Meredith struggled to hear him over the noise. His eyes narrowed. "What are you thinking?"

She didn't like the suspicion in his voice. It put her off that he should be mistrustful of her. She re-grouped and went back to business. "I'm not guessing. It's what I saw."

"Tell me."

"There was a look on Angela's face when she saw Javier." She rushed on; afraid he might not believe in her instincts. "It was more than, 'I'm glad you're here'. It said there was something between them." She searched his face and found what she expected. Hurt and anger fought for dominance.

To himself, he mumbled, "It was just a look."

"A woman has intuition about this kind of thing, not that it took much. Besides, you're the one who says to trust my gut."

Nick's lips pressed together, a closed door. He covered his face with his hands.

Her heart lurched for him. God, the grief he must be going through. She remembered feeling the same way when she found out about her husband Richard's infidelity. Her memory jumped to the moment Nick sat in her living room and told her Richard was dead. Nick had put his arm around her and offered what little comfort she was willing to receive. His support helped her through those earliest painful days of her widowhood. She wanted to offer the same solace now. She reached out, one arm around his shoulders, the other on his knee. There was nothing more to say, so Meredith just kept hold.

Nick twisted toward her, reaching around her shoulder to complete the embrace. He laid his head alongside hers. She heard his breathing quicken like…she thought he might cry.

He didn't. He leaned back and searched her face. Meredith wasn't sure what he was looking for, but from the depths of her soul, she felt a pang of unmistakable excitement. An ache for something long absent throbbed through her. She closed her eyes.

Nick's fingers gently traced her jaw line, then up to her lips. Leaning toward her, he brushed them softly with his own. She turned into him, her lips meeting his with a passion so fierce, she hadn't known she possessed it. Both arms slipped around his shoulders, pulling him to her chest.

His lips pressed on hers—soft, moist, at first—then with growing pressure, matching her mounting urgency. She didn't think. All she did was feel—feel the excitement she hadn't ever remembered, the need she had denied.

The smell of him: two days without a shower stripped him of any artifice. His skin held the masculine scent of sweat from hiking up to El Rancho and getting busted; then sitting in an airport for way too many hours with just a washbasin for clean-up. Yet, it wasn't unpleasant, it was just Nick. Her fingers splayed across the back of his head and through his hair, massaging him closer to her.

He groaned. It was impossible for her to know why. Was it desire? Or the realization of the line he had crossed? Regret or satisfaction?

"¡Alta, alta!" A tinny voice from a loudspeaker blared from behind them.

They fell apart like teenagers caught by their parents.

A gray, torpedo-shaped gunboat loaded with four heavily armed men cut through the waves behind the Mary Elisabeth, 100 yards off the starboard side.

Morris shouted, "Fuck."

Chapter Fifteen

THEY JUMPED TO THEIR FEET, THE TENDER MOMENT DROPPED LIKE A stone.

Morris peered into the salon and yelled over the slowing diesel motors, "Get down! Get into the engine room, like I showed you. They won't search us."

They slid to the carpet, crawling to the center of the room. Keeping low, Nick pulled open the hatch while Meredith shifted to slide down the ladder. When they were both below with the door secured, Meredith surveyed the small fiberglass-encased room. Everything was sparkling clean, smelling of oiled aluminum motor parts mixed with a bit of seawater. At twelve-feet long, four-feet tall, with a three-foot wide walkway, it was shaped like a coffin. They moved on their hands and knees. She led them behind the engine, toward the back of the boat, where they had room to sit.

Even at idle, the noise from the twin motors gave Meredith a headache. Talking was impossible, much less hearing any warning or the 'all clear' from outside. She resigned herself to sitting until the captain got rid of the Mexican Navy. Two feet away, Nick leaned against an interior wall; his head tipped back, his eyes glazed.

Meredith massaged her temples, her mind filled with confusion. What just happened? What almost happened? Nick touched her face, her lips. He kissed her, and she responded. At least her body did. What would have happened had the Mexican Navy not shot the moment to hell?

Mexican Navy. Deal with the most immediate threat. What happens if one of those swabbies with bandoliers searches the engine room? Should she fight? No, no gun. God, she felt naked without it. If it was left up to her, she'd walk out of the engine room, her hands up, and buy a one-way ticket to Santa Rosa. However, it wasn't up to her. She was in it with her partner, no matter what. No matter how futile.

Nick hadn't moved. What did he see in Angela? She painted herself to Nick as a needy woman but hid things, important things, from him to get her way. She had him wrapped around her manipulating little finger. Did he know that?

A relationship with a male partner's spouse was a delicate thing. Angela had never trusted Meredith because of her closeness with Nick. His life depended on Meredith; he had to trust her to be able to do his job. Meredith knew things about Nick that his wife never would—work things, but still, information Angela would never be able to get. Meredith knew Richard had the same reservations about Nick when he was her trainer. Because Nick was who he was, Angela never made an issue of it. Meredith tried to be as friendly as possible without being patronizing, but she never got past Angela's barriers. It didn't matter; Meredith had little in common with her.

Meredith thought about how different she and Angela were. She disliked Nick's wife, more so now that she had shown herself so selfish as to hurt the man she married. Was this who he wanted?

Rigo spat out the dried-up corn tortilla. He was hungry all right, but this was like eating shoe leather. No beans, rice, or meat. What the hell?

The door flew open, slammed against the wall, and bounced back off the hulk of a man who opened it. He stood on the threshold with eyes that didn't move, but said they understood everything. An AK47 rested comfortably in his hands, the wooden stock a dull gleam in the afternoon sunlight. A crescent-shaped clip hung below the rifle, adding ominous fuel to Rigo's fears. Several more clips hung on the man's belt.

In spite of his earlier certainty that he could extricate himself from this predicament, a jolt of fear shook him. What if his ace in the hole failed him? He shook his head to chase away the treacherous thoughts.

The guard grunted and waved the butt of the rifle toward him. Unsure of the man's message, Rigo rolled onto his hip and then to his knees. He wobbled into position, leaning forward with his ankles straining against the rough jute that bound them. With his hands still snugly bound, he pushed off, straightened, and stood. It was degrading as hell, and it made him angry all over again. He must speak to their leader to straighten out this mess.

The guard stepped inside the room, smirking. He slung the rifle over a shoulder and then reached behind, pulling out a machete. He twisted its handle, inspecting the blade's edge, then squinted at Rigo. The steel caught the afternoon rays of sun shining through the open door. As he sauntered toward Rigo, the guard's smile said he was a man who enjoyed wielding his weapons, enjoyed hurting living things.

For the first time, it occurred to Rigo that he might die. A prayer erupted from his lips, a plea from a man who had not believed in God or anything except himself for years. A prayer. He didn't know the words, couldn't remember them. His mind burst forth with appeals made up of emotion. He felt the involuntary release of his bladder and the warmth of his own piss running down his legs.

The guard raised his arm clutching the machete. It was a menace that defied Rigo's version of reality. What would the cutting edge take? His face, his heart, his hands? Rigo raised his arms to ward off the blow. He felt the whisper of the blade as it sliced through the dry air—to his feet, to the jute that hobbled his ankles together and past —an inch into the dirt.

With a smile that telegraphed satisfaction at the terror he had caused, the guard yanked the blade from the earth. Rigo collapsed to the ground.

The guard kicked Rigo's knee with less mercy than he had shown a moment ago. "Get up. The boss wants to see you."

Chapter Sixteen

EL RANCHO FORMED A U-SHAPE AROUND AN ABANDONED PATIO. Rubble from the disintegrating walls spilled across the terracotta tile floor. Picking his way around the debris, Rigo followed the guard from the room he'd been held in. Crumbling adobe walls, an aged tiled roof with the fading sunlight that shone through to long forsaken gardens. Dust, spider webs, and debris were permanent tenants of this house. Most of the windows were broken. Doors were missing or hanging by a hinge.

In a stark contrast, the opposite wing was clean, tidy, and in good repair. Although not painted—no overt sign of occupancy—Rigo had the impression these rooms were being used on a regular basis.

The guard turned, entering a hall, then stopped. He tapped on a surprisingly sturdy interior door. Although still shaken from the display with the machete, Rigo felt stirrings of hopefulness. Maybe now he could speak to the leader and reason with him. Rigo was sure he could make the man see his point of view.

A fortyish man with dyed black curls so greasy his hair looked wet, stood behind a table, smoking a cigarette. He wore a yellow Polo shirt and pressed khaki slacks. His posture said he was an important man and was to be treated as such. Light from the camp lantern played across the walls creating a sinister tableau of evil. Its monstrous shadow sent a chill down Rigo's back.

The guard pushed Rigo inside and slammed the door.

"Mr. Borrego." The man spoke. "I am Miguel Vega." A curt nod of acknowledgment made Rigo wonder at the man's game. His tone sounded like this was a business meeting. All right, Rigo thought. He'd play along.

A polite nod in return. "Mr. Vega."

Vega crushed out his cigarette in an ashtray. "Mr. Borrego, I am a businessman. I am quite successful because I possess a bullshit meter that is calibrated daily. Do you understand me?"

Rigo didn't understand at all, but he nodded furiously anyway.

"Mr. Borrego, you have something that I want. While I am open to some negotiation, there isn't much room for compromise."

Rigo's legs felt wobbly again. He shifted from one foot to the other, wondering where this was going. "Yes? What could I have that you want, sir?"

When Vega reached into his pocket, Rigo held his breath. Certainly, if Vega wanted to kill him, he would have already done so. Rigo exhaled as Vega pulled out a wallet. He flipped it open, picked out a small photo, and pushed it across the table.

"This is my wife, Silvia. I believe you are acquainted with her."

The words on Rigo's lips stumbled, refusing to come out coherently. Silvia? His Silvia? Oh no! What had he gotten himself into?

"You are, I believe, her divorce attorney?"

Rigo found enough volume to grunt, "Technically, yes, sir."

Vega paused, taking time to light another cigarette. "I assure you that Silvia had no intention of divorcing me. In fact, she will not be proceeding any further." Vega's words were civil, but his tone cut through to Rigo's bones. Had?

The force of his recklessness slammed him. His mind scrambled to work out the consequences of his actions. What a fool he was. No wonder she had been so secretive. He had let himself believe that she was mysterious to further her appeal. What a fool. Could he deny it? Was it too late for that?

"My profuse apologies to you, sir. I didn't know she was married to you." Again, the words stumbled from his lips. Even to his own ears, he didn't sound convincing—though it was true. He was in trouble.

Vega's silence told him what he needed to know. The man didn't offer anything. He remained standing, smoke curling above his head like a tiny volcano. Rigo wondered why he was still alive.

"During your rendezvous together, did Silvia ever talk about me?" Jabbing the cigarette out, he eyed Rigo with an intent squint.

There was one answer. "No, sir. She never spoke of her husband."

Vega's fist pounded the table. "Do I look that stupid?" He leaned in. "What about her declaration to the court, financial statements and such?"

Rigo trembled. "She hadn't given me the papers yet. She..." He swallowed, hoping to create enough saliva so his dry lips wouldn't catch on his teeth. "She kept putting me off when I asked her for them." He hated being afraid like this, hated that it was so obvious to Vega. Rigo had to wonder again, why was he still alive?

Vega strolled around the table to stand next to Rigo. "She never told you about my business? People I know?" His voice was smooth as a politician's, but there was such a deep intensity to his questions.

Looking up at Vega put a kink in Rigo's neck. He tried to look him in the eye but couldn't. She had talked about her husband. She had told him things that made him believe he worked within the judicial system. She told him about magistrates, contracts, money. He hadn't paid much attention because he thought she was just a bitter woman—they all were by the time they saw him. It was common to hear preposterous accusations against their husbands. What had she said?

Judges, bonus money... Silvia told him about her brother passing cash to judges in Michoacán for...what was it? He couldn't remember what, but it took little imagination to fill in the blanks. Rigo recalled a news account of an upcoming trial for several La Familia cartel lieutenants in Morelia. Silvia was upset because they were family. One night, she'd handed him a straw cigarette box that contained a journal. She'd told him she wanted to keep it from Vega. It had something to do with that.

Now it made sense. The dates, times, peso amounts, and locations. Clearly, it was something different than what he first believed it was: a wayward wife's records of her husband's scandalous affairs. He'd been so stupid, but there was nothing to reference it to. How did he know she was married to Vega? Silvia hadn't given her husband's surname. And how many Miguels were there in Mexico?

How stupid he'd been. Vega wanted the book. Why not give it to him? No, now he realized he was a dead man in any scenario. The book was in the house. The last thing he wanted was to endanger his beloved family—especially Angela, who had endured so much already. No, he didn't want to die, but for his family and Silvia—he would keep his secret.

Rigo bent his head, trying to keep the tears from breaching. What about his amor? Daring to look at Vega again, he asked, "What about Silvia?" He couldn't bring himself to use the words he was thinking.

Rigo felt Vega's eyes boring into him. "Silvia won't be telling anyone anything." The meaning was clear.

Rigo's heart broke. Never to smell the musk of her hair, touch her pale skin, kiss her lips. With the loss of his love, he couldn't live any longer. Not that he would. Soon, he would be joining her in heaven.

"You, however, will not be so lucky as to die quickly as she did. You have benefitted from the busyness of my schedule. This is the first opportunity I've had to deal with you. You won't have any more reprieves." Vega stared into Rigo's eyes, like he pried inside his soul. "Tell me everything she told you. Your choices are to cooperate and find a swift, merciful death. Or you can make your agony last. I know which one I would choose." Rigo couldn't speak.

Mistaking his captive's silence, Vega gave a sharp whistle. The guard opened the door, smiling, as if the promise of Rigo's pain gave him infinite delight.

Forget about the 'ace in the hole', Rigo thought. Nothing would get him out of this.

Chapter Seventeen

MORRIS OPENED THE ENGINE ROOM DOOR AND SHOUTED, "YOU CAN come out now." The captain turned and stepped up the ladder to the helm.

Nick stood, pausing for Meredith to lead them out. The waiting together had stretched Meredith's nerves taut, a violin string out of pitch. They walked back to the cabin without speaking.

Once in the salon, Nick paused at the door to the bathroom. "That wasn't supposed to happen." His voice didn't drop at the end of his sentence to indicate finality. Coffee-colored eyes shifted from side to side as if he was searching for the right words to explain. Nothing seemed to come, and the silence hung between them.

Nick stepped into the head and closed the door.

Wondering at her own reaction, Meredith dropped to the sofa. She rubbed her eyes with her fingers. His denial swirled around her, mixing with her own feelings. He was right—it wasn't supposed to happen. Partners sometimes fell into this trap, but it never worked out. You couldn't work this job and worry about the safety of your partner/lover. Too distracting. Too easy for priorities to get skewed.

It didn't matter; she sat up with her shoulders back. Nothing more could happen, for either of their sakes.

The bathroom door swung open. Nick came out, eyes averted. He was embarrassed, she thought. Then, before she could stop it, she said, "Nick, what we did isn't the worst thing that could happen."

Nick gazed at her for a moment, his face a mask. "We have to do this thing now." Then he walked past her and hopped the stairs to the deck.

Meredith followed, feeling an uncharacteristic reluctance to face him. See? It's starting already. Still, she had to nail down what they were going to do once they got to land.

A warm breeze whipped her hair into a frenzied assault on her face. Tucking it back into her ponytail, she stood next to Nick without looking at him. Over the wind, she shouted, "Do we have to talk to Angela to find out Rigo's girlfriend's name?"

Meredith felt his sigh rather than heard it. She walked after him into the salon, grabbing an apple from a fruit basket. Nick avoided the sofa, falling into a brown leather club chair. Rubbing his eyes, he waited for her to sit. She slid into the chair next to him. "I still think the best link to Rigo is the girlfriend," Nick said. "We need to find her."

"Why?" She was beginning to think there was another option they hadn't thought about. "What if we can't find her or if we do and she won't talk? What about El Rancho?" Meredith bit into the yellow apple. It was tart and sweet at the same time. A little like her partner. "You think because the crooked cops showed up there, that Rigo isn't in some back room? Seems to me they were pretty anxious to keep us out of there. Why don't we backtrack and check it out first?"

Nick's lips pressed into a single line as he considered her idea.

"I mean, think about it." She had other important points to hammer through his thick Mexican skull. "This could be a pointless chase. We're looking for a woman whose name we don't know. We don't know what she looks like. If we have to go to the nightclub in Sayulita dressed like this, how far do you think we're going to get? Who's going to talk to us?"

"We can buy clothes for Sayulita." Nick rested his elbows on his knees. "I have enough cash for that. We'd have to rent a car or taxi to get there."

"Shopping and car rentals all increase our visibility to the cops."
His mouth twisted with frustration as he agreed. "Damn."

"So we're settled on another hike to El Rancho?"

"I guess. We need to stay under the radar."

She watched his profile: his drooping eyelids, the strong nose, his defined lips, and stubborn jaw. He was good at keeping his emotions under control. There were times he cut loose, and Meredith had been one of the privileged few to witness it. Sometimes, she saw through his façade. She couldn't now, but it was easy to guess what he would be thinking.

She hated to, but she had to ask. "Are you going to contact Angela?"

Nick sat back. "I'm thinking about it."

"Isn't there someone else to talk to?"

"No one I can trust. Emilio and Liliana don't know anything. Can't trust Oswaldo. I'm sure he had something to do with the fiasco at El Rancho. Javier is doubtful. That leaves us with Angela. But I'll wait until we check out El Rancho."

Meredith took a last bite of the apple. "I guess we have a plan, then." She stood and pitched the core into a garbage can.

"I'm going to try to sleep. You should, too." Nick looked away.

"I already tried. I'm going to stay up for a while and keep an eye on our courageous captain." Meredith folded a director's chair and carried it to the back deck. Nick trailed after her. "It's cooler here anyway."

He nodded, then paused as if he was going to say something. He turned and walked into the cabin.

Meredith settled into the canvas chair and kicked her feet up onto the railing. Glancing sideways, she saw Captain Morris silhouetted against the green glow from the dashboard. She didn't like him. She didn't trust anyone these days—even Nick was reacting with questionable sense. It was more than being away from home—being in a foreign country. All this was unfamiliar to her. This wasn't a Sandals vacation. It was Mexico—gritty, impoverished, crime-ridden Mexico. Still, something stirred in her chest at the sight of the last rays of the sun firing orange and red on the water. A wet breeze caressed her bare arms. She understood how this country got under a person's skin. It was the land of extremes—a kind people, gentle and guileless like Emilio, or devious and violent like Oswaldo. The weather—hot, humid days refreshed with turbulent afternoon rains, a Wal-Mart in the same block as a centuries-old cathedral. Then there was the land itself—barren desert scrub, minutes away from lush tropical jungle and inviting sandy beaches.

The boat slowed almost imperceptibly and Meredith's eyes blinked open. The night was ablaze with stars. The moon was almost full in the southern sky. Any place else, and she would have let herself indulge in the magic. It was a captivating scene. The coast was a ghostly profile in the distance, and she saw three small islands off to the starboard. A quiet giggle at her use of nautical language made her think that maybe she might come back here someday. Maybe she'd learn to sail.

Again, the voice of the engine deepened, slowing. She hadn't realized that she'd internalized the engine sounds so efficiently. That was what had awakened her.

She rubbed the sleep out of her eyes, then glanced at her cell for the time. Almost midnight. Stumbling up the ladder to the flying bridge, she greeted the captain. He sat at the wheel, a cigarette dangling from his lips, looking a little like Humphrey Bogart.

"You get some sleep?" His smoke bobbed up and down as he spoke.

"Yeah. I guess Nick is still out." Morris nodded.

"Are we slowing down?" She studied the sea ahead, looking for a reason for caution.

"We headed west for about five miles when we came out of Mazatlán to avoid some islands. Once we turned downwind, the sun set, the moon rose, and the winds calmed, but a nasty 6-8-foot southwest swell is keeping the seas a little rough."

Meredith took a 360-degree turn and saw nothing that she needed to worry about. "It looks like you've got it under control."

The bow dipped deep into a trough, then slammed into a heavy swell. Meredith's stomach flipped, and her teeth clattered together.

"You feel like making a pot of coffee? The stuff's in the galley."

Coffee sounded good. "You haven't had my coffee, or you wouldn't be making that suggestion."

"All right. You want to take the helm?"

A shiver of excitement snaked down her spine. "Yes. That would be awesome." Her fingers curled around the aluminum wheel. She let herself feel the heft of the boat slicing through the waves. "Just go straight?" Before he answered, she wondered how to gauge "straight." At his nod, another thought popped into her mind. "I can't get us in any trouble, can I?"

Morris let a smile escape. "Nah, I won't be gone that long. Use the compass here. Keep it at south-southeast. That's how to stay straight."

Meredith was smiling when the captain returned. A feeling of freedom blew across her face. She felt as if she was flying. The yacht liberated from her earthly limitations and worries. The deep throb of the engine resonated through her as she steered the boat over the waves. The spike of exhilaration surprised her. She'd never known such raw power. "I could get hooked on this."

A rueful grin spread across Morris' face as he took over. "Coffee's brewing now. Be ready in a few minutes."

Meredith leaned against the fiberglass dashboard. "How close are we?"

"About six hours." Morris glanced at his watch. "We should be on the lee side of Punta Mita before seven A.M. We made good time."

"Where the hell is the 'lee side'?" Nick stood at the top of the ladder, rubbing his eyes.

"The side of land without wind." Morris kept his attention on the water.

Nick ignored the captain's tone. "You'll take us in on the motor boat?"

Morris nodded. "I'll get you in."

Chapter Eighteen

ANGELA BORREGO REYES SHIFTED THE GROCERIES FROM ONE ARM TO the other while fumbling for her house key. She could have banged on the door to have her mother open it, but the key seemed much easier. This way, she would slip into the kitchen, put away the food, and then face her parents.

Walking the last block home, she savored the few moments of quiet before opening the door to the doubt and anxiety that would swallow her yet again. The day was warm enough to bake bread in a mailbox, almost the same temperature outside as her own insides. A light breeze drifted in over the two blocks of homes that separated her from the beach, but it offered little relief. Her tank top kept her as cool as decency permitted. She was glad she'd worn her shorts— light yellow linen—her favorites. She needed pockets for her phone, keys, and cash. She hadn't felt like dragging a huge purse with her.

She strolled home, lost in the languorous daydream of having another child. What had she calculated? By February, she would be holding a baby in her arms—but this time, the baby was Javier's. She felt the life inside her growing. At three months, the baby had basic facial features, arms, and legs, while the toes and neck had just begun to develop.

It was time to tell Javier, then her parents. All hell would break loose once more. Her father would tell her she had sinned against her husband; her mother would be thrilled at the prospect of another grandchild. And Javier? How would he react? He told her he loved her, said he wanted to marry her. He should be happy, but one never knew.

Telling Nick was a problem for a million reasons. She didn't want him to know until after he found Rigo, maybe not even then.

Her key dangled in the lock as the front door swung open. Stepping inside, her ear caught odd thumping noises upstairs. Dumping the groceries on the kitchen counter, she walked into the living room. She held her breath as she took in the sight.

Her mother and father were gagged and tied to their chairs in the dining room, near the tipped-over table. Sofa pillows were on the floor, cut open, with the cotton stuffing shredded. Books were dumped from the shelves, and paintings had been pulled off the walls and sliced open.

At her mother's wide-eyed stare, Angela glanced over her shoulder. A burly man with coarse Indian features and thick spiked hair descended the stairs with little agility. As he trotted towards her through the trashed room, Angela's feet rooted to the floor. A numbing shock spread through her. He was coming after her.

Nick? Where is Nick? She reached into her pocket, pulling out the phone. Pushing the icons to call her husband, she slid the cell to the coffee table. Then, too late, Angela tried to run. An iron grasp took hold of her arm and threw her to the floor. A thousand terrors sprinted through her mind. Rape? Oh my God, my child. Please don't hurt my baby.

Hands the size of steering wheels curled around her arms, lifting her like she was a small child.

"Where is it?" His peasant-accented syllables assaulted her. The ugly brown face was inches from hers. "Where did you hide it?" She twisted in his grip, but her effort was wasted.

"I don't know what you're talking about." She spat out her answer.

He pushed her into a chair, drew a pistol, and leaned into her on one arm. The gun barrel met her cheekbone. The sharp blow stunned her. She was trapped. She turned her head away from his foul breath.

"I don't know anything."

"I'll shoot you." He whispered. She tried to formulate words that would persuade him to free her, but nothing came out.

The shot overwhelmed her. The impact of the blast sucked all the air out of the room, the noise causing momentary deafness. Searing pain pierced Angela's left triceps. The shock was physical as well as emotional. Blood oozed from her arm, like spilled red paint. Looking away, she met the fierce expression of the man who shot her. "Bastard!"

"Where is it?" He shoved the hot barrel next to her nose. Cordite and spent powder cut into her sinuses. "I can't tell you what I don't know," she cried. Her chest heaved, gasping for oxygen.

The man's fingers twisted into her hair, pulling her off the chair. She closed her eyes and shrieked, as if she could deny his presence.

Angela heard a choking sound from above; saw a flash of sunburned skin. Then the man's body jerked off her.

MEREDITH GRIPPED the man's beefy neck in the crook of her elbow, her other hand on his gun. She pushed it toward the ceiling, grunting with the effort. Finally, the choke weakened the man, and looked like he might lose consciousness. Careful not to keep him in the carotid hold too long, Meredith pivoted him around to the floor and tucked the gun in her waistband. She straddled his body and sat on his back.

She patted his body down, twisting him to get to his front pockets. Her fingers found something solid, keys maybe? She pulled out a set of keys with a metal Chevy symbol and tossed them on the coffee table. After she finished the pat search, she reached out of habit for her cuffs. She didn't have them. They existed in her other life back in California. The man lay still, wheezing, catching his breath. For the moment, he was immobilized. He had no idea how close he'd been to dying.

Nick thundered through the front door, skidding to a stop at Angela's chair. "What happened?"

Angela shouted, "Nick, Nick!" The tears began. Her pretty face swelled to a red mask of pain.

As a loving husband would, he tried to calm her. Tenderly, he pried her fingers away and poked at the wound. "The bullet just grazed your skin. We'll get you to a doctor to clean it up and you'll be fine. Maybe a few stitches." A bruise was tinting her cheekbone.

Nick grabbed a couple of clean dishtowels sitting on the kitchen bar.

Angela sniffled, wiping at tears with her uninjured hand. "He almost killed me." Her voice sounded small, timid, and accusatory, like Nick failed to take care of her. "I almost bled to death." Tears streamed down her cheeks, her body swayed in the chair.

Wrapping her arm with the towel, he said, "It's not too serious. Some stitches and you'll be fine." Nick reached out to stroke her deep chestnut hair, a gesture so tender that it spiked Meredith's temper. Angela had gone to nursing school, although she'd quit when she married Nick. She knew better. She was playing him again, and he was falling for it.

"Oh, I'm just fine, partner," Meredith spoke up, still sitting on her prisoner. "Thanks for asking." She smiled at the surprise on Nick's face. "You better cut them loose." She tipped her head toward Emilio and Liliana. "They can help Angela, and you can help me. I could use a hand." She might have been giving directions to set the table. She marveled at her own self-control. She wanted to punch Angela in the nose to shut her up.

While Nick freed his in-laws, Meredith shifted and put her knee in the intruder's back. Watching Emilio, she had a funny feeling. He looked embarrassed, like he was ashamed that he hadn't defended his family. She guessed disgrace was a natural reaction for a macho Mexican patriarch.

Nick and Meredith each took an arm, and they yanked the bad guy to his feet. They had to keep a grip on him as he was slow to regain his strength. Nick looked down his nose at the man. In Spanish, he asked, "What are you looking for?"

The man had just enough energy to smirk.

Before Meredith knew what he was doing, Nick had pushed the man across the room. Stumbling over books and pillows, Nick shoved him to the back-sliding door. Meredith figured Nick's adrenaline must have kicked into overdrive—the man was six inches shorter but had fifty pounds on him.

Meredith reached to the door, slid it open, and stood to the side as Nick pitched the man headfirst onto a small patch of lawn. Bouncing across the grass, his face landed in a tub of marigolds. The man rolled, shook his head, and snorted dirt out of his nose. Nick grabbed a handful of his cotton shirt, lifting him back to his toes.

"What are you after?" Nick spat out his Spanish like each word was a curse.

"Your wife." The man's smile was intended as a taunt, but the dirt between his teeth made Meredith laugh. Nick took inventory of the yard, then pulled him to a bare patch of sandy ground next to a shed. Meredith followed, the gun still in her waistband.

Again, Nick shoved the man to the ground. Fine sand sprayed around him as he landed roughly on his back. Meredith knelt on one arm while Nick stood on the other. She leaned over, looking into his eyes. "What were you looking for? This is your last chance." Nick translated, just in case he didn't understand.

The man's eyes widened as Meredith pulled his own gun from behind her. Flexing her fingers around the grip for effect, she made sure his full attention stayed on it. Pressing her index finger on the trigger, she pointed the barrel into the sand, next to his ear.

Three rapid-fire rounds blasted into the ground next to him. Sand spurted into his ear as he winced at the sound and percussion. Sweat and dirt beaded on his face. "What were you looking for?" Nick asked again in Spanish.

No answer. The man's chin stiffened with artificial defiance. Then it quivered. He was scared, no doubt about it. But he wasn't talking. Meredith had a thought. "You're more afraid of your boss?" She didn't wait for an answer. "Man, you picked the wrong family to mess with."

Nick's mouth twisted in disgust. "Where's Rigo Borrego?" No answer. The stink of fear emanated from him.

The partners arrived at the same conclusion. "So, we're done with him?" Meredith asked.

Nick moved toward the shed. "I'll get something to gag him and tie him up with."

The man groaned.

Chapter Nineteen

NICK TIED UP THE INTRUDER SO TIGHT THE MAN CRIED OUT FROM THE pain in his wrists. They used a kitchen towel for a gag, and Nick shoved him into a closet in the house until they figured out what to do with him. Emilio hovered over his daughter until Nick pushed him away. He knelt at Angela's side.

Angela, eyes half-closed, slumped in the chair while Liliana dabbed antiseptic on the wound. At Nick's silent inquiry, his mother-in-law said, "She appears fine. Her father has called Oswaldo. We will take her to the clinic to see a doctor. The bullet caused little damage, as you said." Wiry tendrils of gray hair curled around Liliana's hairline. Her cheeks still showed patches of red from the duct tape, and her eyes were drawn with exhaustion. Nick thought she looked too drained to get hysterical.

Whatever the reason, Liliana thankfully hadn't complicated a situation so incredibly messed up that little of it made sense. Nick turned to Meredith. "This has changed the game. They've taken it from a simple economic transaction—to something far more personal. There's more to this than we know." He turned and studied Angela. "What were they looking for?"

Angela's eyelids snapped open. Her mouth twisted into a snarl.

"It's just like you to believe that I know what that fool was asking about. Don't you think I would have given it to him rather than being shot?"

"Nick, don't excite her. She's been injured." The plea in Liliana's face was the reaction of a mother tending to her injured child. And Liliana was a good mother, but something was off here. Nick was mad. Most people who got shot had it coming. There were too many gaps in the story. He couldn't help feeling that Angela had hidden things from them. Armed with the truth, this whole situation might be in a better place. His question was reasonable and necessary. He hadn't accused her of anything to make her so defensive. He'd heard that tone before. Why didn't he see this earlier? This might be why Angela acted so…spoiled.

Nick held his frustration in check. He turned his attention to Meredith. "Let's talk this through. What do you think?"

Meredith grabbed a banana and spent a moment reviewing the past hour. Peeling her ideas like the fruit, she said, "You're right. This isn't a simple ransom situation. The fact that there is no money complicates things. But I'm curious: why haven't they called to tell us where to bring the money? And then, who is the punk searching the house, and why?" She glanced up at him. "Remember, they changed the rules, not us. Not that it makes any difference, but now the stakes are different."

Angela chirped, "You can't mean you're going to leave us?"

Nick almost laughed at the thought. Yesterday, she didn't want him back. Now, she couldn't live without him. What did she want?

"No, we're not leaving." His voice was slow and measured. "Meredith, any guesses what he was looking for?"

He watched her swallow the last of the banana and drop the peel into a trash bag Emilio carried while he tidied up. Nick needed her ideas. She always came up with something useful, something he hadn't thought about. Behind her deep, coffee-colored eyes, he saw intelligence and common sense. She hadn't lost it. She hadn't felt sorry for herself over the trauma of the past year. Her growing edge hadn't eclipsed her logic. She was a good woman—a woman to kiss. Even if the kiss was a perfect example of bad timing.

Enough, he thought. Back to the problem.

Meredith shook her head, then eyed Emilio. "I'd like to search this house."

Emilio sputtered a protest. Nobody wanted their house scrutinized. Meredith didn't give him any choice. "We'll be considerate. With your help, Señor Borrego, this will go faster." Emilio looked to Nick. His father-in-law would go with whatever he suggested.

The wisdom of Meredith's suggestion was obvious. "Papa, she's right," Nick said. "Maybe there's something that doesn't belong here. Maybe Rigo hid..." His head tilted to encompass the universe. "God knows what he might have hidden here. We have to look. You and your family know what is normal and what isn't. We need you."

The lines in Emilio's face seemed deeper, like he'd aged five years over the last three days. "I suppose you are right." He met Nick's gaze with unyielding strength. "I—we—will help."

ANGELA'S ARM THROBBED. She needed something for the pain. Oh, but the baby. What could she take? Tylenol, just Tylenol as a pain reliever. She hoped this baby appreciated the sacrifices she had to make. She'd never been good with any kind of suffering. Even though she'd never show her mother's dramatics, Angela understood the enormity of her emotion. Hers were almost the same.

Her arm tormented her, but she decided to wait until they were at the clinic for the Tylenol. She needed her health card. It was right that Nick's insurance should pay for this. After all, he'd been responsible.

She needed her purse. She pushed her mother's hands away. As Angela rose, Oswaldo hustled through the open front door. He treaded around debris in the house to her, his eyebrows pinched together with worry. His concern registered, and she filed it away in her mind. It might be useful at another time if an opportunity presented itself.

"Angelita," His voice was hushed as he grabbed her good shoulder. "Are you all right? Your papa said you've been shot." He surveyed her from head to toe. "You look pale."

Angela thought he might try to hug her, so she pulled back. "Be careful."

At Oswaldo's elbow, Emilio's voice trembled at first, then got stronger. "She needs to go to the clinic downtown. Dr. Frank will help her. You take her. Keep her safe."

Oswaldo snapped out of his single-minded focus on Angela and glanced around the room. He looked to where Nick was searching a bookshelf loaded with toppled books, boxes, and baskets. Angela was dismayed her husband hadn't reacted to Oswaldo's display of concern. She wasn't intentionally trying to make him jealous but—okay, maybe she was. Nothing wrong with that. He's still my husband, she thought. He seemed to ignore Oswaldo altogether, but Angela knew he'd seen it. Nick didn't miss things like that. A reaction from Nick would've been satisfying.

"Come on." She nodded to Oswaldo. "I need my health card." She brushed aside his offer to find it himself. "It's in my purse, and I don't want anyone going through it." Especially when there was a receipt from the farmacía where she bought the pregnancy test kit. "Help me upstairs." When he hesitated, she snapped, "They're looking for whatever it was that criminal who shot me wanted. They're searching the whole house."

Oswaldo said, "Since we are going up, we will go through Angela's room." Without waiting, he followed Angela.

The room was a mess. The dresser stood on its side, drawers cracked and thrown against the wall. Mattresses were pulled off the bed and sliced open. Anger swept through her, competing with the throb of her arm. Over her shoulder, she told Oswaldo, "Look for my purse, but if you find it, just give it to me." She didn't care what he thought, but she didn't want him to hear about the baby before Javier.

Shoving a toppled lamp and some books aside, she worked at sounding disinterested. "Where is Javier today?"

"At the bank, talking to someone about Rigo's accounts." Oswaldo's voice carried the petulance that she saw in his eyes. Damn him, she thought. Damn them both. They should be with her, keeping her safe.

Oswaldo turned abruptly into the closet. He began sorting through clothes ripped from their hangers and thrown to the floor.

Angela knew the last time she saw her purse was earlier this morning when she had gotten grocery money. She'd dropped it on her bed. Now the whole room was upside down. Her nightstand lay on its side, the drawer pulled out and the contents spilled on the floor. She dropped to her knees, shoving papers around until her fingers touched a pink book. She clutched it to her chest like a silk-covered baby. "Mia," she whispered. Another pain heaped on her bruised soul. Her attention fell on the white leather cover of her wedding album, where gold leaf calligraphy announced Nick and Angela's names and the date of their wedding. Months ago, she'd tucked it away, unwilling to look at it but unable to part with it.

She called to Oswaldo. "Pull the mattress over so I can look underneath."

He grumbled something she didn't hear. She let it pass. "Pull it that way and I'll move the box spring. I'll bet my purse is under here."

He pulled, and the mattress shifted. "Hold it up, I can't see under it," she said.

He lost his grip and the mattress slid to the floor. The coiled edge caught the drawer and flipped the nightstand over.

Both Oswaldo and Angela stared. Secured under the drawer was a colorful straw box reminiscent of an old souvenir cigarette case. Oswaldo saw it, too. Angela's mind dismissed a hundred things the box could be. They wouldn't know until they looked. Without a word, she reached for it. She tugged the lid for a moment, then Oswaldo's massive hands took it, yanking out the staples that held the lid in place.

Angela snatched it from him. "This is what that man was looking for." She ran her good hand over the cover—a woman's book with gold embossed fleur de lys. Full of expectation, she pulled it open.

"What is it?" Oswaldo's voice was breathless.

"It's a book—with handwriting in it."

"What does it say?"

"Let me see." She waved aside his questions as she studied the pages. "It's like it's in code or something." She flipped a page. "There are names, dates, and peso amounts. Like a ledger."

Oswaldo looked over her shoulder. "It's a record of payments."

Angela held the book open. It seemed to have its own particular gravity.

"Give it to me." Oswaldo's voice held a resolve that surprised Angela. "With this, I can negotiate Rigo's freedom. I know how to contact Vega. I will do it."

"No," she snapped. "No, remember what happened last time you tried to negotiate?"

His dark face grew even darker. "That is why I will do this. For Ishmael."

"No." She turned away from him. "I called Nick to do it. He's good at this kind of thing."

"Maybe in Cali, but here he's bungled everything. He even got you shot." Oswaldo's eyes narrowed. "He speaks the language, sure; but he doesn't know anything about our lives, how things are done."

Angela considered this. It was true. Nick had visited Mexico but never lived there. She and Oswaldo had grown up here. Oswaldo knew the neighborhoods; the nuances of life lived on the brink of crime or poverty. He knew the people: who looked out of place, who fit in—who was a hoodlum, a turista, or the policía.

Oswaldo pitched his last fastball across the plate. "He doesn't even have a gun. I do."

Angela put her misgivings aside and handed the book to Oswaldo.

Shoving the book back into the cigarette box, he dropped to a knee. "No one found it the first time. It will be safe here for now, until I can trade it." Fishing out a pair of paper clips from the drawer, he rigged the box into the base of the drawer, much like they'd found it.

Chapter Twenty

"THERE'S NOTHING HERE." MEREDITH SHOOK HER HEAD AS SHE descended the stairs. "Unless you want to go through Angela's room after she's gone, we're done." She studied Nick's bloodshot eyes. She hated to pile on bad news, but there was no reason for optimism. There was nothing good here—nothing she saw, anyway.

"No, we don't need to do that." Nick glanced around the room with a shrug. "If it is here, it's hidden well. We don't even know what 'it' is. We're wasting our time."

She was either too suspicious, or Nick was too trusting when it came to Angela. Dismayed, Meredith thought she knew what was coming—a trip back to El Rancho. She asked anyway. "What next?"

"We go back up the hill. I'd like to scout around while it's still daylight, see if we can find Rigo or anything that might tell us where he is." He glanced at his watch. Eleven-thirty. "Time to leave."

"Are you going to leave us here?" Liliana's tiny voice reminded Meredith of a crying baby. "Maybe we should go to my sister's in Puerto Vallarta. We would be safer." The old woman's hands kneaded a dishtowel.

Emilio stood. "Yes. That is what we will do." The old man

glanced at Nick. "Mama will go to her sister's house. I will drive you up the hill to El Rancho."

Nick's face flushed. "Papa, are you sure you want to do this? You could get hurt."

Emilio's lined face beamed with resolution. Where there had been resignation was now strength. "I do. And I want Mama somewhere safe—with or without Oswaldo." Emilio seemed to have found the mantle of a patriarch. His posture straightened, his eyes glinted with purpose.

"It's your choice, Mama." Nick was all out of sympathy. "The last time we left, Oswaldo was supposed to be watching you. Where did he go this morning, anyway?"

Liliana shrugged. "He got a phone call, then left." Her eyes sought her husband's, then returned to Nick. "We thought he would be back soon. But he wasn't…"

"Where is he? He's supposed to take Angela to the clinic."

"Angela! Oswaldo!" Emilio's voice boomed. "Come down here." Meredith was surprised to hear the strength and command in Emilio's tone. She began to re-think her first impression of him as ineffectual. There was power in the man, and now he was using it. Why now?

Oswaldo followed Angela into the living room, smug and smiling. "We searched her room, looking for her purse. We found nothing."

"Before you go, this needs to be settled." Nick motioned them into the room. "Oswaldo, since you made such a mess of your job this morning, we're making other arrangements for the safety of the family."

Oswaldo pulled himself taller. "I would have been here, but Javier needed me at the office while he went to the bank for Rigo's accounts. Angela isn't working; he had no one else to answer the phone. Emilio said he could handle their safety."

"You're out of it now, Oswaldo. We'll take care of the family. Emilio is going with us, and we will put Liliana in a safe place." Nick's jaw looked like it was set in granite.

Oswaldo's mouth turned down in disapproval. He wasn't a big

enough man to stand up against Nick. "Javier is on his way now. He can take Angela to the clinic, and I'll take Liliana to a safe place."

"No, Angela will come with us." Emilio shook his head. "I have been thinking about this. I will drive Nick halfway up the hill to Las Pulgas below the old silver diggings, and she and I will wait for them, nowhere near danger." At Oswaldo's protest, Emilio's hands spread out to calm him. "It's not that I don't trust Javier, but he is so busy all the time. We need someone to watch Angela with full attention. There is no one more capable to defend my daughter than Nick, her husband."

Oswaldo's face darkened. "How's he going to do that when he's supposed to be rescuing Rigo?"

"You have no say in this," Emilio was out of patience. "I will call my friend, Bernardo, to take Liliana."

A thumping noise came from the living room closet. The gangster was coming to. He was making entirely too much noise. Meredith looked at Emilio over her shoulder. As the patriarch, he needed to be included. "We'll take out the garbage, Señor Borrego. Let's find the Chevy that goes to these keys. We can use his car."

JUST AFTER NOON, a blue and gray primered 1959 Chevy Impala came to a sudden stop next to a rough stucco building on the corner of Matamoros and Avenida San Juan, the Bucerias Tourist Police building. The coupe doors flew open. Wearing bandanas across the lower half of their faces, Nick and Meredith got out. Emilio stepped from behind the wheel, also with a bandana. They opened the trunk and pulled out a limp body. Nick grabbed one arm and Meredith the other to drag it to the building's front stairs. Nick tossed the keys back to Emilio, who fired up the Chevy engine.

The man they carried had duct tape sealing the mouth and rope binding his wrists. He groaned as Nick dumped him against the steps. Meredith secured a loop of the rope to the iron railing at the front door.

She stuffed a paper inside the man's pocket. It said, "I shoot defenseless women."

Then, they ran back to the Impala.

As one would expect, no one saw anything, heard anything, or knew anything. Mexico.

Chapter Twenty-One

RIGO BORREGO'S MIND SWAM UP FROM THE MURKY ABYSS TOWARD A faint light. If he'd had the sensibility, he would have likened it to an enclosed chamber filled with water, where his body and mind hung weightless. Then, his consciousness became aware of an innate struggle to keep moving upward. He didn't want to fall back into the depths, where he was suspended in the dark, unknowing and unaware. He had to make it to the light so he could breathe, see, hear.

Brightness grew until it overwhelmed him. Clenching his eyes against it, he took stock of his senses. He heard nothing, although the hiss of white noise played in his ears. A dull pressure on his hip and shoulder told Borrego that he lay on his side on a hard surface, not concrete, but something like packed dirt. His arms and fingers throbbed in every joint. He smelled dust, and a coppery scent. Blood. His blood.

Rigo was afraid to open his eyes. When he tried, he discovered something held them sealed shut—crust, dried tears. He moved to lift a hand and rub it away, but shards of pain cut through his muscles. His bones throbbed like they were broken.

Wincing, he broke through the crust and opened his eyes. He was in the place where he'd been held captive for the past six days. He searched the room, looking for the source of his pain.

No one here. He was alone. Nothing but scorpions and rats—including the human variety, he thought. Human scum that would do this to a person—for no reason.

At first, Rigo thought his punishment was a result of his infidelity with Silvia. But as Vega had soon made it clear, the book she gave him was more important than her life—or his. Then, when the guard had begun to hit Rigo, he had been too absorbed in the pain to think. Now, lying here, beaten and flat on the dirt, he had time to consider Vega's questions. If it was important to Vega, it was important to him.

Think, think. The book.

What had Silvia said? She'd told him that she never loved Vega, that the marriage had been arranged to cement the family business. Her brothers had pressured her to marry. She had grown tired of being made a fool by her husband's infidelities and had kept a book of proof. What was the business? He couldn't remember—investing, she said. No, didn't she say pharmaceuticals? What was it? Maybe it was both. Maybe it all—everything with Silvia—had been a lie.

Pharmaceuticals? Oh no. Why hadn't he seen it?

He hadn't been thinking, had he? At least not with his brain. The first time she glided into his office, she took his breath away. She was a beautiful, elegant woman and knew it, wearing her beauty like a crown. Regal and untouchable, her expensive scent swept him away from his miserable little office. Her surprisingly blue eyes drew him into the depths of her mysterious allure like a siren. Now he knew he'd been doomed the moment she walked in—doomed to love her.

He would never know if she had planned it that way.

Silvia gave him the book then, saying it was proof of her husband's fraud. She had told him to keep it somewhere secure. She objected when he wanted to put it in his wall safe. Lost in a fog of infatuation, he told her he would take it home and stash it where no one would find it.

And he had, but not before looking at it. She'd told him it was records of infidelities, but the pages he scanned looked more like payoffs. He saw no women's names, only businesses. It could've been a code for a woman, but...

Never mind, he thought, drifting in the dreamy cloud of expectation she'd presented. Silvia wanted the book stored in a safe place. Therefore, he found one—under the nightstand drawer in the guest bedroom, the room where Angela slept. He'd tucked it in a souvenir cigarette holder and stapled it to the bottom. Safe and secure. So small and well hidden, even he had dismissed it from his memory.

Was he going to tell Vega? Why? He wouldn't be released if he told. Vega had promised a quick death versus a slow, painful one. Rigo tried to take a deep breath, but it felt like a rib was broken, like an ice pick stuck in his side that someone cruelly twisted every time he moved. A shallow breath and certainty settled into his heart. Telling him Vega would bring gangsters to his house, jeopardizing Angela and his parents.

What difference would it make to give up the book? He remembered one of Silvia's brothers was on trial in Morelia. If the book was some kind of evidence, Rigo had no wish to make things worse for his beloved Silvia's family.

No. He would keep it to himself.

ANGELA STORMED through the front door of the Borrego home, knocking over her mother's suitcase. She was annoyed at Javier and did nothing to hide it. She should have been the center of his universe. He'd told her he loved her, but now he was so distracted she couldn't hold his attention long enough to tell him about the baby. Damn him, she thought.

Javier trailed behind her, busy on his cellphone, his voice low enough that she couldn't hear what he said. Angela flopped down on the living room couch and let her mother fuss over making her comfortable. Her father was not home, but Oswaldo sat on a barstool, watching.

Liliana fluttered like a hummingbird around a flower, brushing her daughter's hair out of her eyes. "Why don't you go upstairs to your room? Your father and I set everything back the way it was. You can lie on your bed. He had to take that criminal to the policía. Nick will be back in a little while, then you will have to go with them to Las Pulgas. You need some rest, dear. You have been through so much today."

As Javier snapped his phone shut, Oswaldo stood, "I'll take her up, Javier. You can go back to the office."

Javier's attention focused on Angela. He leaned over the couch. "The doctor said you will be fine. Now you are with Oswaldo, you will be safe." He squeezed her hand.

Angela yanked it away, glaring at Javier. "What do you know? You weren't even here!"

Her words didn't seem to have any effect on him. He smiled indulgently, patting her shoulder. "You need rest, Angela." She knew his smile was more for everyone in the room than her.

Angela's frustration rose. She couldn't make a scene like she wanted because her mother didn't know she had been seeing Javier. As far as her parents were concerned, she was still married to Nick. The whole idea pissed her off. She lifted her head. "Yes, Javier. Leave so I can rest."

He didn't look as surprised at being ordered out as Angela thought.

With a look at his phone, Javier mumbled, "I need to take care of some business out of town." Although he didn't appear to be hurrying, Javier was soon out the door.

As Angela watched the front door close, Oswaldo bent over and scooped her up in a swift movement. He carried her up the stairs, whispering in her ear. "I got a message to someone who will put me in touch with Vega."

Angela nodded, too weary from the day's events to think about Oswaldo's news. She was tired and grateful to be heading to bed.

Javier was right. She needed sleep.

Chapter Twenty-Two

OSWALDO SAT ON THE WOOD RAILING SURROUNDING THE BEDROOM balcony, his brow filled with glistening beads of sweat. He rubbed moisture away. The afternoon was warm, no question, but his situation was hotter. He used the back of his hand to mop his sweat while Angela thought about what to say.

"You're going to meet with him tonight? Did he say anything about the ransom for Rigo?"

"I asked, but he didn't answer." Oswaldo leaned toward her. "It's best not to push men like that."

Angela sniffed her indignation so Oswaldo could see what a failure he was. She folded her arms across her chest and turned away. "That may be true, but you cannot let him think you are afraid of him. Men like that are mad dogs, insane with the smell of blood."

Oswaldo didn't speak. She heard the sounds he made while pulling out a cigarette and lighting it.

Her head whirled around. "Don't smoke out here—anywhere near me!"

She was delighted by his surprised face. Wouldn't he be shocked by her news about the baby? This foolish clod, who always had a crush on her—like she could even be interested in someone as brutish as him.

His lower lip shined with saliva. "You never minded smoking before."

"I do now. Put it out." She walked across the deck and leaned on the wood railing. "What time tonight, and where?" Her fatigue drifted away. "Tell me everything."

"I am to meet Vega tonight on a road off the highway to Sayulita. He said to bring the package, but it sounded like he didn't know how big it was."

Angela mulled this over. The gangster had torn the house apart looking for something he didn't know the size or shape of. He'd even said as much.

"I have to go with my father tonight. Text me after your meeting."

"Of course, querída." His coarse face glistened in the moonlight.

"Don't call me that." She hated when he presumed too much—like now, calling her his loved one.

His face slipped into his usual detached demeanor. "As we agreed, I'll leave the book here for insurance. We will arrange to trade it when we see Rigo."

As she nodded, she heard her father's voice from downstairs. "Angela. We must leave, Angela."

"In a minute, Popi." She entered the living room, then started back up toward the stairs. "It gets cold in the mountains at night. I have to get a sweater."

THE SKY WAS ABLAZE with sunlight reflected off bulbous cumulus clouds. They bumped up against the tree-laden mountains behind El Rancho. The sun hovered over the westernmost ridge of the Los Lobos Hills. Closer to earth, the afternoon thunderclouds had dumped a wet bounty on the countryside, dampening Meredith's resolution. Her clothing was saturated for the second time that day. This morning, Morris had made them wade in the last few yards to shore. Later, when Nick got the call from Angela, they were damp through and through. At least this wasn't salt water.

Both had dry clothing tucked in their backpacks, but neither wanted to take the time to change. The sky was darkening, and the cicadas were buzzing like bees in a hive. Mosquitoes swarmed in the gloom of the trees. They weren't enthusiastic, but they had to move out. Nick chewed on a corn tortilla—Meredith knocked rocks out of her sandals, swatted at flies and everything else that flew into range. She hated bugs.

They hiked to the same place where the Federales had detained them. On the far side, Nick explored the slope beyond the trees. He found a rocky track to a perfect vantage point on an outcropping. The boulders were flat on top with a few scraggly weeds struggling for survival on a windy rock. The plants gave enough concealment for them to observe El Rancho.

Finished eating, Nick wiped his hands on his pants. From their vantage point twenty feet above El Rancho and fifteen yards away, they could see the entire house and surroundings. The U-shaped building was set up so the central part of the house faced the ocean in order to catch the cooling breezes. Both wings pointed away from their observation point and toward a distant valley. The house was in mid-stage decay—on one side, adobe bricks tumbled to the ground around half the structure, some holes revealed the interior. Holes the size of Volkswagens punctuated the tile roof. With the binoculars, Meredith saw into some parts of the house.

The other half of the wing was intact.

They saw one guard doing a perimeter check after the squall. Nick's voice was quiet. "With any luck, a light should come on soon." Nick lifted the small pair of glasses to his eyes. "That should tell us where the guard is."

"I don't like going in unarmed." Meredith felt compelled to say it — as if Nick didn't know.

He studied the house. "Me, too. But we don't have time to get new firepower." He dropped the glasses to his chest. "We can take weapons off the guards." He fixed the binoculars to his eyes again, rolling the dial with his middle finger to adjust the clarity. "You only saw the one guy, right?"

"Um, hm. There's the light. Looks like a lantern in the east wing."

"Ok, got it." He slipped the glasses into his pack. "We'll go in from the hillside. He would expect trouble to come from the road. I'll take point."

"When?" The nervousness that grabbed her before a mission came on fast. It always happened. It wasn't fear, exactly, but there was a dose of that, along with the anxiety of trying to figure out all the variables, the moves, and counter moves. It wasn't even the fear of getting hurt. It was more worry over letting Nick down or letting the bad guy get away. She'd done both before and didn't want it to happen again.

Her first major case in Violent Crimes Investigations had been a homicide—a grandmotherly victim raped, beaten, and murdered. That suspect, Earl Redmond Sutton, had escaped her grasp three times. Twice, Nick had to stay behind to help her with her injuries instead of chasing Sutton. In the end, Nick caught the murderer by himself.

She would have analyzed it, but as soon as an operation was over, she tucked the memory away in a distant corner of her brain. Best left there, too, despite what the shrinks said.

"Now. Before it gets too dark." Grabbing a weathered oak branch from the ground, Nick rose to a crouch. The branch looked like a baseball bat. "Here, take these. We may need them." He held out a pair of two-foot lengths of jute rope. "We'll come back for the packs."

Meredith shoved the rope into her back pocket. She followed, thankful that the earth was saturated enough to keep the dust down. She didn't want a dust cloud announcing their arrival. The last rays of the sun cast a reddish glow—and enough light to see.

THEY WORKED their way down a track that led to El Rancho. Now that she was moving, she was fine—confident and focused, yet aware of the surroundings. The bugs buzzed, birds sang in the distance, and the breeze blew wisps of hair into her eyes. She cleared the strands with a knuckle, glancing from side to side. Everything looked ordinary—except for the mission they were on. She hoped Rigo was inside and that they could get to him without getting themselves in trouble. She hoped he was still alive and fit enough to walk out. She hoped...

Nick reached the west wing and turned so his back was against the wall, next to a door. Meredith reached it and flattened herself in the same manner on the other side, pushing her adrenaline rush back down where it came from. She took a deep breath for control. Nick twisted the loose doorknob. The door swung open a few inches.

He made eye contact with Meredith and used his finger to signal that he was going in. After her crisp nod, he stretched out his leg and pushed the door with the toe of his tennis shoe. The hinges ground out a high-pitched squeak, cutting through the silence. Nick peeked around the doorframe, then pulled back. He flexed his fingers around the stick, then pivoted into the space. Meredith peeled in behind him.

The hallway was dark, but their eyes were already acclimated to the dimness. Dusky light came through holes in the roof but did little to illuminate their way. Meredith saw two doors on each side, one closed. She primed herself for hand combat, ready for anything. Damn, she wished she had her Beretta. She felt naked without it.

At the first doorway, Nick rolled into the room, the stick held like a bat close to his body. Following, still reining in her adrenaline, Meredith looked behind them, then met Nick's glance. All clear.

They searched the next two rooms the same way—Nick leading, Meredith following, covering him and watching their rear. The last room had a closed door. Down the hall, Meredith saw a huge cooking and eating area. A half-dozen opened cans lay on a tile counter. Flies buzzing in a cloud above them. Maybe more than one guard here, she thought. To make sure Nick saw the threat, Meredith touched his shoulder softly and pointed.

He nodded, then focused on the closed door. She took a position across from him so she saw the kitchen and the hallway. Nick turned the knob. She wondered at her automatic action. She couldn't shoot an aggressor. They had always done it this way. Throughout her training and afterward, even when she was on her own, she followed the procedure. Allowing for inevitable variables, none so debilitating as being without a gun, this was the safest way to search a house.

The door was locked.

Meredith sidestepped toward the kitchen and cleared the room. Satisfied it was vacant, she slipped first beside Nick, then to the other side of the doorframe. Nick gripped the stick, raised it above his head, and rammed it into the knob. The sharp metallic thud was loud enough to wake the dead. The knob was so flimsy it took two swings before it fell apart. Wishing with a vengeance that she had her Beretta, Meredith followed Nick in.

Chapter Twenty-Three

A MOUND OF CRUMPLED CLOTHING LAY IN THE CENTER OF THE ROOM. From the middle of it, a man's head raised enough to see them, then thumped back down. Dark hair plastered to his skull with sweat and blood. His eyes glazed over with pain. If this was Rigo, he didn't recognize Nick.

Meredith whispered, "Is that him?" Nick nodded.

She scanned the room, listening. "Heads up," she whispered. At Nick's inquiring look, she nodded towards the kitchen. Rigo moaned. They hurried to either side of the open door. Nick's gaze met Meredith's. He pointed to her, then held his index finger up at chest height. His thumb tapped his sternum, then flashed his index and middle finger. Her chin dipped in acknowledgement. She'd go in first; he would follow.

Heavy combat boots pounded down the opposite wing. Meredith couldn't see anything. The silence of the hilltop magnified the sounds of men approaching. She figured there were at least two.

Meredith crouched, her body charged with strength and purpose. She had to fight harder and dirtier than a man. When it got physical, there was no such thing as dirty or clean. A woman battled with everything she had. It was a thought she always had before things turned to shit. A dozen scenarios of what could happen darted through her mind.

Before she knew it, her target was a step ahead of her. A small man with wavy hair, wide shoulders, and an AR-15 with the stock jammed in his armpit.

Perfect.

She used the wall to launch herself toward the man. Right where she wanted him, she caught his knees with her shoulder. The guard gurgled what might have been a curse had it not been cut short by impact. He folded backwards like the legs of an ironing board. Ready for his fall, Meredith spun sideways. She drew up a knee and kicked hard at the rifle, making it skitter across the floor. The guard rolled into a coil, preparing to get to his feet. Her heel shot out and met his cheekbone with a sickening crunch as it shattered. Blood spurted out his nose.

The blood mesmerized her, and time was suspended. It looked like the burst of blood from Rusty Webber—a man she'd killed over a year ago. The blood had the same color and viscosity…

She didn't have the luxury of time to fight her emotional phantoms. She had to move.

The man's eyes narrowed with fury. His voice ground out an ungodly growl. Pushing off with her right foot, Meredith dumped her entire weight on his chest, and her elbow found its mark when it gouged into the soft parts of his neck. Stunned, he lay gasping for breath. She flipped him onto his stomach and tied his wrists with the jute rope from her pocket. She unsnapped his holster and pulled out a shiny new Glock—same make and model as the one used by the gangster who shot Angela, but this one had two notches in the grip. It wasn't rocket science to connect the two thugs. Another one of Vega's guys.

A glance toward Nick showed he was also in control. The guard Nick had been fighting lay proned-out on the dirt floor, drooling spit and blood into a little mud-pie under his mouth. Meredith searched the room and found a dusty T-shirt lying next to Rigo. The cloth ripped easily enough for her to fashion strips to use as gags. After tying up her soldier, she strode across the room and thrust the rag and jute at Nick. She picked up the AR-15, slinging it over her shoulder.

With both men out of action, secured, and silenced, Meredith leaned against a wall, calming her heaving chest. Adrenaline still surged through her body, but the fight was over. Her legs felt wobbly. Her pulse thundered in her ears. Keeping an eye on the inert figures on the floor, she assessed her body for injuries and tried to settle her whirling brain. Her damage inventory turned up nothing more than a sore heel.

Nick padded softly to Rigo and knelt beside him. Brushing flies away from the dried blood on his lacerated cheekbone, Nick whispered. "Hermano."

Rigo's eyes fluttered open but still showed no recognition. He turned his head away. Nick winced as he glanced over his brother-in-law's body, inspecting the cuts, bruising, and blood. "I can't touch him. I can't see where he's hurt." It was basic first aid, not to move an injured person until you knew the extent of the damage. But this wasn't a classroom, and the rules didn't, maybe couldn't, apply.

Meredith crossed her fingers that Rigo wasn't too busted up to walk out of here. Wait. She studied his body, then the floor. He had moved. "Try again," she said to Nick. Meredith pointed at scrapes and loose piles of dirt on the floor. "Look, he must have dragged himself away from the fighting."

Nick leaned into Rigo's ear. "Rigo, it's Nick. Wake up, buddy."

A groan worked its way to Rigo's lips as he made a pitiful struggle to consciousness.

"Nick? Where am I?" His cracked lips worked to form words. Flies and gnats swirled around his head. Nick brushed them aside again.

"You're in trouble, that's where you are. I wanna get you out of here, but first, I need to know where you're hurt, and how bad."

Another groan rumbled from Rigo. He lifted his head again, trying to focus on Nick. An arm moved, then a foot and leg. Rigo's head dropped to his shoulder.

Meredith fought back her feelings of contempt. She banished the image of carrying this guy down the hill. Why didn't he participate in his own rescue? Sure, he was busted up, but they were there to help him get away. "He's sound enough to crawl under his own power. I wouldn't worry about a neck or spine injury."

Nick's frown told her that he agreed.

"It's my head, my arm, and hands. My chest hurts, too."

"My partner and I are going to get you up. Try to help."

With Nick and Meredith on either side, they pulled on his belt placket and the shoulder seam of his shirt until Rigo was on his feet.

He trembled and dipped unsteadily.

Nick tightened his grip on Rigo's shirt.

Rigo looked around. He grunted and asked, "Is this El Rancho?"

"Yeah."

"Where we going?"

"Down the hill. Back to your house. We've gotta figure out what they wanted."

"It's Vega," Rigo panted with the exertion of standing and talking.

"He wants a book that Silvia gave me."

Nick stopped. "A book about what?"

Rigo's eyes watered. "It has facts and figures in it that prove Vega's been doing something illegal."

Meredith couldn't help herself. "Everybody is doing something illegal in Mexico."

"No, you don't understand," Rigo said. "It has info that Vega wants, badly. He killed her for it, and he'll kill me if I talk."

Nick pushed Rigo. "Let's get out of here first, then you can tell us about it."

A grimy hand caked with dried blood grasped Nick's forearm.

"No, not that way." Rigo pointed in the opposite direction. "That way."

"No, Rigo. We have to go down the hill. We have a car at Las Pulgas."

"Listen to me. I've been thinking about getting out of here." Rigo closed his eyes for a moment, then opened them, focusing on Nick. "The mines. I know the way down. A tunnel—comes out at Las Pulgas. There's a decent road from there."

Chapter Twenty-Four

THE FARTHER OSWALDO GOT UP THE ROAD, THE HARDER IT RAINED.
The wipers on his Explorer couldn't keep up with the volume of
water the storm threw at the windshield. The thunderclouds broke
open minutes after he left the Borrego house. Oswaldo cursed his
bad luck. He was to meet Vega on the road to Sayulita, a turn-off on
the coast side of Highway 200. He hoped they would talk in a car or
some other shelter. He hated standing outside when the rain came
down this hard. Moisture soaked his skin, chilling him no matter
what the outside temperature.

A bad omen, to be sure. He shuddered, anticipating his misery.

THIRTY MINUTES LATER, turning at an abandoned gas station, he came
to Mesa Quemada, a scab on the elbow of Mexico, just above Las
Pulgas. The jungle had swallowed up almost everything crafted by
man, leaving no building standing more than four feet tall. The half
dozen structures were almost undetectable, a corner here, a shingle
roof caved-in on itself, weathered wood with lichen and moss
growing so lush, it was hard to tell where the wood ended.

Following directions, he turned right off the pavement at a derelict gas station and drove over the bridge that crossed a creek. The rain forest threatened to swallow the road that graduated to a steeply ascending rocky lane. After twenty yards, the way became tougher to traverse. Rainwater from one side of the road built into a mudslide carrying mud, sticks, and rocks downslope toward his car and across the road. The slide had inched into the ditch on the other side of the narrow road and was now like a huge serpent with a full belly, slithering down the hill. If the rain kept up, travel would become infinitely more dangerous. Worry about flooding joined all the other concerns in Oswaldo's already crowded mind. Flash floods happened in the mountains all the time. Another evil sign. Maybe coming here to barter was a bad idea.

He pulled onto a slight rise, out of range of the mudflow. He parked, hoping the ground might be more solid than the road. With the headlights on, he saw little ahead. There was nothing on either side but trees and rain. Even the bridge and the abandoned gas station behind him were obscured. Goosebumps raised on his scalp. He'd never felt so alone in his life.

Then, in his rear-view mirror, lights. The dawning of relief eclipsed the reality of his enormous peril. At least he'd left the book in a safe place. That it remained hidden was his insurance policy that Vega wouldn't kill him immediately.

The lights were so bright Oswaldo couldn't see what kind of car it was. Both doors opened. The two men who trotted to Oswaldo's Explorer were soaked by the time they reached him. They were mere shadows and waited one on each side of the car while Oswaldo unlocked the back doors.

The doors slammed with finality. The man sitting on the passenger side spoke first. Was he Vega? "Tell me where it is —now."

Oswaldo swallowed. "First, my conditions…"

Rustling came from the seat behind him. The second man gripped Oswaldo's chin, tipping it upward. The point of a very sharp knife traced a line across Oswaldo's throat.

Oswaldo held his breath. He'd known there would be a risk, but he wasn't expecting the brutality so soon in their negotiations. He took a breath. "It's a book—with figures in it."

The first man snapped. "Figures, like circles and squares? C'mon. What's in it?"

"Money—paid to who, where, and when." Oswaldo was sweating again. The SUV felt closed, like the two men had fouled the air. Moisture trailed down his chest.

The first man growled. "Did it have any names in it?"

Oswaldo would have nodded, but he was afraid to give the knife an opportunity. "Yes, sir. But I didn't see any of them. Really."

"You think I am a fool?" The man—still just a shadow—sat back in the seat. "Did you bring it with you?"

Oswaldo gulped. "No, sir. I left it someplace safe until we can exchange Borrego for the book." He realized what a mistake he'd made. Oh, God, if you get me out of this...

A sarcastic laugh erupted from the back seat. "Don't worry about Borrego. Tell me where the book is. You've run out of time."

"I will take you there." Oswaldo offered without much hope. If they bought it, though, he could do just that. The Borrego house was empty. No one would see him turn over the book. "Tell me where it is—right now."

Chapter Twenty-Five

THE KNIFE POINT MADE A GENTLE POP AS IT BROKE INTO OSWALDO'S skin. With something less than a surgeon's skill, the man sliced slowly, then paused for impact.

Oswaldo whispered. "Please, Señor Vega."

A sour laugh from the man in the back seat. "Wrong players, man."

If not Vega, who? Someone Vega told about the book.

After the first inch, the knife paused. The pain wasn't as unbearable as Oswaldo expected. It was the shock of what would happen next. He felt the warmth of his own blood oozing down his neck to his shirt. His chest heaved inaudibly as he tried to calm himself. He was a dead man if he told them where the book was. Hell, at this point, he was minutes away from meeting his maker.

None of this was fair. All he wanted was to redeem himself for his failure in negotiating his Cousin Ishmael's release. Since then, his family shunned him. It seemed like everyone in Mexico had heard about it. Javier even took heat from some of his attorney friends. It took months for Angela to spare a glance at him. The shame almost consumed him. He loved Angela. He couldn't bear to disappoint her.

When Vega's men had snatched Rigo, Oswaldo had made a

stupid move. He'd found Rigo's cell phone on the driveway. Thinking it was a sign for him to take some initiative, he called the Borrego home as if he was holding Rigo. He'd demanded a ransom. He hoped to bankroll the money and use it to lure Angela to him.

It didn't take him long to realize the family was broke. His feeble effort embarrassed him. The good thing about it was that no one knew he'd made the call. He wouldn't have to stand before Angela filled with shame—again.

And now, this deal for the book was backfiring. He couldn't tell these gangsters where it was. He had to hold out until he got to the Borregos', then he would try to get away.

Feeling emboldened, he glanced in his rear-view mirror. Surprise shot through him. The man he'd thought was Vega moved closer to him. Instead, he looked into the blue eyes of a male version of Silvia Guzman. These guys were her brothers. Knowing their brutal reputation, a larger dread crept over him.

"Where is it?" The knife tip cut through another inch of Oswaldo's skin. Two inches now, he estimated, the blade going deeper as it moved. Blood dripped down his neck in an agonizing tickle. His body fell into shock, so he didn't feel much pain—yet. Soon the cut would reach his windpipe. If they stopped cutting now, he might survive. The knife was sharp, but sometimes it caught on his skin, puckering along the incision. He recalled a time when he and his father had been hunting in the Sierra Madre mountains above Puerto Vallarta. They'd killed a wild boar. Even though Oswaldo's knife was sharp, it hung up on the pig's hide. This blade dragged just like the one on the pig...just before its guts fell out of its stomach onto the grass.

"I'll show you." Oswaldo clenched his chattering teeth.

"No, I want it now." Blood seeped through his shirt, the warmth clinging to his skin. "Tell me, and you die quickly. It would give me great pleasure to kill you slowly, Oswaldo. But that would be a bad choice for you." Images of the pig guts sped through Oswaldo's mind.

He would die looking like that poor animal.

He wasn't going to make it out of this. A collage of images fluttered through his mind—his mother praying in the nave at her church, the first time he saw Angela, watching Rigo's soccer game, target practice with a new gun. Now, none of them held much meaning.

He'd lost his chance to have Angela. He'd lost. Period.

"The nightstand in Angela's room, under the drawer." He sighed, searching for the right words to save his soul. "Hail Mary, full of grace."

Chapter Twenty-Six

MOVING STIFFLY AND WITH NICK'S HELP, RIGO LED THEM TO A weedy meadow nestled in the steep ochre-colored walls of a rock canyon. As large as it was, this stadium-sized area wasn't big enough for smelting and processing. The mine sat with a rocky ledge at one end while the sagging skeleton of a small ore crusher kept watch. Pressed into service to break down the ore for transport, the crusher was still freestanding, threatening to collapse at any moment. Underneath it, rails crossed the meadow for fifty yards and disappeared into thick underbrush. Nick knew there had to be a road the miners used to remove ore for processing. Maybe the jungle had swallowed it. They circled the field on a muddy trail that led to a shelf in the cliff. A hundred years ago, the area might have been a beautiful meadow. Today, it was a long-forgotten dumping ground for the detritus of spent labor.

Tucked into a ledge on the cliff stood a portal framed with rough timbers and thick with spider webs—more uninviting to Meredith than the torrents of rain. The weathered planks nailed across the opening were no challenge for Nick, who kicked them away from the casing.

Just inside, and out of the downpour, Meredith helped Rigo onto a boulder. She searched her backpack for a small Maglite flashlight. "Are you sure you remember how to get around in here?"

Rigo nodded, catching his breath. He'd been winded most of the way from El Rancho. It would be slow going—and easy for the guards, if they followed. Meredith glanced over her shoulder toward the broken wood. "Nick, let's prop the planks up so they look undisturbed. It wouldn't survive a close inspection, but it could buy us some time."

The beam from Nick's flashlight illuminated a patch of floor. "Yeah, and they won't be able to track us inside. The floor is rock and gravel."

Rigo used the filthy shreds of his sleeve to wipe blood from the lacerations on his forehead. "We'll find some water, too."

Nick turned toward the meager light from the opening of the mineshaft. Meredith followed. Together, they found enough rain-soaked boards to cover the opening. They put the last one in place from inside the mine. She hoped it would hold.

Returning to the injured man, Meredith ran her flashlight over the 12x12 beams bolstering the entrance. "Rigo, how'd you know about this?"

"My father was an engineer with his degree in geology. When the state hired him, they put him to work as a traffic engineer." Rigo's closed his eyes. "He made a career out of it, but his first love was always rocks." He smiled, and his eyes opened to look at Meredith. "He and Mama used to bring us to these mountains when Angela and I were kids. We explored all over up here. When Mama wasn't with us, he'd let us go inside the mines."

Meredith clicked off the light. "How long since you were up here?" She wasn't sure this was a smart move. Would the tunnel go all the way through?

"Hmmm. About fifteen years. Not much could have changed. These old mines have been abandoned for years. In this economy, any chance of them opening again has evaporated."

Meredith sighed, not making any effort to hide her doubt. This just got better and better, she thought. "Are we going to have to do any climbing up shafts or anything?"

"No, this is a horizontal mine with tunnels built off to the sides. It goes downhill for a mile or so, but it's a slight grade. It will be easy going."

"You said one of the tunnels dumps out somewhere down the hill?" Meredith suppressed the thought that it might have collapsed.

"Las Pulgas. A few shacks that used to be a village for mine laborers. I don't think anyone even lives there anymore."

"Let's head out." Nick's voice cut through the darkness. He flicked on his flashlight. Meredith wrapped Rigo's good arm around her neck, flicked on the light, and took the lead.

They walked for twenty minutes, rested, then picked up their snail's pace again. He wasn't growing any stronger, but Rigo walked longer between rest breaks. He seemed to learn that his brother-in-law would push his limits. An occasional grunt of pain was all she heard from him for hours.

Meredith mentally crossed her fingers. She didn't think they had been followed. Sometimes, they heard the sound of raindrops pounding the corrugated aluminum shaft covers on the tunnels that ran perpendicular to the main trunk. The rain hadn't let up, and the ventilation inside the tunnel was well thought out. Meredith had no trouble breathing, although Rigo's chest heaved with the exertion. She stopped at an intersection populated with rusted ore carts. One sat on its side. "Nick, time to let Rigo take a rest." She steered Rigo to the cart, sat him down, then stepped away to stretch her back.

Nick sat next to Rigo and ran the light over his brother-in-law's face. "How you feeling, dude?" The cuts on Rigo's forehead had scabbed over, but his eyes sagged with fatigue.

"Like shit, bro." Rigo hunched over, closing his eyes. "I haven't slept much."

"Me, either." Nick looked toward Meredith. She wondered why he'd left her out. She thought for a moment, then figured something was coming. He was always aware of their partnership, and if he kept her out of the conversation, he had a reason...

Nick rooted around in his backpack, coming out with a fistful of bent energy bars. "I know they're crap, but better than nothing." At their grunts of approval, he handed one to each and ripped his open.

"Be sure to police your trash. We don't want to leave a trail."

They ate and drank a few sips of water from Meredith's water bottle.

Nick stuffed his wrapper in his pocket. "So, Rigo. Who would kidnap you—and why?" He said it so casually that it took Rigo a moment for the question to sink in. He didn't move, but Meredith saw that something in his eyes had changed.

Nick sat, waiting.

Rigo sighed. "Miguel Vega. At first, I thought they picked me because of my car. Kidnappers like to go after guys in flashy cars—it usually means money. This wasn't like that. They left me alone for days, tied up in a room. No one spoke to me, so I didn't know anything until I met with Vega—yesterday, I think."

He made it sound like it was a business meeting. Like people repeated this kind of thing all over the world, thousands of times a day, maybe more. Did she think he was lying? Well, maybe not. But, he was hiding something.

"Didn't know what?" Nick prompted. Meredith wondered if her partner saw the same thing in his brother-in-law. She didn't ask.

He'd been somewhat distant since—the boat.

Rigo bowed his head, looking at the wrapper in his hands. "I figured out that Vega picked me specifically—because I was seeing his wife."

"Holy Christ, Rigo." Nick's eyes bulged. "You couldn't find someone who wasn't a drug lord's wife? You have an epic sense of self-destruction, don't you?"

"It wasn't like that..." Rigo's voice trailed off.

Nick stood one hand on his hip while the other ran through his hair. "Christ, Rigo. It's always like that. Married women are a nightmare at best. At worst, you picked the one who could get you in the most trouble."

Rigo's voice was so low that Meredith almost didn't hear it. "I didn't know who she was married to. It's a common name, and he's new to this area. Besides, I loved her."

"Whoa," Meredith said. "Loved?

"She's dead."

"How do you know?" Nick's voice was stiff with tension.

Rigo took a moment to answer. The wrapper floated to the ground. "I don't know, but Vega killed her." He used a wrist to rub his eye. "He killed her. He said so."

"Why?" This didn't sound right to Meredith. It wasn't unheard of for one spouse to kill the other when infidelity was involved, but they were missing something. Usually, those dead women's husbands were easy to catch, with blood still on their clothes. The whole package sounded fishy.

Rigo looked up at her. In the faint light from the flashlights, she saw his tears cut through the grime on his face. "She gave me a book. It was after she hired me as her divorce attorney—it was in a straw cigarette case. She said to hide it, and we would use it later in court as evidence of his fraud and infidelity." Meredith saw the pain in his eyes—he suffered at Silvia's death. A tick in his favor.

"Did you look at the book?" Nick asked. "What was in it?"

"Yes," he sighed. "It was filled with dates, places, first names, and peso amounts. It was a ledger."

"Marking some kind of transactions?"

Rigo nodded. "To make sense of it, you would have to know what the merchandise was."

"Any ideas?"

"No. It made no sense to me, but it was important enough to hide."

"Okay." She almost heard the gears turning in Nick's head. As he picked up the wrapper, he asked, "Where did you hide it?"

"In Angela's room—under a drawer in the nightstand. No one could find it."

Nick's gaze met Meredith's. He shook his head. "You wanna bet?"

Chapter Twenty-Seven

TWENTY MILES OUTSIDE OF BUCERIAS AND DOWN A LONG-abandoned asphalt road, Emilio drove the primered '59 Chevy Impala to the edge of the ragged blacktop, then pulled off. They parked in a turnout that formed a ledge over the creek alongside the ghostly ruins of Las Pulgas. Angela squirmed in the front seat. The white tuck and roll leather groaned as she shifted impatiently. Her father slouched behind the wheel, a toothpick rotating between his lips. The world was dead black beyond the faint glow of the dashboard. Emilio plucked the knob that turned on the headlights. He barely made out a manmade structure on the other side of the creek, the tunnel exit. To the right of the chiseled opening, tentative frame boards from the remnants of a shack leaned against the cliff. He had parked on a shelf that dropped off into a tangle of brush. Trees that stretched across a broad arroyo bent under the weight of the rain. The sound of rushing water made the hair on his arms stand up. This wasn't normally a creek. It was more of an overflow route for the water.

They'd gone as far as they could drive. They were to meet Nick at Las Pulgas, but Emilio wasn't sure his son-in-law could make the trip from the tunnel to where they parked. Rigo, if he was alive, was probably injured. It would make for slow going. Even with Meredith's help, it would be dicey. What if Nick and his partner were able to rescue Rigo, but they were lost escaping?

ANGELA WAS ANGRY. The entire situation was unfair and ridiculous. All her father's worries were just the product of an idle mind. She didn't care, anyway. She avoided looking at him. He was upset—no doubt about it. Over a hundred different things. She wanted to get Rigo and just get out of there. Then she and Javier could be together. And she needed a divorce from Nick. With the baby on the way, time was crucial. She wasn't sure how much longer she could deceive her father. Or Nick. She would have to go away—and soon, before she started showing. Lying to them both was necessary because she knew they wouldn't understand. They would be disappointed, which was an annoyance she didn't need. She wanted to be left alone. She wanted Javier. She wanted the baby.

"I'm going to get out. It's stuffy in here." Angela opened the door.

"Are you crazy? It's pouring rain."

Rain drenched her arm as she paused. "There's a rock over there. I'll stand under the overhang."

"Don't be stupid. You'll get soaked."

"Popi, I just want to breathe for a moment. I'll be back. I won't even be out of your view."

Emilio's shoulders drooped. She knew she'd gotten her way when his wrinkled face sagged in resignation. She'd spent a lifetime working her way around his orders. When she was a child, she always finagled what she wanted by using a sweet smile and a soft embrace around her Popi's waist.

As Angela got out of the car, her father put a hand on her arm. He held her in a surprisingly tight grip. "Angela, get in and close the door." She'd been wrong. She wouldn't get her way this time.

The timbre of his voice was completely out of character. He sounded firm, unyielding. What was on his mind? She thought back to the scene with Oswaldo at the house. He almost sounded like he was giving orders. He was a little late for that.

Irked by his manner, she closed the door. "What?"

"You're hiding something." He released her and sat back, gazing out the windshield.

"Me?" Warmth rose in her face. "What are you talking about?"

"I mean, there is something that you are specifically not telling Nick or me."

Angela did not look at her father. Both her secrets would shatter him. "You're seeing things that aren't there."

"You look away when Nick asks you a question. I can see it. I hope it isn't anything that will hurt him."

Damn it. She felt like a little girl again, when she committed a venial sin and then lied about it. Damn, damn, damn. She was almost thirty years old, married and…damn it. Why the hell was her father worried about Nick? He should worry about her. She'd always been annoyed by how Emilio loved Nick like a son. She'd heard him on the phone talking to her husband after she'd moved back to Mexico. She almost understood the affection between the two men. Nick's father died when he was a child. When he married Angela, she came with a ready-made family. Her parents took Nick into their hearts because they saw how much he loved their daughter.

None of them understood. She lost her trust in Nick after Mia died. When she needed him, he wasn't there. His consolation was his work, but she had nothing. She was in her first semester of nursing school, and she didn't have the friends he did. He'd left her alone when she needed him the most.

She'd told her parents she was considering divorcing Nick so that it wouldn't be a surprise. Her father disapproved. To him, marriage was a lifetime commitment. She felt that way, too, but sometimes life was just unfair—things happened, people changed. There was no reason to keep two people miserable together when they had a chance at happiness apart.

"Nick is just hurt. He wants…"

"It's more than that." Emilio didn't let her finish. "Yes, Nick is wounded. But you're lying by omission. I can tell. Is this about Javier?"

She inhaled sharply. She hadn't expected that. "What about Javier?" Did they know about the baby?

Lightning flashed above the meadow on the other side of the hill. His gaze met hers. In the dark, his eyes glowed in the dashboard light. "Don't patronize me, hija. I see how you look at each other." Thunder rolled over them.

Angela thought this might work for her. "Yes, Popi. Javier wants to marry me when the divorce is final."

Even in the darkness of the car, she saw him wince. Maybe she felt it. Once again, he sided with Nick. She couldn't tell him about the baby. He couldn't know about the baby until after she and Javier were married. It would kill him. She decided to give him something substantial.

"I found what the gangsters were looking for." She spoke as if she was in a confessional box. In a sense, she was—telling some of the truth to appease her father. "It was a book."

Emilio rubbed his eyes. Angela almost heard him formulating his thoughts. He was a smart man. Educated and intuitive. Normally, she respected his opinion. Now, she dreaded his next words. She knew she had upset him—and she was tired of getting disappointment from him. She had to give him something to get him off her case. He'd seen through her, but he didn't know what she was hiding.

"What kind of book?" Suspicion thickened in Emilio's voice.

"Like a journal, with entries of names, dates, cash amounts."

"Where'd it come from? Who does it belong to?" Her heart jumped at his urgency. Like Nick, he didn't miss much.

"Rigo must have hidden it—I found it in the nightstand in my room. A woman wrote it. We—I—don't know whose it is."

"We? Javier? Oswaldo?" His wiry hand stretched across the seat, grabbing her wrist. "Who are you scheming with—and what do you hope to gain?"

Twisting her bandaged arm, she whimpered. "Ouch, you're hurting me."

"I'm sorry." Emilio released her abruptly.

Angela rubbed her wrist, feeling for the bandage to be sure it was still holding. She had to give Oswaldo up. Besides, what could her father do now?

"Angela, tell me who you're in this with." "Oswaldo," she sighed.

"Oh no, hija." She saw the whites of Emilio's eyes.

"He made me, Popi," she lied. "He said he would use the book to ransom Rigo. I don't know whose book it is, but Vega wants it."

"What were you thinking? Oswaldo has no tact, no cunning. He means well, but he's too weak, too stupid. He can't talk to someone like Vega in this sensitive situation." Emilio's dark eyes were pinpoints of fury. "You have sent him to his death. A man like Vega will not negotiate—especially with Oswaldo."

"I have not." Angela pushed her hair out of her face. She swept aside the tiny tendrils of guilt that tried to gain a foothold in her heart. She simply didn't care. "Besides, it was his idea. He begged me to let him go."

Her father was silent for a moment. "And the book? Where is it?"

Angela patted the side of her huge purse. "It's here, Popi. I have it."

Emilio leaned his forehead on the steering wheel, trying to sort it out. "How is Oswaldo supposed to exchange it for Rigo? Does he know where it is?" He groaned. "This isn't good. And what about Nicholas and Meredith? What happens when Vega finds out your brother has been rescued? You could have compromised them, also."

"Popi, you are assuming Nick can free Rigo." Angela had no faith this would happen. Her hand caressed the side of her purse. "I want to keep our options open."

"Querída, you are playing both ends against the middle. It is too dangerous, this game of yours. Someone will get hurt. Nick could die."

A distant rumble announced more rain and maybe lightning, too. Instead of fading, the noise grew. The ground began to vibrate.

What was happening? What had her father gotten them into? "Popi, it sounds like a jet plane is landing on top of us." Angela wailed against the noise of the storm.

"No, it's a mudslide. The ground beneath us is shaking. It'll take the car and everything else in its path. Go; get to higher ground— over there." He pointed at a rock outcropping. "Go!"

"Popi!" She couldn't hear her own voice. Terror invaded her and she couldn't move. The roaring noise grew louder. "¡Popi!"

The sedan slid sideways with a lurch, slamming them both into the passenger-side-door.

Chapter Twenty-Eight

MEREDITH STOOD SENTRY, LEANING AGAINST THE ROCK WALL—cradling the AR-15—listening. Overhead vents with rusted iron grates every hundred feet allowed faint light inside the tunnel. Not that there was much to see. The rock walls were gray and the boulders they slept on were the same colorless shade. She wondered at the men who had chipped the angular wall with hand tools, working and sweating under this chunk of earth. What an existence.

Meredith watched Rigo's chest rise and fall in his troubled sleep. His head propped on his backpack, Nick lay in an uneasy catnap beside his brother-in-law. Fatigue nearly lulled her to sleep, too.

Meredith rested the rifle against the wall, stood, and stretched, trying to stay awake. She inhaled the warm, dry air, trying to draw more oxygen to her brain. She was exhausted—they all were. Nick had to be just as tired. She wanted a shower and a full charge on her cell phone. Such easy things, always available in California. Her phone was almost dead. A small, bitchy part of her nature yelled for a conclusion to this mess. Soon. She was frustrated with Nick for the lengths he had gone to help Angela. His soon-to-be ex didn't have a shred of loyalty for Nick, nor give a rat's ass about him, except for what he could offer her.

Did that make her sound jealous?

Rigo had little more to recommend him. He was an extravagant philanderer who put himself in a dangerous position by accepting this book that put his life in peril. He had unwittingly endangered his whole family. The one spark in his character was the obvious love he felt for the woman, Silvia.

Meredith felt sorry for Emilio and Liliana. They were good people. They raised two kids and tried to instill morals, only to have their children reject their values and embezzle their retirement. How long would it take Rigo to give them that news? What would their response be?

Nick shifted against the coarse gravel and dirt floor. Meredith watched him. Nick was a bear—big, suspicious, and slow to anger, but nobody you wanted to mess with. The beam from the flashlight weakened. She flipped it off to save the battery, so they sat in absolute darkness. As frustrated and tired as she was, she understood why they were there. Nick was loyal to a fault. No matter what happened between him and Angela, he would honor his word—and more. Nick would think ahead to the family's safety after Rigo's return. She loved that about him. It was his bulldog-like attitude that had saved her last year. Even after her bosses failed to support or protect her as the judge stalked her, Nick stayed by her side. The judge killed almost everyone dear to her, and almost Meredith. But Nick risked his life, ignored the department. At his own peril, he'd been there for her.

She owed him the same. Now, there was something more. Glimmerings of feelings she didn't dare admit threatened to push past her barriers. Her chest warmed with memories of his kiss—was it just yesterday? So much had happened. It was hard to force her mind in another direction.

"Are you still awake?" Nick whispered.

"Um, hm. I'm supposed to be."

"Just checking." He rustled in the dark, then his flashlight flipped on. "I'll take over so you can get some sleep." Nick stood over Rigo, hooding the light with his hand. Rigo lay dead still. It was hard to believe he'd made it this far. Nick came toward her, bouncing light in one hand, his other balancing on the grip of the pistol in his pocket. "Go ahead and take 20 minutes. It'll help."

"What makes you think I can sleep?" Worry needled her. So many things could go wrong, so many variables over which they had no control. She rubbed her eyes, knowing her question was ridiculous. She'd been running on adrenaline for an hour. She knew her body well enough; she'd crash soon. Sleep was what she needed to recover from the huge expenditure of energy at El Rancho.

"You're worn out. The nap helps—really. Here, have the last of my water."

Meredith pushed it away, then settled back against the rock. She shoved her pack in a position where she rested her head, thirsty. Her water bottle was dry. Rigo had been wrong about finding water. So far, anyway. "Doesn't seem like anyone's following us." "For now."

Nick's damned Mexican pessimism—always thinking the worst. However, he might be right. Someone said Vega was new to the area. She found it odd that he would use El Rancho without securing his get-away route. Any gangster worth his bullets should know about that. However, Vega didn't seem all that organized. "Do you think Vega knows about the mine?"

"If he doesn't, he will soon. His goons look like locals."

"You can tell?"

"Just a guess—the two boys we've seen so far have been pretty primitive."

Rigo's even breathing softened the silence that hung between them.

She tried to drift off to sleep, but her gut churned with questions. Would the Borregos be safe when Rigo came home? When would this mess be over? Did Nick hope to reconcile with Angela? That had all the earmarks of a disaster. Whatever he decided, Meredith would be there for him. Watching her friend get sucked into the vortex of Angela's selfishness gnawed at her sense of loyalty. If they did get back together, it seemed to Meredith their love was a one-way street—in Angela's direction. Or was this some distorted version of faithfulness that he took so seriously? She'd been as honest with Nick as she could be with her opinion—that helping

Angela was a waste of time. In any case, he would be hurt in the end.

What about her and Nick? She wished she could say their bond was as strong as before—professional and solid friends. But she couldn't. What happened on the boat came from nowhere. It was like all the hints from her heart were strings that had banded together in a bunch. Suddenly, they were strong enough to knock her over. Then, all the doubt, plus excitement, forced those strings into a crazy braid that ended in a relentless knot. Nick and Meredith couldn't go back to the way they had been. They'd turned a corner and gone to a place from which there was no return. Their relationship would always be changed. At the worst, their stability was damaged—but not destroyed. They knew each other too well and had been through too much together to tear that down. She wished for a normal feeling, just be happy that she'd kissed this man.

What was the best-case scenario?

"Nick?" Her whisper drifted away in the cavern.

"Go to sleep," he said, sounding like a parent, cross with a child.

Chapter Twenty-Nine

THEIR BODIES HAD BEEN THROWN TOGETHER AS THE IMPALA TIPPED at an acute angle. Her father freed himself quickly. Fighting gravity and the slickness of the upholstery, he grabbed Angela's bad arm to pull her across the car seat. Keeping a tight grip on her purse, she screamed with pain. She braced her feet against the steering column. Satisfied that she was in a better position, he let go. Opening the door, he gathered himself into a ball. When he pushed off the threshold, he was airborne across the mud. He landed close enough to solid ground to get a firm footing.

She collected herself at the open driver's door. Her father held on to a gnarled oak branch and reached a hand toward her.

The sedan rocked, pushed by the mud, its nose tipped down. Angela stood in the doorway, her arm stretched toward her father—his hand a mere six inches away. She was scared, afraid to jump. She might fall and hurt herself or, even worse, the baby. A glance at the mud told her there was nothing to stop the car from sliding down the hill to Bucerias. It would take the path of least resistance, finding gullies and washes already cut into the hillside.

"Jump, hija," he yelled.

The car slithered on, gradually gaining speed. There was no hope if she stayed. Scared or not, she had to move. The car pitched again.

Her feet left the floorboards just as the bumper caught in a downed tree. She landed a few feet from her father, mud sucking at her sandals and holding her down. "¡Popi! Help me!" She wobbled until his hands drew her to him.

Still clutching the purse, she buried her head in her father's shoulder. He brushed her off. "We must get to higher ground." He searched the moving hillside and shouted over the storm. "Follow me!"

The Impala shuddered as it spun under the weight of the overpowering mud. One by one, the windows burst into shards as the car, now filling with mud, tipped on its side, slipping down the hillside and away from them. It looked like a half-sunken ship, falling down with the rest of the jungle debris carried by the river of mud.

Angela didn't want to follow her father, but there was no other choice. She wouldn't make it without him.

The lightning lighted their way over the ridge. After a flash illuminated the hillside, they zigzagged as far as they could. Sticking to the rocky edge of the bank until they could see again, they moved alongside the flowing mud. Fist-sized chunks of mountain grass flowed with more treacherous debris, including pieces of trees as large as their lost car. Moving cautiously, Emilio found a sturdy stick to test the soil before them. A tree limb swept by, almost ripping the pole from his hands. He wrestled it back, disentangled the stick, and steered his daughter out of the range of hazards.

The rain let up and slowed to mist. The path was no easier, except Angela didn't have to wipe water from her eyes every step. Suddenly her father stopped, his gaze on something in the distance. They waited. Soon, the night lit up with a distant flash.

"There it is!" Emilio pointed higher up the hillside. "Did you see it?"

"What?" She felt his excitement.

"It's a bridge." He faced her. "It's been there for many years. I hoped it would still be there."

Angela sighed, not making any sense of his words. "What difference does it make? It won't get us home."

"No, hija, but it will get us to the other side of the mudslide. Your brother should be waiting for us there." Even in the darkness, his smile was brilliant.

Emilio turned, yanked a sodden bough aside, and moved on.

SOMEONE NUDGED MEREDITH'S FOOT. She snapped awake. It was Nick. She wouldn't have believed that she fell asleep. Even exhausted, her mind was in constant debate. Now Nick—her partner and best friend—cut her off like she was a precocious kid after a moment they both obviously enjoyed. Man, it pissed her off.

She eyed Nick, a smart remark about waking her percolating in the back of her mind. His index finger was perpendicular to his lips. Quiet. What had he heard? Whatever it was, it couldn't be good. She stood, slinging her rifle over one shoulder, the backpack over the other.

Ready.

Nick shook Rigo awake. Meredith walked the tunnel looking for something, her fingers touching the wall in the dim light. There, ten feet from where they rested, she felt a rocky seam. It was a long one, cut at an angle, almost 45 degrees from the ground to the roof, and deep enough to conceal all three of them. Peering inside, she decided. Running was not an option. Rigo had trouble enough walking. Meredith had gambled with their getaway time—staying instead of running—and it had paid off. If you didn't know it was there, the hole was invisible. She waved for Nick and signaled him to come to her.

With Rigo's arm draped over Nick's shoulders, they scuffled along the rough rock floor as they made for Meredith. Following her hand, Nick steered Rigo toward the crevice.

Meredith heard a scrape—gravel against rock floor, echoing from some distance away. She had no way to determine how far.

Nick backed into the chasm first, his shoulder under Rigo's

armpit. They shuffled in quietly. In seconds, they pressed against the wall surface, tense and waiting. Meredith hugged her rifle. She couldn't aim and shoot in their tight space without showing herself. If they were discovered, the best she hoped for was a good swift strike with the rifle butt. Something cold and metal touched her elbow. Nick handed her the Glock. She forced herself to breathe deeply, slowly, and gripped the pistol.

They didn't wait long.

The two stocky guards they'd tied up in El Rancho skulked by in an arrogant trudge. Both men followed a narrow flashlight beam. The guy with the spiked hair—the guy Meredith had clobbered—had a rag wadded up his nose, and his reddened eyes already sported purple smudges underneath. He carried a pistol. As his comrade had no sidearm, Meredith speculated that he had given it to Spike, putting their armaments at a rifle and pistol, maybe a knife, as well. The other man kept an AK-47 pointed straight ahead.

The guards walked by.

They stayed hidden, waiting. When Rigo wanted to sit down, Meredith whispered they had to stand for a while longer. She hoped the men would return and not go all the way through to the end of the tunnel. With luck, Emilio and Angela would be on the other side waiting with a car. She didn't want the guards to find them.

It was hard to tell how much time passed—an eternity, or ten minutes. Meredith felt a little disoriented not knowing the exact time. Here in Mexico, it wasn't relevant. It didn't matter how long something took. It took what it needed. Time lumbered on, unencumbered by human wants or needs. She missed having her phone available. She had ditched her watch a few years ago, when her phone became an extension of her work. She disliked redundancy. Now she missed them both.

When the guards returned, Spike sulked while his partner's rapid-fire Mexican reverberated off the walls. Meredith's Spanish was iffy, but their tone told her they would be in trouble if discovered. She heard Vega's name more than once.

The guards passed the seam. If they turned around and looked, they would see the three of them hiding.

Meredith held her breath.

The light beam went wild as the flashlight clattered to the rocky floor. Spike pitched forward with a half groan, half cuss. The other guard froze with a "what the fuck?" grunt. On the ground, Spike was immobile for several heartbeats. He must have sensed no threat because he spat a command to the other man. After some rustling around, one of them picked up the flashlight. Both men, now on their feet with guns pointed, turned as one to follow the light.

On the ground, in front of the guards, a boot, then another near the wall, splayed out as if occupied. A shovel, pick, and lantern lying in the dirt, then pants, a shirt, and a dusty, yellowed bone—an ulna, radius, and…

He'd tripped over a skeleton.

Meredith clamped a hand over Rigo's mouth, a preemptive move in case he felt the need to yell.

Spike took a wild aim with the pistol and fired at the corpse. The report echoed within the rock walls, battering Meredith's ears, the percussion a shock. She felt Rigo's body jump.

"¡Madre de Dios!" Spike yelled. The other man backed away.

In these close quarters, the odor of cordite was overwhelming. The cloying smoke made it difficult to breathe. Releasing Rigo, Meredith took shallow breaths.

The guards snapped out of their shock. Spike stared at the skeleton, stretching out his boot to tap the phalanges. A small cloud of dust rose; he drew back as if the bones had come to life.

Abruptly, the other man slapped Spike's shoulder, an unmistakable message of retreat.

After the guards' footsteps died away, they came out of the chasm. Rigo flexed his fingers. He winced as he rubbed his arm. He looked at the corpse in the dim light. "Poor guy. What a way to die."

Nick shone a light over the remains to see if there were any weapons. Finding nothing, he turned to Rigo. "How far?"

"Not too much longer."

Meredith focused her flashlight beam down the tunnel. The light withered away into darkness, at odds with Rigo's estimate. "Let's get moving." She led the way, keeping the light off unless needed.

It took ten minutes to reach the barricaded exit of the tunnel, although it felt longer. Meredith had given up trying to estimate time. Her phone was dead.

Faint rays of yellow light traced the outline of boards and corrugated aluminum. They framed an eight-by-eight rectangle of beams and braces. Flipping on the flashlight, she ran it over the entire wall. The barricade work had been done from the inside. The tools were left where they fell, as if the workmen couldn't be burdened as they hurried to get out. How many years ago, she wondered. Ten? Fifty? Empty canvas bags sat piled in a corner, barely recognizable under layers of fine dirt.

Nick walked Rigo to the bags, easing him down in a puff of dust.

They listened to be sure the guards weren't returning. Meredith handed Rigo the flashlight and rifle.

"This is going to make a lot of noise," Nick said.

She shrugged and lifted a pickaxe. "We don't have any choice."

Nick took the first swing, wielding a sledgehammer. The wet, rotting wood disintegrated under the power of his blow. Ignoring the noise, Meredith concentrated on prying corrugated aluminum sheets away from the wooden braces. They worked together as they always had, each assessing needs, then one diving in to take action, while the other picked up the balance of the work. With zero-to-no discussion, they did the job. She savored the moments like this when they clicked.

When the aluminum sheet peeled away, meager light and damp, fresh air greeted them. Meredith leaned on the pickaxe and gazed at the scene before her. It was almost dawn. From below the Sierra Madre Mountains, the sun's early rays streaked upward into the clouds. Above, the sky was a crystalline blue looking so crisp it could shatter at a breath of wind. Verdant moisture-saturated foliage matted the hills below them in a brilliant tapestry of greens. Breathtaking, she thought. A land of contrasts—Mexico.

She looked for brown or gray—a road. Nothing. Glancing to her feet, her breath caught. Nothing. No hillside, no trail, nothing. Whatever was on the other side of the barricade had dropped away, a landslide. Grabbing a moisture-swollen brace, she leaned over for a better look. Below was a sheer drop, about thirty feet to the closest solid earth. She saw the outline of a pair of struggling conifers, and a fallen deciduous tree, with brush crowding its trunks. A huge branch had torn off, and it rested on the ground below. Rails, wood ties, and vestiges of decades-old mining equipment were strewn about the meadow. The arroyo began as a narrow cut through the cliff on one side and exited as a broad swath of mud.

Behind her, Nick whispered, "What the…"

Chapter Thirty

"LAS PULGAS IS CLOSE BY," RIGO INSISTED.

"Okay," Meredith said in that voice that said she didn't believe him. She pointed for him to look outside.

Nick was dismayed when Rigo peered out the tunnel opening and seemed confused. Below was an oozing mess, but at least it was no longer sliding down the hill. He wondered what had been there but decided it didn't matter.

"Look for a road," Rigo insisted. "There used to be shacks around the diggings." Nick had a sinking feeling that all Rigo's landmarks had been wiped away. Still, from the tunnel opening, he scanned the jungle for Emilio and Angela, or guards from El Rancho. Nothing.

Meredith leaned out, studying the terrain. She turned back to Nick with a wry smile. "Easy. We can climb down the cliff, through the brush, to the other side of the valley. Looks like a cut through the ridge may be a road—if the jungle doesn't kill us."

A breeze blew through the mountains, a hint of a cooler day. A gust blasted into the mine, a welcome relief to Nick's already sweat-soaked body. He supported Rigo as well as he could within the narrow space while they surveyed the countryside below. Although not easy, the route Meredith outlined was doable. He was sure Rigo could make it with help.

Meredith stepped out onto the lip of the cliff. Limestone outcroppings provided solid hand and footholds. Rigo went next. Nick used the leftover length of rope and tied it under Rigo's arms to hold his brother-in-law steady. It was slow going, but with Meredith to guide them to footholds, they made it with nothing more than a few new scrapes.

A downed tree rested at a gentle angle from the base of the escarpment, its trunk disappearing into a tangle of brush. Here, Rigo moved under his own power. When they crawled over the exposed root ball of a huge fallen laurel, its leafy boughs swallowed them up. The stout trunk, its limbs reaching toward the Sierra Madre peaks, provided concealment and a navigable passage. Even better, when solid earth appeared, the laurel offered smaller branches to stair-step down.

The trail had been partially washed away, but they found enough rocky ground to walk on. "We keep moving." Nick's glance didn't rest on Rigo for long. His brother-in-law had to know they were in a tough spot because of his guidance.

"A machete would be nice," Meredith suggested, staring at the undergrowth. Sometimes her statement of the obvious irritated Nick. They didn't have a machete, and they had to keep going. Standing still and analyzing their situation wouldn't get them out of it. "When we get to the buildings, we'll rest until Angela and Emilio show."

It would help to know what they were getting into between the trees and the shack. Rigo was tired; so were he and Meredith. Nick didn't know the local geography, but if the gaping hole at this end of the tunnel was any gauge, the terrain had changed very dramatically, very recently. He wasn't confident that Rigo could find their way over the changed landscape, but he was all they had.

"I'll scout the path." Meredith volunteered. She didn't wait for an answer. Nick watched her pick her way through the leaves. He kept his eyes open for any movement out of the ordinary. What was abnormal in the jungle? Nick wondered, not for the first time today, how a city girl like Meredith ran around on tree branches like Tarzan, er, Jane. His momentary irritation evaporated as a swell of admiration filled him. That woman could do anything.

He pushed Rigo on to follow her through the leaves.

RIGO STUMBLED, clutching Nick's shoulder and falling heavily into him. The path was wet and slippery. Nick dragged his brother-in-law on. They'd reached a boulder the size of a garbage truck, Nick bent a limb aside to get by, then motioned for Rigo to sit down. They would rest here until Meredith returned.

Nick slapped a mosquito from his neck. God, he hated this. He hated feeling like his life was suspended above a fire pit on a fraying rope. Angela was showing a side of herself that he hadn't seen in six years of marriage. She seemed so different. It would be a normal assumption to attribute that to her family's problems but, excitable as the Borregos were, they were good people. Angela though, had grown nasty and self-centered. Maybe Mere was right about his wife and Javier. Angela seemed like she belonged with Rigo and Oswaldo. Nick had never felt that from her before. She was under the influence of her brother, where the truth varied from one audience to another, and moral life was questionable. Would she ever return to Nick? Would she ever again be the sweet woman he'd married?

Meredith was back. "I didn't go too far because I knew you'd need help here." She glanced at the boulder, tree trunk, and rocky landslide below. "It looks like more of this." She held up her hands, pointing to the heavy undergrowth.

She climbed past them and placed herself above Rigo. She slipped her arms around him from the back, joining one hand with her other wrist. In a slow movement, she helped the injured man slide down the rock to a sitting position on an angled tree trunk. Nick placed Rigo's uninjured arm on his own shoulder to brace his weight. Wincing, Rigo slid to the rocks below with Meredith following. Panting, they worked at finding their footing in the small, loose slide. Once on solid ground, they paused long enough to catch their breath.

While Rigo stretched his good arm, Meredith leaned to Nick's ear. "I think I saw the roof of that shack he's been talking about." She nodded toward a ridge.

"You want to lead, then?"

Adjusting the straps on her backpack, Meredith set off.

A path soon emerged from the ruins left by the slide. Meredith scanned the soggy trail and stepped back into the trees, motioning for them. Approving of her tactic, Nick followed. They had no way of knowing if the guards were following them. If they were, the trail would be easy to follow. Trees offered some concealment, and forging a new trail left few tracks in the decaying leaves and humus.

In less than half an hour, they broke through the undergrowth to a clearing. A handful of abandoned buildings sat in crumbling disrepair. Some looked like they had been storage sheds, but only one had been used for living quarters. Meredith glanced at the ground, then shook her head. No footprints in the steaming earth. No one had been here recently. She shouldered the AR-15 and she moved in. Nick watched her search the interior of each building. Soon, she waved them into the one that looked the most stable.

Nick was looking forward to letting Rigo rest. He also was ready to take a break. Hunger clawed at his empty stomach. He was thirsty, too. Once he got Rigo settled, he'd search the grounds for some way to catch rainwater from the storm. Both Nick and Meredith's water bottles were empty.

While the structure Meredith had found had an intact roof, moisture still trickled down the interior walls. The window had long since lost its glass, and the door dangled on one hinge. Still, the inside was the most habitable of all the buildings. Nick wondered if the place ever dried out. A few broken wood chairs sat in a corner, along with a table tossed on its side, and a mattress that looked like mice nested in it.

When Nick pulled the mattress outside, a half dozen rats scattered. He smiled at how they made Meredith shiver, then watched with surprise when she kicked a long, wiggling rat down the hillside. Inside, using the shovel, she cleared the floor and set the table upright. The chairs were a lost cause. Not great, but better.

They moved Rigo in and got him settled. Propped up against the rough wooden wall with their backpacks, he was asleep almost immediately.

At the door, Nick leaned against the jamb. "I'm going to look for some water. Maybe find something to eat."

"I'll stay here. You want the rifle?"

"No, you keep it. Give me the pistol and your water bottle."

Nick took stock of the area. Broken pieces of a metal aqueduct lay scattered near the buildings. There should be a cistern or some other system to catch and hold rainwater. Following the corroded remnants, he hiked up the hill until he found a stone reservoir. The wooden cover was half-rotten and had fallen away, but leaning in, he was able to reach the surface of the water. After dunking both bottles, he looked around for a bucket or something else that might hold more. The jungle tended to reclaim men's artifices with a minimum of noise and effort. Wherever he saw, the brush and vines encroached on the structures and crept onto the surrounding clearing. It wouldn't be too many generations before the vegetation grew over all of it.

Back down the trail toward the clearing, he found an area once used as a scrap pile. A heavy mist dripped down his head and off his nose as he worked, finding oil cans, pipe fittings, and other industrial toss-aways. His catch consisted of two vegetable cans. He trudged back to the cistern to fill the cans and then back down to the shack.

Meredith offered her bottle to Nick first. "What about you? Aren't you thirsty?"

"Thanks, I got some up there." He nodded toward the hill. "But I'm hungry. I'm going to scrounge around and see if I can find anything."

Meredith gave him a funny look. "Nuts and berries? A banana, perhaps? Isn't there a 7-Eleven on the corner?" He shook his head. Wiseass.

Nick gave up his quest for 7-Eleven type-grub when he couldn't identify any of the fruits or berries he saw. After all the trouble they went through to find Rigo, poisoning them had no appeal, so he passed on food for now. Not trusting Rigo's memory, Nick paced the bottom of the hill, looking for a trail or road. Maybe he could find an easier way to get back to civilization. From this section of the mine area, there should have been a road for the laborers to take ore down to a crushing mill.

Farther down, the brush fell away to stubby grass and ratty wild-flowers. He walked on, feeling more encouraged that he might find an easier way out. A rail cart axle in an advanced state of rust hinted that a track was nearby. Dropping down the gentle slope, he followed the rails for a hundred yards until they were swallowed by the jungle.

Leaves brushed against his clothing; he stopped. He wasn't sure what he'd heard. Then he identified it—voices.

There was a man's low growl, then, to his surprise, a familiar feminine taunt. "We're lost, Papa. Admit it."

Angela.

Chapter Thirty-One

IT WAS ALL HE COULD DO NOT TO SHOUT HER NAME. ENVISIONING Vega's thugs following them and hearing his voice, he kept quiet. He couldn't see through the thick wall of green. A few steps further, the bushes followed the line of a shallow ravine. Picking his way past a mass of thick vines and thorny scrubs, Nick listened. He focused on where he thought the voices came from and hiked toward them. When he felt close by, he whispered her name.

The movement in the brush stopped a mere ten feet away. Then, Angela yelled, "It's Nick!"

He rushed around a thicket to them, shushing his wife. She ignored the caution and lunged against his chest, sweeping her arms around him, her huge purse banging into his side. Shock at her welcome dashed through him. It was a second before he could put his arms around her.

Emilio touched his shoulder, smiling. Nick released Angela, then grinned as his father-in-law told them he knew right where they were. Relief obvious in his eyes, Emilio reached up to embrace Nick. Nick's chest swelled with affection for Emilio. He was the quiet one in the family, yet here was the strength. He'd proven himself as a father.

"Rigo?" Emilio's voice trembled, afraid to hear the answer. Nick tipped his head toward the shack. "He's not far."

———

TEN MINUTES LATER, at the shelter, Angela brushed past Nick and hurried through the door. Nick followed Emilio inside. Angela threw herself at her sleeping brother. "Rigo!"

Rigo's eyelids fluttered open as he pressed against the wall.

"Rigo, it's me, Angela."

"Angela!" His voice sounded raw. Joyful tears erupted from both as they struggled to hug each other with their injured arms. Now able to see him through Angela's eyes, Nick understood how messed up Rigo was. Even so, Emilio stood above his children with a wide smile.

Soon, they sat on the floor, sharing stories of the past twenty-four hours while Meredith took their bottles and the vegetable cans to go for more water.

When Angela finished her account of their adventure, Emilio stood, pointedly looking away from her. Nick noticed instantly. Something was bothering Emilio.

"Emilio, we'll make it back okay. It'll be a long hike, but we can do it. Don't worry."

The creases in Emilio's face softened. "I know, Nick." He looked at his daughter, sighing with disappointment. His chin dropped and his shoulders sagged.

Nick recognized a hint of panic in Angela's voice. "Popi…"

Emilio's chin snapped a not-so-gentle nudge. "Give it to Nick, Angelita."

When she didn't move, his tone dropped. He spoke with a command Nick hadn't heard from him before. "Do what I tell you."

"I'm so tired, Popi." Tears appeared, coursing down her cheeks, as she clutched at her purse. "Later. Let's do this later. I need to rest."

Emilio squinted at his daughter. With a disgusted shake of his head, he turned away.

Nick scrutinized his wife, noting her attempt at a distraction. "Do what, Angela?" What was she avoiding?

Angela turned to Nick. "Aren't you happy to see that we made it?" She pulled back, her neck stiffening at the indignity. "Am I intruding with your partner?" The word 'partner' was used as if she was referring to Hitler. "You didn't expect to meet up with us like we planned?"

Where did this come from?

Jealousy of Meredith?

It was Nick's turn to be surprised. Rigo laughed nervously from his seat on the floor. Emilio barked at his daughter. "Angela, enough."

"The book." Meredith stood in the doorway, holding their water.

"She's got the book." It was an accusation.

Emilio stood inches away from Angela's nose. "Give it to Nick."

Her lip quivered. "¿Popi, really?" She waited for a response and got nothing but a cold stare from her father.

She fidgeted with the snap on the huge bag, then slipped the purse off her shoulder and fumbled inside. Reaching deeper, the contents rumbled as she swept her hand around. Peeking into it, she tsk'ed impatiently. She drew a compact out, tossed it back in, then drew a folding mirror. Tossing that back, another tsk, then a mumble. "It was right here. Maybe it fell out."

A quick step and Nick was in front. His patience fled. "Hand it over." He reached toward her.

Angela twisted a protective arm over her purse. "No. It's mine." Her voice was a whine.

Grasping the straps, Nick lifted it off her shoulder.

She reacted like a lioness protecting her cubs. With a wince, she grabbed the bag, pulling it to her. The action caught Nick by surprise. He released the straps and the purse tipped, dumping the contents onto the dirt floor.

"No," Angela wailed as Nick dropped to his knee to sort through the items.

Angela fell to her knees, scrambling to push her things back into the purse. Her shoulder nudged Nick away. "No."

Off balance, Nick shifted to steady himself. His hand flattened a small cardboard box. The pink color caught his attention. Even the book they'd been fighting over wasn't as interesting as this. His fingers curled around the empty box. "Angela?" He held it up to her face.

Emilio choked out a protest. "Hija."

Angela spoke in a furious stream. Lies dripped from her lips like spit. Nick didn't even hear them all. After her transparent lie, "it's not for me", he stood, hardening his heart to her. She'd betrayed him, for sure. There was no doubt. He'd questioned her word and motives before, but this was so much worse.

Emilio's tired face knotted in distress. He covered his face with his hands.

She pulled something out from the mess and offered it to Nick. A small, soft-cover book. The size of a deck of cards, it was embossed in gold filigree.

"I found it in my bedroom," Angela whispered.

Rigo sat up. "Silvia's book."

Nick took the book and stuffed it in his back pocket. There was much more to this. Nick thought. He hated what he knew already. What was she doing with the book? Why was she reluctant to give it up? Was she covering up for the pregnancy test?

"Tell Nick the rest." Emilio slumped against the doorframe as if he had lost all the energy in his body. Disappointment oozed out of his pores.

"Oswaldo and I found it in my bedroom." Angela ran her tongue along her lower lip. "That's the truth."

Behind her, Rigo nodded. "That's where I hid it, Nick."

"What about this, Angela?" He held out the cardboard. Nick's chest tightened—could there be news worse than his wife hiding something so important from him? He wondered how he would ever trust her again. What kind of relationship could survive without faith in the other?

She walked to her only ally in the room, sat down, and sagged against her brother. "I don't want to talk about it. I'm too tired."

Nick's anger clouded his thoughts. His attention tunneled in on his wife, all periphery vision lost. He was across the room and his fingers curled around her arm before he knew it. He pulled her to her feet. "Are you pregnant?"

"Nick, you're hurting me."

Meredith stepped between them. She pushed Nick's arm from Angela's. Her face inches away from his, she said, "let's look at the book. You can talk about this later." She'd broken his concentration on purpose, interrupting his rage. A quick finger of anger pushed at him, then slipped away. He wondered what he would have done had he and Angela been alone. My God, he thought. He had wanted to shake some sense into her, shake the truth out of her, and he'd come close. He glanced at his hand like it had a life of its own.

Meredith had done the right thing. This needed to be settled, but not here, not now.

"The book, Angela." It was all he could say.

Angela rubbed her forearm with a grimace of distaste. She looked at her father, then faced Nick. "Oswaldo thought he could make a deal with Vega, trading the book for Rigo. It was Oswaldo's idea. Really, Nick. It was." She pleaded with him to believe her. He didn't even know if he wanted to but he knew he didn't.

"You didn't have enough faith I'd find Rigo?" He ran his fingers through his hair. He couldn't look at her. Through the glassless window frame, Nick saw an acre of earth damaged by man, scarred beyond what nature could recover. It was a metaphor for what Angela had done to their marriage. "You went behind my back. Hid things from me. You don't trust me." What else had she lied about? He should have known about this before she ever asked him to help. No trust, no relationship. It was what Meredith had been trying to tell him.

Angela stood and pawed Nick's arm. She pleaded in her most innocent voice. She was the poor little girl who needed to be cared for. "No, Nick. It wasn't that way at all."

Nick yanked away from her as if her touch burned him. He glanced around the room. Rigo cleared his throat, studying his feet, but Emilio stubbornly watched his daughter. Meredith put the water down and stood next to Emilio.

"Where is Oswaldo now?"

"He didn't tell me." Angela wasn't convincing. Nick felt he was seeing her for the first time—as she truly was, not how he wanted her to be.

Emilio answered. "He made a meeting with Vega to trade the book for Rigo."

Nick straightened, pushing Angela's deceit away for another time. He couldn't help Oswaldo. He had to focus on what move to make now. "We decide what to do next. Medical care for Rigo should be the priority."

"Vega will be watching the clinics for him." Meredith went to Rigo and gave him water.

"I have an idea." Emilio waved his hand. "We have a family friend who is a veterinarian, Bernardo. He lives outside San Vicente. No one would look for an injured man at a horse hospital. Bernardo drove Liliana to her sister's house yesterday, and he is discreet. Nick, if we walk to the highway, there is a bus."

Nick nodded. "All right." His glance took in his wife and brother-in-law. "I have the book now. It's my responsibility. When you are all safe, I'll see what Vega's up to."

At Emilio's quizzical look, Meredith said, "Vega won't take this lightly. He wants the book back. Your family won't be safe in Bucerias."

Chapter Thirty-Two

"I'M HUNGRY." ANGELA SOUNDED LIKE A PETULANT CHILD.

Meredith walked in point position, four yards in front of the raggedy procession. "We're all hungry, honey." The words came out before she could stop them. They were true enough, but her tone was rude. She worried for a moment over the unwritten rule—not to talk crap about your partner's spouse. If Nick wanted to, that was one thing, but no one else was allowed. Technically, though, it wasn't talking smack about her. She was nasty to the woman's face. That was different.

Different, but still a no-no.

From the front, Meredith couldn't see Nick's reaction. She sighed.

Well, so what? They were in Mexico. Mexico sucked.

No one else said a word.

The sun was high, a blistering mass that made them sweat like it was raining. They were in what Meredith considered the jungle—trees so foreign to her they could have been on postcards. Lush, vibrant green trees, bushes, and shrubs lined the road and stretched beyond as far as she could see. The stillness felt peculiar—not a breath of wind. It was eerie. The sound of their shoes scuffling down the gravel road was all they heard.

They had walked for hours. Emilio relieved Nick and half-carried Rigo. Nick had dropped back after the first hour, telling Meredith he was checking to see if they were followed. Meredith thought he might just want to be alone. They continued their slow progress until Nick caught up with them after three hours. He'd been somewhere rough. His clothes were dirtier than when he'd left. Meredith thought he might have gone back to the mine, or somewhere to hide the book. She'd ask him later.

"We can rest down this road," Emilio spoke to his daughter. "There used to be a gas station and store at the turn-off for Sayulita, it may be abandoned, but I can't remember. Maybe we can find something to eat."

No one spoke. Hunger rolled in Meredith's belly. Perspiration dripped from her head to her toes. The water barely slaked their thirst from the rationed bottles.

Thankfully, most of their way was downhill. The road was solid gravel and dirt. Beside it, a river of mud ran through a creek bed. Where it overflowed to the shoulder of the road, slime covered the dirt. The gravel roadbed was elevated enough that it hadn't breeched the road—so far.

THE SUN WAS STRAIGHT OVERHEAD when Meredith noticed the handmade wood plank. Nailed to the trunk of an oak tree, it dangled sideways. In rough printing, it read, "Sayulita." An arrow underneath pointed to the left.

"Emilio, do we turn here?"

Emilio's voice reflected his exhaustion. "We stay on this road. We'll find help sooner."

The road turned into a pot-holed asphalt slab.

Angela panted, "I think I see the store. There, through the trees." They all looked. No roof, the walls were gaping holes between rotting frames. There was no hope for food or water at a wreck like that. Their pace didn't change.

Ten minutes later, in the afternoon stillness, a shadow spun across the road. Meredith stopped, glanced up, then trotted to a tree close by. She propped the rifle against the trunk, then climbed onto a low branch, peering upward through the leaves. "I've got a bad feeling about this." Her voice cut through the silence. Vultures circled in the air current above, their grace a contradiction to their mission. "Nick, c'mere. Leave everyone else there."

She dropped from the tree, grabbed the rifle, and crept toward the store, keeping behind the trees as long as she could. She was in a crouch, waiting, when Nick appeared by her side.

"What d'you have?"

"A white SUV parked behind the store. Looks like someone behind the wheel, but the head's at an unnatural angle." Meredith pointed to the vultures. "Look lively."

The Explorer sat in the weedy clearing twenty feet from the shell of the store. Encircled by the jungle, the area had once been a dumping ground. Patches of dirt where oil had been poured formed circles of dark scabs. Not even weeds grew there. Rough wood pallets and weathered cardboard were scattered. The car sat with both back doors hung open, but the hulk behind the wheel sat immobile.

Nick raised his eyebrows. He nodded toward the SUV. "You first."

Meredith raised the AR-15 to her shoulder. She stole around the last tree with Nick behind her. He was graceful at this, like a stalking bear. He moved weightless and quietly, clearing the area. They checked the tree line, the back of the store, then circled the car. No one around, but footprints in the drying dirt led to where another vehicle had been parked. With the rain during the night, it was hard to tell how long the tracks had been there.

Checking the person inside was next. He hadn't moved.

Crap, the car looked familiar. A white Ford Explorer, like the one Oswaldo drove when he picked them up at the airport. Explorers are a dime a dozen down here, she thought. Still…

Nick moved toward the passenger side of the Ford. He slipped to the rear fender and popped his head up to sneak a look inside. Returning to Meredith's line of view, he put up his index finger, indicating one occupant.

A thin breeze whispered through the spiked palm leaves. Then, she smelled it. It was a scent like no other—one that no one ever wanted to breathe, much less cause. It would be in her sinuses for days. Whoever was behind the wheel was long past help.

Meredith padded along the tree line toward the driver, still poised with the rifle, watching Nick out of the corner of her eye. Figuring her angles to avoid a crossfire situation, they danced their purposeful waltz around the car. She was ready for anything. No movement from inside—except the circling flies.

At the driver's side door, she fought the rising need to puke. She slung the rifle over her shoulder and pulled up the neck of her T-shirt to cover her nose.

Oswaldo sat—stiff and pale—with his head tipped awkwardly off to the right. A bloody slice creased from one side of his neck to the other. Globs of coagulated blood collected at the wound site. The rest of his blood had pumped itself out, pooling in his lap and under his body. Meredith noted punctures against his neck in the same vicinity as the fatal cut. "It's Oswaldo. He's been tortured."

Nick was beside her. He studied Oswaldo's throat, then straightened. "I'll bet I know why."

"Let me guess. It has to do with Angela." She backed away from the car.

This never got any easier. They cleared the rest of the area as methodically as if they were in Sonoma County. They moved together as they always had. It took the smallest tic of a finger for her to understand his signal, and he responded the same. There was a security in their routine—no surprises, while expectations of the other were always met.

When they were done, she stood looking at Oswaldo's mutilated body. "This guy was a douche, no doubt about it, but he didn't deserve to die like this. You think Vega did it?"

Nick nodded. "Vega or one of his gorillas. He wants the book. Do you have any more juice in your cell?"

"Not much."

"Try taking some pictures."

Meredith stared at her partner, trying to remember to breathe through her mouth and wishing she had some Vicks to pack up her nose. A light breeze dispersed the smell, but it was still bad.

"Do it. I'm going to move him, and then we're going to use his ride to get out of here."

"Wow." Meredith turned on her phone, touched the camera app, and took a dozen photos of Oswaldo and the scene. A "low battery" alert forced her to stop. She turned the phone off so she wouldn't lose the data.

By the time Angela called to them, Nick and Meredith had pulled Oswaldo's body from the car and stashed it at the base of the trees. Nick searched the store and came up with some cotton rice bags wadded up in a back room. He hurried to the Explorer and began mopping up the congealed blood.

While Nick tried to make the SUV presentable, Meredith went back to the others. "We found Oswaldo. He's dead." She watched closely for reactions. Angela's brows drew together. She dropped to the boulder she'd been sitting on. "What?"

Emilio crossed himself, uttering a prayer. "Heart of Jesus, once in agony, have mercy on the dying."

"Poor Oswaldo." Rigo's head dropped in a pose of grief. "How did he die?"

Meredith had considered the question. It would serve no purpose to sugarcoat it.

"He was tortured. Someone cut his throat. He bled to death."

Angela gasped and bent over, her chin to her knees. Emilio made a reverent sign of the cross.

"We're going to take his car. Emilio, can you drive?" The old man nodded. "Okay then, take Rigo and Angela to your veterinarian friend. If you'll drop us at a bus stop, Nick and I will take the bus back to Bucerias to find out what Vega's up to."

Angela straightened. "What about Oswaldo?"

"He's going to stay here." Meredith worked to keep the irritation out of her voice. "You don't want a body in that car, and we're not going to bury him."

"I don't want to get in that thing." Angela's voice rose an octave. "He was murdered—maybe even inside. I'm not getting in it."

Meredith turned away. "Then I guess you'll be walking to San Vicente."

Chapter Thirty-Three

ANGELA DIDN'T WALK, OF COURSE, BUT SHE SAT IN THE BACK—AS far away from the driver's seat as she could. She stopped short of saying "ew, ew," but Meredith heard her thinking it. Meredith had found some weathered cardboard that she put on the driver's seat. Emilio met her gaze. "Thank you, my dear." After another sign of the cross, Emilio got behind the wheel and started up the car. Wipers clawed across the windshield. Even with the windows open, the cloying, coppery smell of blood was heavy in the air.

Meredith appreciated Emilio's thanks. With all the crap going on, manners seemed to suffer with the rest of his family. How could someone so nice raise two such self-serving kids?

They drove to the crossroads, where another gas station stood next to a store. When they entered, the three people inside averted their eyes from the strangers. Their disinterest surprised Meredith, until she remembered they were in Mexico—not the US. Here, interest in something or someone unusual could cost them everything.

Fortunately, cash wasn't a problem for Nick or Meredith. Nick had the foresight to carry his ATM card, and he'd gotten over $63,000 pesos, $5,000.00 in cash after they arrived in Puerto

Vallarta. The money was limp from humidity after being stashed in a zippered pocket of his backpack, but usable. They grabbed some food and filled the gas tank.

Emilio inquired about buses from an aloof, mustachioed señora behind the counter. Yes, a bus that will take you to Bucerias is due along here very soon. Yes, there is a place to wait. It's over there under the shade of that tree.

A young woman with a yellow bandana entered the store and found herself face-to-face with Rigo. Her eyes widened, then her gaze swung away as she ducked down an aisle.

Meredith found sugary pan dulce cookies. Some of the fruit was past its prime, with flies circling. She couldn't identify any of it. She settled for a banana and knowing she needed the carbs, the cookies, and then a carbonated drink. Outside, she found the beverage was too sweet for her liking, so she gave it to Rigo. One by one, they collected beside the store at a grayed picnic bench. They finished off their food, then sat in a stupor. Nick finally spoke, the edge of their hunger sated. "Meredith and I will take the bus when it comes. You guys should beat it into San Vicente. Rigo needs to be looked at." Emilio nodded, looking at the AR-15.

Meredith had considered what to do with it. They couldn't carry it on the bus. "I'll unload the gun and put it under the back seat of the car." She kept the Glock she'd taken off the guard in her backpack.

Emilio rose, somber. "We should go now."

The Explorer kicked out dust as Emilio steered it out of the parking lot. Meredith sighed and sat on a rickety chair chained to the bus stop sign. Rigo was safe, and so were Angela and Emilio. Liliana was safely stashed in Puerto Vallarta.

Oswaldo wasn't so lucky. Even though the bodyguard certainly had a hand in bringing on his own death, Meredith couldn't help wondering how many more people associated with Angela would die. How much more trouble would they get into because of her? Meredith wished she could keep an eye on the woman, just to thwart whatever selfish plan she had set in motion.

THE BUS PULLED to a stop with a squeal of brakes. Relatively new, the side decorated with a vibrantly painted mural of the Virgin Mary. Her peaceful face and outstretched arms rested under a film of dust as thick as a finger. Above the tailpipe, graffiti in red and black showed the Norteño star.

In Spanish, Nick told the driver where they were going. Meredith fell into a seat with an open space for her backpack. Nick paid and sat behind her.

The bus lurched on, hit a pothole, and lurched again. Powder blue dingle balls mounted on the valance over the windshield danced wildly. A stoic middle-aged driver wrenched the colorfully wrapped steering wheel, urging the bus side to side, dodging ruts in the road. Religious picture cards were taped to the interior like wallpaper around the driver. A passenger in the back spoke machine-gun Spanish to another, but after a short conversation, the passengers settled in in silence. Nick leaned toward her to interpret: "They were wondering why we were sitting in different seats."

Meredith nodded, then eased into the monotony of the rocking bus. Inside, it smelled like spices, maybe cumin, and the unadulterated sweat of working people. Looking out the window, she saw more jungle and the river of mud that ran parallel to the road. Nick tapped her shoulder, pointing out the gangster's Impala that Emilio had driven. It sat, nose tipped down into the muck, and cocked off to one side. The cat-eye tail lights blinked faintly as wet ooze threatened the electrical system. She thought it was eerie, like the car resisted its imminent demise. It wasn't moving—it looked hung up on something, a rock or submerged tree trunk. Then the creek and mudslide veered off down a sharp embankment and was lost to her view.

She thought of home with a longing she hadn't expected. The Russian River flooded every couple of years. Mudslides were common in the steep redwood-lined canyons. As a deputy, she worked them all—evacuations, roadblocks, and rescues. These spectacles of nature weren't foreign to her, and she never underestimated them.

Even so, she missed how much easier life was at home. A wry

smile crept to her lips. She didn't have a home. As soon as escrow closed, her house was sold. It felt so far away—the house that was hers, but wasn't. She didn't have a place to go after this adventure.

The bus rumbled toward Bucerias. To the west, occasional homesteads came into view in varying stages of occupancy and decay. The closer they got to civilization, the more litter she saw on the side of the road. Fat cattle defied the obvious poverty of the locals, roaming the small green meadows. For a while, she listened to a bird squawking in a cage in the back of the bus, thinking that she could never sleep with that racket going on.

The driver yelled something Meredith couldn't make out. From behind her, Nick grumbled back at him, then nudged her shoulder. They'd both fallen asleep.

Las Palmas. They got off and walked the mile back toward the Borregos' house. Two blocks away, Nick sniffed at the air. She smelled it, too. Acrid, she thought, like burned chemicals. "Smells like a house fire."

He stepped up his pace. "Let's split up. You take the alley at the back."

She looked sideways at him as she hustled to keep up. "What are you thinking?"

"I want to be ready for anything. I wish we had that damned AR."

"Do you want the Glock I took off the guard at El Rancho?"

"You keep it for now."

"I don't hear any sirens, so either it's unreported or already history."

Nick's jaw flexed.

Chapter Thirty-Four

THE BORREGO HOUSE WAS IN RUINS. A PARTIAL WALL STILL STOOD, but you couldn't tell there had once been two stories. A pair of fire-fighters in heavy boots and turnouts poked at a pile of smoky debris, scattering ashes. Wisps of steam hissed in the afternoon sun. The pungent odor of car exhaust surrounded the house. With the Glock in her pocket, Meredith approached from the alley along the backside. She ducked under a plastic banner that announced, "Peligro"—danger. Entering the property, she saw that even the backyard shed was in ashes.

Nick waved down one of the firefighters. Meredith walked the perimeter of the property as they talked. Sooty water oozed into her shoes as she waded through the mess. Next door, she heard a child's voice calling, enticing a pet. She picked through the mess, stopping at the cinderblock wall separating the neighboring property, and peered over. In the next yard, a young woman lured a wet and disheveled gray cat to eat.

At least the Borregos' cat would be safe.

After a short conversation, Nick and the firefighter shook hands. The fireman went back to his work, shoveling over smoldering debris.

Nick met Meredith near the front gate.

"Obviously, it was arson. The fireman said they used gasoline—lots of it. That's why this place is so decimated." The look in Nick's eyes was a hard, thousand-yard stare. He sighed and faced Meredith. "He also said Javier Davalos was here. Javier told him that Rigo was out of town, but he'd try to get in touch with him."

"Wow. Javier thinks pretty quick on his feet."

"Or maybe he knew about it before it happened." Nick shoved his hands into his pockets. "Let's go see what ol' Javier has to say about where he's been the past few days."

"Where? His office?" How far this was going to go. What did Nick suspect Javier of? Setting the fire—probably not. He saw no purpose for that. Messing around with his wife—definitely. Nick might be mad, but Javier had a lot to answer for. He was "away" when the gangster broke into the Borrego home, searched it, and shot Angela. Where had he been? Javier's partner was kidnapped, his girlfriend assaulted. The whole family was in danger from Vega and his gangsters. Oswaldo told her Javier was at the bank trying to get money. If the family had already tried, why would he bother asking again?

Javier's actions didn't add up.

"Let's go there first."

EMILIO'S VOICE was earnest with worry. "Bernardo, please understand harboring us can cause you much trouble. Be sure of what you are doing."

Bernardo Castillo stood well over six feet tall, an anomaly in Mexico. As he looked down at his short friend, Angela thought the man's compassion magnified his size. Bernardo draped a long, thin arm over Emilio's shoulders. "You and your family will be quite safe here. There is plenty of room, and we have many outbuildings where you can hide if needed." He glanced at Angela's bruised cheek and bandaged arm, then pointed to a closed door. "First things first. Let me look at Rigo, then Angela. Come in here to the surgery."

Emilio and Angela half-carried Rigo into the room. They sat him on the examination table. Rigo wobbled, then slumped over. Emilio caught him before he rolled off the table. With Bernardo's help, Rigo stretched comfortably on the examination table.

Bernardo fired out orders. "Angela, use those scissors to cut off his clothing. Emilio, get that tray of tools over there. And find a thermometer. There should be one in the big white cabinet."

"Yes, but first, I must use your phone to call Liliana."

"In a minute, friend. Let's get your son fixed up." Bernardo focused on Rigo's head laceration.

"Yes, yes, but I must warn my wife. She might be in danger." Bernardo's gaze caught Emilio's.

"Then, go."

———

THEY CAUGHT a cab on the Jalisco-Puerto Vallarta Highway and directed the driver to Javier's office, off Avenida Las Palmas. They could have walked, but Nick was in a hurry, and they were both tired. The street was a frontage road to the traffic whizzing by on the highway. A sea breeze blended with the aroma of cooking and a hint of exhaust and road dust. The neighborhood was a mix of shabby but colorful shops, with utility wires draped across the facades and the odd modern office building on every block. They found the building they were looking for—the modern one—a narrow two-story stucco structure open on the bottom floor to a brightly tiled real estate office.

A sign on the side of the building said, "Davalos y Borrego Abogados." Davalos and Borrego-Attorneys. An arrow pointed around the corner and up. Palms and locust trees shaded a gravelly dirt parking lot in the back. Meredith walked the cracked concrete sidewalk for a look around back. The law office appeared to occupy the entire second floor. Another set of stairs opened from the back lot to a second-story patio. Looked like there was an apartment upstairs.

The sound of a car approaching distracted Meredith. An older blue Porsche Carrera 911 roared into the lot, Javier behind the wheel. When he saw Meredith, he jammed on the brakes, and the car fishtailed in the gravel. Meredith stood her ground, staring at Javier. He sat motionless, as if debating his chances of getting away from her.

Through the dusty windshield, Meredith caught the look on his face—he was going to bolt. To a cop, it was a sure sign of guilt. When Javier saw Nick leaning against the stairs, she watched his face fall as he realized that it was too late to avoid them. Javier jerked the car into gear, then pulled into a parking place near Meredith. He could've gotten away, but he seemed to sense the inevitability of confrontation.

With what Meredith thought was superior control over his mind and body, Nick walked to the convertible. The plan was to press Javier about his frequent and insufficiently explained absences. These made him a suspect in this puzzling adventure. Was he involved in the kidnapping, the ransom, or the book? What else did he have his fingers in? Oh yeah. Angela. That was definitely on Nick's mind, too. Probably too much.

Javier got out of the car. He was smartly turned out in a charcoal designer suit, his Oxford shirt open at the neck. As he leaned on the Porsche door, Nick faced him, Meredith by his side. Instead of greeting them, he pulled a pack of cigarettes from his jacket and lit one.

"Javier, we have some questions for you," Meredith spoke first. "We need the truth—and now."

"That's a joke." Javier exhaled a blast of smoke. "You two wouldn't recognize the truth if it bit you in the ass."

Nick grabbed Javier's lapels, pressing his face inches from the attorney's. Meredith enjoyed Javier's wide-eyed expression as the lawyer dropped his smoke in the dirt. She made no attempt to stop Nick. "Listen, you moron: you couldn't tell the truth if your life depended on it. Right now, it might. I want answers, and I want them quick. Where were you when Rigo was kidnapped?"

"You're making a mistake." Javier struggled to regain his poise. He seemed oddly ruffled, like roughing up his lapels wasn't the only shock he had.

"The mistake I made was letting my wife come down here." Nick's face was dark, his eyebrows drawn together.

It was silly, Meredith thought. He had no interest in 'controlling' his wife.

"Oh, so that's what this is about." Javier tried to pull away.

The situation was getting away from them. Meredith said, "Let's get back on track, Nick." He stepped back while Javier smoothed his hands over his hundred-dollar haircut and Brooks Brothers' jacket.

"C'mon. Take this out of the parking lot and into the privacy of your office," Meredith snapped.

Chapter Thirty-Five

THEY MOUNTED THE STAIRS TO THE OFFICE OF DAVALOS Y BORREGO Abogados. Javier used the key, shoved the door open, then strolled into the front office—a waiting room with an empty receptionist's desk. Meredith glanced at the plaque, then did a double-take. Another glance at Nick's stunned face told her he'd seen it: 'Angela Borrego'. No 'Reyes'.

They walked down a short hall with three doors; one with Rigo's name engraved on a brass plate, another stenciled 'Baño.' The third was Javier's. Meredith thought it odd that Javier's name was painted, not an elegant brass sign.

Javier's office was small and sparse. Meredith had formed an impression of him—a slick, sophisticated ambulance-chaser. She expected lavish furniture and a stylish decor. Nevertheless, she allowed her sense of the room to settle in: The desk was a Formica-topped refugee from the '80s. Two client chairs were ladder-back with worn split-rattan seats. A file cabinet in the corner sat under a small, lifeless, picture tube TV. The walls were stark white. Judging from the chipped surface, it looked like the original paint. Two document-sized frames held Javier's diploma from law school and his certification to practice law, a licenciado en derecho. Javier's desk faced a window—the two client chairs had their backs to it.

The incongruity of Javier and his office struck a nerve. Something was off here. She wasn't sure what, but she kept her radar on for anything—and everything. She didn't trust Javier. No way was she sitting down in a client chair in front of the window.

Javier sat down at his desk, busying himself with opening drawers. Nick moved across the room in a heartbeat, at Javier's side, watching. They didn't want to be on the wrong side of a gun. The attorney's hands flew up in a gesture of surrender. "Wait, wait. I'm putting my keys away."

Nick whirled Javier's chair around and planted a foot on the chair seat right between Javier's legs. Nick gave it a violent push away from the desk. "Just give me a reason..."

Javier leaped up, his spine rigid. "You'll get nowhere posturing like this."

One of Nick's eyebrows twitched. It was Meredith's sole clue that he had been surprised. She watched the two men. Javier was right—they were dancing around the elephant in the room. Angela.

Nick's muscular arms dangled at his side. Javier's eyes seemed aware of the threat.

Nick asked, "What is your relationship with my wife?"

Meredith had considered breaking up this scene to get on with the important business. This was long past due. Nick wouldn't be able to concentrate on Vega until he got answers. While she knew her partner would wind up being hurt, this needed to be settled—at least for now. Meredith moved to lean against the wall near the two men —just in case things got physical.

Javier looked to Meredith as if she would deliver peace. Cocking her head sideways, she said, "Man asked you a question."

"Yes," he answered. "But it's not what you think." He dropped to the chair with an air of resignation.

"It doesn't matter what I think. She's a married woman...married to me. Leave her the fuck alone." Nick's hands curled into fists. He was ready to blow. His back muscles flexed under his T-shirt.

Meredith almost read his mind: Couldn't he hit him? Pound the shit out of him? Start thumping, and the answers will come.

Meredith propped a foot against the wall. If things went south, she'd break them up.

Javier looked down. "Look, man. I'm sorry this happened—for your sake."

Nick's body went stiff. Where did this Javier-nice-guy stuff come from?

"I didn't mean for this to happen." Javier sounded apologetic. He rubbed his eyes with manicured fingers. "Believe me; it's made things very complicated around here."

"You better un-complicate things fast, Davalos." What was he saying? Did he really want to fight for Angela?

"Angela decides, no?" Javier sighed as if he was breaking bad news. "It's not up to you or me."

The logic was sound, the message was clear. Nick had no say. His shoulders slumped as he glanced away. He had to be wondering if he even wanted Angela back.

Meredith had expected hot Latin tempers flying, and a punch or two, but this was a surprise. It dawned on her that Nick hadn't anticipated any manipulation from this creep. She caught a glimpse of Nick's face—drawn and dejected in exhaustion. Her heart thumped in her chest for him. She wished she could take the pain away.

It took the prick, Javier, to say it, but it looked like Nick got it. Angela had decided already.

Meredith pushed past Nick and dropped her palms on Javier's desk. "Give us a minute."

Javier nodded somberly.

TRAFFIC RUMBLED past the Davalos building. Outside the office, Nick sank to the top step. Afternoon heat pressed on Meredith's shoulders. She considered, then re-considered, words of comfort. Nothing came to her. She reached out and put a hand on his shoulder.

She hadn't thought of touching him before it happened—it was like her hand had its own mind.

It seemed to be what he needed. He leaned his cheek against the rough skin on the back of her hand. She wished she had some magic to take away the sting. He had to face that he had lost Angela. It was excruciating, but there was no way to dodge the reality any longer.

Finally, Nick straightened, his attention on the mirage-like blur of traffic. "I guess I should have known."

What could she say to that? Yes, you were blind to what your wife was up to. Meredith withdrew her hand. She leaned back against the stucco half-wall that surrounded the stairs. She watched Nick's back. No matter what she said, it would be wrong. If she disrespected Angela, Nick would feel defensive and make her the bad guy. If she came to Angela's defense, well, he wouldn't appreciate her taking his ex-wife's side. He wouldn't buy it anyway.

She kept her silence.

The muscles in his back swelled beneath his T-shirt as he inhaled. He sighed. "Let's finish this Rigo mess." He stood and turned toward the office door. She thought she glimpsed redness in his eyes.

NICK AND MEREDITH returned to the office. Javier stood backbone straight with an unspoken protest. Nick pulled his thoughts together as Meredith closed the door behind them. Somewhere in the building, the air conditioning throbbed, blasting a cool draft across Nick's sweat-soaked shirt. His first thought was the most pressing matter at hand. Could the Borregos stay in Bucerias safely?

Nick was still curious about Javier's absence at several key events—Rigo's kidnapping, as well as when Meredith and he were caught by the policía and sent back to LA. Where was he when Angela was shot? When he showed up—late—he didn't even take her to the clinic—he left that chore for Oswaldo. Why?

The bigger question was where? Where did Javier go? When Angela got shot, he was supposed to be at Rigo's bank, inquiring about the accounts. That had been done before he and Meredith ever got summoned down here. Why call Oswaldo to the office? To leave Angela and the family unguarded? Did he tip off the policía that Nick was on his way to El Rancho? Did he leak intel to Vega about their plans? If so, why? Did he have a stake in Rigo's kidnapping? As business partners went, Rigo was beyond irresponsible. A partner could justify radical action to recover lost income. Nick wanted a look at their finances to see what kind of money Javier generated and what Rigo spent, but it seemed too late now for that to do any good.

"Where were you when Rigo was kidnapped?" Better just get to it. "You suspect me?" Javier crossed his arms. "Are you kidding?"

Javier's deflection instantly pushed Nick's button. "I'm dead serious." He still would like to take this clown out back and thump the crap out of him. "Why are you always MIA when things turn to shit?"

"You better think about what you're saying to me." A sheen of perspiration appeared on his broad forehead.

"Answer me." Nick leaned across the desk.

Shoulders squared with Nick, Javier met his gaze. "I don't have to." Javier poked his own chest, then pointed to Nick. "What's more, I'm going to tell you something. You better get out of here. You're messing with things you know nothing about."

"I know that my wife asked me to help her." His voice broke on the word 'wife'. "That means more to me than cartels or the Mexican judicial system." His breath was forced—slow and steady.

"She was wrong to have involved you." Javier pouted like he was the wronged lover.

"That's history. This is now." Nick rested his hands on his hips and leaned toward the lawyer. "Someone torched Rigo's house. Burned it to the ground. I'm not going anywhere until I'm sure the Borregos are safe."

Javier lifted an eyebrow. "They'll be safe. You don't need to concern yourself with Mexican citizens. We can take care of our own…as soon as we find Rigo."

"Really? Because if you're an example of taking care of Angela's family, you've done a piss-poor job." A bell rang in Nick's mind. Javier kept saying, 'we'. "Who is 'we'? Who's in this with you?"

"Your interference has caused too many problems." Javier's jaw twitched. "Go back to California. Leave this to us."

"Who? You?" Nick took a chance—a hunting expedition, where truth was the quarry. "You're nothing but a slick shyster, and you're cooperating with crooked Federales."

"You think because they caught you sneaking around private property, then threw you out of the country, they were crooked? You better think again."

Nick went for Javier's throat. Meredith dove into action and grabbed Nick's arm. She wedged herself between her partner and Javier and asked, "What do you mean—they were straight?"

Javier was silent, his lips pulled taut against his teeth, his breath coming in shallow bursts.

"Why did they want us gone?" Nick squinted. Bad news was coming his way. He had to know, but he didn't want to. "Who told them we'd be there?" Leaning toward Javier, his last words were a shout. He knew Angela had told Javier.

Javier didn't answer right away. He held his hands loosely behind his back, his chest out. He met Nick's gaze and held it.

Nick had watched the attorney's movements, trying to read his body. Everything he'd seen so far said he was righteous. The man believed in what he knew. Damn. Nick wanted him to be lying, to justify a swing at him. Any excuse. Any excuse at all.

Nick felt Meredith's hand fall away from his arm. They waited for Javier's answer.

The lawyer's jawline softened. Javier pulled his chair out and sat. He leaned toward them, palms on the desk, then nodded to the chairs. Nick's cop radar was at peak performance.

He sat. Something big was coming, and he wasn't going to like it.

"Let's be honest. We're both here for the same thing—to find Rigo. And to make sure Angela's family is safe." Javier clasped his hands together, a self-satisfied politician.

"We already have Rigo." Nick settled in his chair, relieved to be able to deliver some good news himself.

Javier stood up so fast the chair kicked over behind him. "Where was he? Is he alive?"

Go ahead, Nick thought. Ask about it, so I can show you we were good enough to find Rigo—a cop and his female partner from Cali.

Nick drew out the enjoyment of besting Javier. "He was held and tortured at El Rancho—the place where your comrades took us into custody. And, he's alive—safe for now, getting medical treatment. If you and your buddies had left us to do our stuff, we would have found him sooner."

"You don't know that."

"Maybe not," Meredith said. "But tell me why your guys didn't search El Rancho."

Javier waved the question aside. "If you insist on staying in Mexico, you can ask them yourselves."

"We're not leaving." Nick's voice was hard, a promise. "Not until we know the Borregos won't wind up in a ditch with their throats cut."

Javier leaned back into his chair. "Would it help if there was official representation from the government of Mexico? Then would you leave it to the professionals?"

Now, it was Meredith's turn to be offended. "We are professionals."

Nick raised a hand to stop her. "Are you saying that you are 'official government representation'? What does that mean, Javier? You're a Federale?"

"Federales were officially re-structured in 2009 by President Fox. They are now the Ministerial Federal Police, of which I am not a member."

Suspicion swept into Nick's mind. That wasn't an answer. What was this guy? A mercenary? A US agent? A cop?

Meredith picked up the question. "So, what are you?"

Javier stood and turned for his lawyer's certificate. Pulling the frame off the wall, he laid it on the desk. A white legal-sized envelope was taped to the cardboard backing. He slid a letter opener under the flap and opened it. He handed a card the size of a passport to Nick.

The hair on the back of Nick's neck stood up.

The ID card read, "Policía Federal Ministerial." A silver emblem imprinted with the same words stood above—"Procuraduria General de la Republica." Inside another silver band, fine lines of filigree were set around "PGR" with a native Mexican shield, and flames shooting out three sides. The photo was of Javier, but the name was different. If he was undercover, that made sense. Nick wasn't sure what a real ID card looked like, but this was close enough.

Nick tossed the ID back on the desk. "Crap. He's with the Attorney General's Office."

Chapter Thirty-Six

"I DON'T MIND TELLING YOU: YOU'VE MADE MY JOB A HELL OF A LOT more difficult," Javier said, looking outside the window.

Meredith didn't feel a damned bit sorry for him. A Fed? Javier wasn't making any friends here.

"Were you the asshole who sent the military after us at El Rancho?" Nick leaned back in his chair.

"I had no choice. We had intel that Vega had used the house." Javier held his shrug. "We didn't know who or what was there, but we couldn't run the risk of you two blowing our observation. We had to get you out—preferably out of the country."

"Yeah, well, you did." Meredith's face warmed. Maybe he had a point—except that it ran counter to Rigo and the Borregos, even Angela's best interests. "We out-smarted you, though." She choked back a bitter laugh. "I'm not sure how much good we did for the Borregos, Nick. Rigo's safe, Angela is in one piece. But the family—they'll always be looking over their shoulders."

The small office made Meredith feel like an animal trapped in a cage. "What exactly was your operation?"

Javier's sophisticated polish evaporated, revealing a hardness Meredith hadn't seen before. His shoulders were stiff; his lips tightened until they were a mere slash. Silence hung like a Kevlar drape. Meredith waited. Nick would hold onto this question until Javier answered.

"You are not—" the agent began.

"Don't use that with us." Nick cut him off. "What are we getting into?"

"We have to check out Vega," Meredith said. "He's behind all this. What do you know about him?"

At the silence, Nick urged him. "It's a matter of officer safety, Javier—or whatever your name is. The officers being us—we have to be read in."

"Use the name Javier for now." He bowed his head, then sat, as if he was still considering what to say. "You know that Vega has started up his own crime empire in Bucerias and PV." When the partners nodded, he went on. "He's been fishing around for different families on the west coast to sponsor him. We have solid information that he married Silvia to work his way into her family business."

"How did a snake like Vega get Silvia to go along with the plan?" Meredith couldn't imagine Vega had any appeal. She'd seen a newspaper clipping taken from a distance. Even the man's expensive clothes didn't hide the mercenary set to his shoulders. There was nothing attractive about him.

"Who knows?" Javier shrugged, holding it a moment. A quirk, holding the shrug like that. "Maybe he charmed her. She has all the money she could want, and with her family's clout, he couldn't intimidate her."

"Had." Nick corrected Javier.

At Javier's mystified look, Nick said, "She's probably dead." He ran down all that had happened since Javier had left the Borregos' house.

"Angela? Is she safe?" Javier's first question ripped from him without a trace of self-control.

Nick's face darkened, so Meredith answered for him. "We wouldn't have left her unless she was safe. Now, your turn to brief us."

Javier nodded, then stood again, looking out the window. When

he faced them, he spoke as if he was conducting a task-force briefing. "Miguel Vega emerged from nowhere two years ago. He has an
accent from the southern states, but no one has claimed him, nor
does he speak of his past. Since he arrived on the coast, he's been
specializing in Foco. You know it as crystal meth. He's been steadily
building his empire, cooking his poison in abandoned homesteads in
the countryside. His operation moves regularly, so he is difficult to
catch."

"What other crimes is he good for? Isn't kidnapping a stretch for
a meth magnate?" Nick asked. "How does Rigo's abduction fit in?"

"His people were sticking to drugs until Rigo was taken. About
the same time, two new guys showed up. We don't have any ID on
them, but there's a rumor they are from the Guzman cartel." Javier
sat at his desk, leaning back in the chair. "The abduction deviation
still has us stumped. I have come to believe that it is a personal grab
—to get the book, not ransom money."

"I think I can help you with the motive. But finish the briefing
first."

"Silvia Guzman Cardenas is the daughter of Carlos Guzman
Herrera. He's a powerful boss in La Familia. She's a wild one—
educated and stylish, but has a serious stubborn streak." Javier's eyes
clouded, then the look was gone. "Anyway, after she began seeing
Vega socially, I tried getting close to her. She wouldn't have anything
to do with me. I guess I was too boring. Regardless, she married him
after a short courtship. The rumor was that Vega had bought into her
family, and her three brothers pressured her into the marriage. It
sealed the deal."

Meredith shook her head. "Hard to believe a woman would
stand for that. Especially if she was as educated and stubborn as you
say."

"She had her angles, too." Javier's eyes narrowed. "I'm sure he
offered her something that would make living with him acceptable.
Often women in these cartel families are used as pawns in the drug
world. It's not so different from old-school European arranged
marriages. They were for business reasons, too. These women are
raised knowing this will be their fate."

Nick nodded. "Did the brothers have any other motive for pushing her into marriage?"

Javier shrugged. "We can only speculate. We think because Guzman is in his seventies, the boys look like they are moving in on his action. We don't know if it has the old man's blessing or not." He leaned against the wall, his arms across his chest. "There are three brothers. One is in jail in Morelia to stand trial for drug trafficking; the other two are twins. They have a bad reputation for doing anything to get their way." His eyes were distant. "Very violent men."

"Seems weird they'd be a party to their sister's disappearance and maybe murder."

"They may not know." Javier shrugged again. "Or they may have more allegiance to the peso than family."

Nick stood, stretching. "How do you play into this soap opera?"

"My cover was as an estate attorney looking for a sponsor. I hoped to get on retainer for the Guzman family to get inside their operation, but they already had an attorney—an army of them. When Silvia started seeing Rigo on the sly, I faked an association from college with him so he trusted me. I made a deal to work with him as a partner here. He was naïve. I didn't have to tell him much, as long as I subsidized his business. It wasn't the optimum, but with Rigo's help, I got Silvia's attention." Javier cleared his throat. His earlier arrogance was replaced with a surprising air of contrition.

"It must be a powerful feeling, moving people around like they're chess pieces." Meredith's voice betrayed her disgust. She'd seen it before at the Sheriff's office—where high-risk employees were moved around to places where they could do minimal damage. Still, this was way worse—none of her sergeants ordered her to marry a criminal, then spy on him.

Javier looked like he was lost in a world of his own making. "Silvia saw Vega was building an empire. That was the plan from the beginning, but she grew to believe there was no boundary to his greed and hunger for power. I planted the seed in her mind that he might be working to take over her family's branch of the business. It was an easy conclusion to draw. Her information on Vega's activities proved he concealed cash from her father's operation. It didn't take much from there. She put the figures in a diary and hid it, with the goal of giving it to her father. I tried to convince her to give it to me, that I would keep it safe and be sure the proper authorities would take action. But she doubted me, and she had suspicions about her brothers' loyalty to their father. It seems they were becoming frequent visitors to Vega's house. So, for safekeeping, she gave Rigo the book."

The afternoon sun cast a wide beam on the desk. Motes followed a lazy path to the Formica surface. When the air conditioning kicked on, they jerked into a frenzied dance to keep up with the air current. Meredith knew what was coming next.

Javier cupped his hand around his forehead. "Then last week, it was Wednesday, Silvia went missing. She didn't answer her cell. No one had seen her at her usual places, and she failed to meet Rigo for their appointment. I have someone in Vega's house in Sayulita—not an agent, but a person who told me what happened. Vega and Silvia had a hell of a row. They told me she fought so hard it took three of his gorillas to carry her to his car. I knew what came next—Vega's men like to torture people. And, I had to watch Rigo—he acts without thinking—while trying to find her. Then on Friday, Vega snatched Rigo." He rubbed his eyes. "Silvia must have died without telling Vega where the book was."

"Yes, I think so. Now his soldiers have turned the Borregos and the whole state upside down looking for it." Nick said, "And people have died for it."

"Everyone wants that book." Meredith counted off with her fingers. "Vega wants it because it's proof he was skimming from La Familia. He needs to keep it away from them. You want it so you can prosecute him and break up the cartel. Rigo needs it to bargain the safety of his family." An idea popped into her mind. "Does La Familia know about it?"

Javier's eyes widened. He shook his head. "I don't think so. They'd be in the thick of things if they did."

Nick stiffened. "Do you know where the book is now?"

Javier shook his head again. "One of the Borregos has it, I think."

"Really?" Nick tipped his head sideways, his eyes wide.

"After you all left for El Rancho, I searched the house again." Javier explained. "I found a place where it might have been stored in Angela's bedroom nightstand. Something had been stapled to the bottom."

Nick watched Meredith glare at Javier. "So, what are you going to do now?" He was glad Javier was the target of her focus and not him.

Javier waved a hand. "I'm not sure yet. I have suspected that Angela found the book and she has it now. She doesn't understand its significance."

"You're more right than wrong." Nick glanced at Meredith, and she nodded her approval. "Actually, she and Oswaldo found it." Nick crossed his arms and leaned back, getting comfortable for the explanation. "Oswaldo saw an opportunity to redeem himself after the disaster with his cousin, so he took it."

Javier's body jerked. "But I need it. It's crucial to prosecute this criminal."

"Wait for the whole story before you get excited," Nick said.

Javier strained in an obvious effort to calm down, but he wasn't going to. He looked like a fighting cock, drugged and edgy, ready to fight.

"Oswaldo contacted Vega's people and arranged a meeting. He left the book at the Borrego home because he was sure they would kill him if he brought it along." Nick fought away the image of Oswaldo's lifeless, milky eyes staring at him. The gaping wound at his throat, the flies buzzing, so many it was almost one voice. "Well, they killed him anyway. We have to presume that he told them where to find the book. The Borrego house is toast."

Nick wasn't sure why he didn't tell Javier of Angela's complicity. He was embarrassed by her immorality, and maybe saying the words would make him feel worse. Down deep, he knew Oswaldo had done this in an attempt to impress Angela. His infatuation with her was common knowledge. He wondered if Angela had used Oswaldo, manipulated him—like she said, hedging her bets to get Rigo back.

Javier's flat black eyes moved from Nick's face to Meredith's. "So, where's the book?"

"That depends on what is going to happen to it." Nick's voice was even. He'd spent some time thinking about this answer.

"What?" Disbelief crossed Javier's face. "Are you kidding? If you have it, it's going to the Attorney General's Office. That's what all this has been about." He waved his hand in the air, taking in all that had happened.

"The Borregos might as well move to Siberia." Meredith's voice was filled with disgust. "Consider the role that Rigo and Angela played in this nightmare. La Familia won't forget it. I'm not even Mexican and I know that."

Nick picked up the thought. Sometimes Nick felt Meredith knew his mind better than he did himself. "When we go to pick up the Borregos, I will let them have a say. They should decide." Nick said.

"After all, they all have lost everything."

Javier's face flushed red. "Those are the terms?"

Nick nodded. "For now. We'll see tomorrow what changes. In the meantime, can I use your phone? I want to arrange for Liliana to be with her family."

Javier pushed his landline to Nick. "Use caution, my friend. Use caution."

Chapter Thirty-Seven

HOT SHOWER WATER RAN DOWN HER SAGGING SPINE AS MEREDITH leaned her face against the cool tile. How long had it been since she'd slept in a bed? She couldn't remember. Her mind went blank as she soaked in the steam. All she knew was she wanted to see the back of her eyelids—and soon.

It was unexpected, but most welcome, when Javier offered them the apartment at the back of his office. A safe place to clean up, and rest, were at the top of Meredith's list. For the moment, that crisis was resolved. Yeah, there was still an angry drug lord prowling around the state. Yes, the book was still very hot, with no likely home in its immediate future. That would wait until tomorrow.

Javier had left for San Vicente, and Nick was on his way down the street to buy some dinner. She'd put in her order for chile rellenos and sent him on his way so she could clean up. When he returned, she wanted to eat and fall into bed. They'd flipped for the bed and Nick had lost—he would have to sleep on the couch. Nick seemed satisfied with his luck. Meredith was sure this place was where Javier and Angela met. So maybe the bed wasn't the greatest idea for Nick.

Turning off the water, she reached for a towel. A vigorous

massage sopped the dampness from her hair, then she mopped her body dry.

Rubbing fog off the mirror, she glanced at her reflection. Her eyes drooped with fatigue and—

Movement behind her cast a blotchy image in the blurred reflection.

Nick? No, it was too soon. Besides, he wouldn't come in while she was taking a shower. Would he?

Before she could look, a fist swung toward her, connecting with her temple. Fireworks blasted in her eyes as splinters of pain exploded. Her legs gave out, and she fell to the floor. Hands reached for her...

THE LATE AFTERNOON sun weighed on Nick's shoulders as he trudged up the stairs of Javier's apartment. In the distance, thunder rattled among the clouds cloaking the mountain peaks. The air had a heaviness that pressed on his already dark mood. The gun and holster Javier had given him stuck to the small of his back. Nick should be content. He and Meredith had rescued Rigo. The Borrego family was safe for the moment, and the book was hidden.

He wasn't happy—not at all. His marriage was over. Angela hadn't even given him the courtesy of telling him, nor waited for a divorce to start another romance and get pregnant. She had used him without shame. She'd called for his help, knowing he would drop everything. It was almost worse than divorce, knowing that he'd fallen for her manipulation. It made him question his definition of love and loyalty. Was he blinded by his love for Angela? Did he still love her at all? Would he come if she called him again? What about Meredith? How did he feel about her?

Well, Mexico wasn't the place to figure any of that out. He shifted the bag in his arms and pulled out the key Javier had provided. Unsure if Meredith had locked the door behind him, Nick tried it with an elbow. The door swung open.

"Hey," Nick shouted toward the back of the rooms. The scent of coconut shampoo came from the open bathroom door and mingled with the smell of dampness from the shower. Meredith must be dressing.

Pulling the Styrofoam boxes out, he yelled, "Soup's on." No answer. What was she doing in there?

The aroma of roasted peppers, an overture of spicy cumin, and the flat starch of pinto beans threatened to overwhelm him. The mole reminded him of his mother's cooking. His stomach growled. Snacks they ate from the store at the turn-off to Sayulita had worn thin.

He dismissed a brief thought about opening his dinner and diving in without waiting for Meredith. That was just rude. Yanking a few drawers open, he found forks and pulled two out. "Meredith. Come on. Dinner's ready."

No answer. Nick didn't care if he pissed off Javier or his agency. In fact, he relished the discomfort and inconvenience he'd caused them. Fed or not, Javier was an asshole.

"Mere?"

The wisp of a memory flitted to his conscious mind: the front door was open—unlocked and ajar. That wasn't right. She wouldn't have left it like that while she was in the back rooms. This was all wrong.

Adrenalin spiked through his system. Reaching around, he unsnapped the stiff leather holster clipped to his waistband. He gripped the stock of an old but immaculate Smith and Wesson .38 revolver and pulled it out. Even if it was a wheel gun, he'd get off six shots if he needed to. At close quarters like this, he shouldn't need more than six rounds. He silently thanked Javier for the gun as he moved toward the back of the apartment. No sound but the road noise from outside.

He cleared the bedroom, Meredith's backpack sat where she'd left it on the floor. He dipped his hand inside and felt the hardness of the Glock Meredith kept with her. Nothing else looked out of order. Maybe she went for a walk. No, not without the Glock.

The bathroom was next. A glance at the misty mirror showed the room was empty, but just. He checked behind the shower curtain and found nothing but wet tile. He swept the room again and spotted a toothbrush on the floor near the toilet, then a plastic glass upturned on the counter. The bath mat flipped over and not put back, towels dropped on the floor. Whatever happened began in this room.

Nick studied the floor tiles but couldn't tell if the scuffs were from normal activity or...

Standing in the living room, he studied the apartment, hoping for some detail to tell him what happened.

In the kitchen, Meredith's cell phone sat on the counter, still charging.

She wouldn't have gone anywhere without a gun or her cell —voluntarily.

A noise that didn't fit the traffic pattern came from the back of the building—outside, maybe. What was it? Yelling? A woman's voice—Meredith?

Nick was in motion quicker than thought. Out the front door, sliding down the steps—two, then three at a time. It might have been Meredith's voice, he wasn't sure. Then, the scrape of tires on hard-packed dirt and gravel. A surge of acceleration, rocks flying up from the rubber, and the metallic thump as the fender hit a parked car.

There. A big SUV—a Ford? A navy-blue Expedition, fishtailing out the driveway of the adjoining lot. Too far away to make out the license plate. With blacked-out windows, he wasn't sure if Meredith was inside.

The world dropped out beneath him as the certainty settled in. Something told him she was inside.

Shoving the gun into the holster, Nick raced after the car. One foot in front of the other, each landing on the dirt with an almost weightless step. Sprinting over potholes and rocks, he crossed over the uneven concrete sidewalk, following the SUV as it lurched into traffic. Horns blared as it cut in front of drivers moving with the flow. His pace settled into a rhythm, fueled by the desperate knowledge that he needed his own stamina to keep up the chase. The Expedition swayed across two lanes, dodging a scooter. It was three cars ahead of him.

Fishtailing again, the SUV thumped onto the raised median, passing cars, wobbling but moving forward. Four, now five cars ahead. Nick followed for a block, his veins throbbing in his ears. Then, the Expedition clipped a small green sedan, jumping a stoplight. The SUV shot into the intersection as cross-traffic screeched to a stop. It barreled onward to a clear lane. As the car accelerated, a black smudge of carbon blew out of the exhaust.

Nick watched the SUV pull away, wrenching his heart. His chest heaved with the exertion, and dread sucked what little energy he had left. He dropped to his knees on the sidewalk, and a sob ripped from his throat.

They had taken Meredith.

Chapter Thirty-Eight

WHEN MEREDITH OPENED HER EYES, SHE WAS BEING LUGGED DOWN the stairs over someone's shoulder. From her upside-down view, she saw they were going out of Javier's office. Her head throbbed with each step, while every nerve ending in her body spiked with alarm. Someone was taking her from the apartment.

Her confused mind sought a way to free herself. She felt an ocean breeze blow across her back. Crap! She was naked!

Someone tossed her damp towel over her as they thumped down the stairs. My God. This was everyone's worst nightmare. Waking up naked in public. Abduction in Mexico! The entire trip had been this way, hadn't it? Mexico, a place where the worst-case scenarios came true every ten minutes. Nick's effort to help his family was failing; people weren't who they claimed to be, and now this.

This was the last straw. If she got out of this, she was heading back to Sonoma—with or without Nick. Mexico was the land of surprises, and none had been to her liking. She wanted out.

Through her loose hair, she glimpsed a sign-pole in the parking lot, giving her an idea. If they went by it close enough—all she needed was two feet away. She could do it with her outside hand. When they passed, she reached out and grabbed the pole while jabbing her knee at her captor's face. She made contact, and with a howl, he let go. Meredith tumbled to the dirt. Her wet towel fell on top of her, along with her jeans and her T-shirt.

A small rock dug into her hip. Her injury inventory told her she had a headache, but she was alive and planned to stay that way.

Grabbing the clothes, she pivoted, ready to take off. She brushed the hair out of her eyes to see. A sweaty, muscular arm swung around her chest and pinned her to a solid body that smelled of sweat, tequila, and too much cologne. Grunting, rapid-fire Spanish flew between the two men. The guy who'd pulled her from the bathroom secured her wrists behind her, then slung her over his shoulder again —and this time, the other man tied her ankles together.

She squirmed, trying to wrestle her way loose again. Someone took hold of her bound ankles and slugged her ribcage. The blow knocked the wind out of her. Gasping for breath, she fought the urge to cave in. She gulped for air while kicking against the second man.

Then a car door of a big dark SUV opened. A third man, with a prominent gold front tooth, materialized to help stow her in the back. It took all three of them to hoist her writhing body over the seat and dump her onto the bench. Her wet bath towel and clothes fell on her again as she tried to slow her breathing to minimize the pain in her ribs.

The men's laughter echoed in her ears as they got in the car. Spanish ricocheted around the cab. The two men who were not driving leered at her nakedness with salacious smiles. They almost drooled, for God's sake.

This indignity rose in Meredith's chest as a lump of fury. Struggling against the flex cuffs that secured her wrists, she sat up. Twisting, she used her teeth to drag her T-shirt across her torso. Her eye caught movement from outside.

Nick!

He barreled down the stairs, his head swiveled, searching around him. He was looking for her.

Meredith heard what sounded like a shout of caution from the front. They'd seen Nick.

The SUV lurched, knocking Meredith against the seat. She

dropped her head against the leather for a moment, trying to collect herself. Nick had seen her—she hoped. It all happened so fast, she wasn't sure he'd seen inside the car.

As her breathing steadied, the men up front got quiet. Nick wasn't a threat to them anymore. They didn't seem to enjoy a passive captive who didn't struggle. She was too busy trying to stay in as least a vulnerable position as possible.

The SUV sped along recklessly, pounding over rough roads and hairpin turns. Without a seatbelt to secure her, Meredith soon rolled off the seat onto the floor. Her face skidded on the dusty, littered mat as cigarette butts, empty soda cans, and fast food containers rubbed against her skin. She propped herself sideways, anchoring her knees against the steel seat supports and the front of the back seat. It was little relief but enough for her to begin wrapping her mind around this new disaster.

Who were these goons? Vega's men or policía? What did they want? The book. If this was about revenge, they would have killed her. They must want something. The book was the solitary thing of value. So, what now? She never was good at a "wait-and-see" attitude. She went over scenario after scenario in her mind. What would she do if they tried to rape her? With her hands bound or free? Meredith calculated her moves and the consequences with every variation. Her instinct was to fight with every breath. But as the SUV raced along, she began to think she should be smarter than that. She'd planned on biting any flesh that came close, but decided to "wait-and-see" after all. Maybe an opportunity would present itself and she'd have a chance to escape.

She couldn't figure out how long they traveled. The road improved, like they were on a highway, and she was glad the smooth pavement allowed her aching ribs a rest. Then, the road turned to ruts and potholes again. An hour? Or three? Time was so distorted, she couldn't tell.

The SUV slowed. For miles, the tires rumbled over what sounded like gravel. Then, it slowed even more, eventually swaying to a stop.

Psyched for more trouble, Meredith ignored the dull throb in her ribs and tightened her abs, waiting for the goons to reach in for her.

She ground her teeth when it happened, in the effort to resist biting the hairy, brown hands that grabbed her arms. She was lifted, repositioned, then again slung over a man's shoulder. Just as before, another man held her ankles so she wouldn't kick. She squirmed and pushed against her captor's shoulder, knowing that because she wasn't blindfolded, she was disposable. As soon as they got what they wanted—whatever that was—she was of no use to them. This was a one-way trip. She stopped resisting for the moment, knowing that if the gangsters freed her, she couldn't run. She'd have to wait for a better opportunity. She went limp, thinking about how to free herself when the time came.

They carried her across a tiled courtyard into the back of a pale terra cotta-colored building. It looked like a single-story rancho, much in the style of the abandoned structure in the hills. However, this place had plush, overgrown tropical landscaping that surrounded the buildings, with a lawn in the middle where a fountain sat, dry. A building—a shed or garage—sat back, twenty feet away from the main house. The place was lovely—even upside-down.

Beside the driver and her two kidnappers, she counted at least six others, all dressed in dark BDUs. All had side arms; several had automatic rifles.

Her retinue made its way around to the back door. They hauled her through a huge kitchen, then down some ancient wooden stairs. They dumped her in a dark room with a rough cement floor. Someone threw her clothes on her head, then muscled her onto her stomach. The ties around her wrists tightened. She heard a click, and the plastic dropped away. The same snap, and her ankles were free. Then, muffled laughter, and the door slammed shut.

Meredith rolled onto her back, and reached for her clothes. She couldn't get her clothes on quickly enough. She slipped on her jeans and T-shirt and wished the douchebag gangsters had grabbed her sandals. Rubbing her ankles where the restraints had been, she tried to get the circulation going into her feet. The pain in her ribs had faded, but her head pounded from the blow she'd received in Javier's bathroom.

She surveyed the room—windows too high to access with

nothing to stand on. One door, which was undoubtedly guarded. Cardboard boxes and straw baskets lined the walls.

The door swung open. Gold Tooth stood there, his face blank.

With an open hand, he curled his arm. She was to follow him.

Meredith rose. Blood was returning to her feet. She shuffled toward him. When she drew close to him, she hesitated. He motioned again, his voice deep and rumbling, "El jefe quiere verte." All she understood was "El jefe." She was going to see the boss.

Chapter Thirty-Nine

NICK'S MIND WENT BLANK FOR A SECOND. WHAT WOULD HE DO now? How would he ever find Meredith? Who took her—the cops or Vega? A jolt of understanding jumpstarted his brain into functionality.

A girl from a shop rushed to his side, but Nick stood and brushed away her attentive hands. A growing anger whirled in his chest. His jaw set as he considered his options. Javier? Did he trust him? Even if Javier was honest, that didn't mean others in his agency were. The alternative was to go it alone. Nick spoke Spanish, but he didn't know much about cartels. Plus, he wasn't familiar with the area. This cartel business was beyond his scope. It would take too much time to catch up on the players to even the field. He needed someone who knew about these things. Intel. He had no choice but to call Javier for help. Nick's anger forged the steel core of purpose that he needed to get Meredith back. It was time to go to work.

"Javier." Back at the apartment, Nick panted into his cell phone.

"Where are you?"

"Almost to San Vicente. What's up?"

"Somebody just snatched Meredith."

"Are you kidding?"

"No." Nick ground his teeth. He wanted to scream at him, the same man he needed to ask for help. "I don't know who took her. I need your help."

At the other end of the phone, Javier sighed. "Yes, you do. Look, I'm almost at Bernardo's. I'll send Emilio to fetch Liliana by himself. I'll be back at the apartment in less than an hour. Don't be alarmed if you can't reach me. The cell service here is spotty."

Nick grunted into the phone, then slammed it shut. Javier was going to see Angela. What could Nick do about that? Go crazy, that's what.

Get a hold of yourself, he thought. Figure out what to do next.

His mind flooded with possibilities, he found himself shuffling into the bathroom. He studied Meredith's few toiletries scattered on the counter, trying not to think of all the bad possibilities. He found her backpack behind the door. Mechanically, he pushed her phone and belongings into her pack, zipped it up, and dropped it by the front door so he wouldn't forget it.

She would need it when he found her.

His gaze fell on the bag of take-out food. He couldn't predict his immediate future, but he needed to eat to keep up his strength. Nick forced himself to chew and swallow the cold fish tacos.

Javier was still thirty minutes away—at least. Nick plodded through the empty rooms, searching for something undefinable, feeling lost. He smelled her shampoo, touched the still-damp towel he'd picked up off the floor.

Meredith. What if they didn't find her in time? What would his life be without her? He dropped into a lumpy recliner and buried his face in his hands. God, he was so tired.

"Reyes." Javier's voice cut through the darkness of his mind. "Hey, wake up."

A bump to his foot snapped Nick's eyes open. "You took your time."

"Yes, but it was profitable. Get your shoes on. I'll fill you in when we're on the road."

NICK STASHED both his and Meredith's backpacks in the Carrera 911's small back seat. He slid into the leather of the passenger side. The compartment surrounded him like a space capsule. For a moment, he allowed himself to appreciate the car. "Nice that your government will spring for an undercover car like this." He glanced at Javier with a half-smile. "I drive a ten-year-old Taurus."

"It's old, a 2000 model," Javier maneuvered the car onto the highway. "Neither the Federales or the locals pulled any kind of kidnap. I talked to several people who would know these things."

"How sure are you?"

Javier stepped on the gas, and the sports car jumped ahead. "As sure as I can be." He kept his eyes on the road. "I spoke to people I can trust."

Nick sighed. Half the quandary solved. "If not the cops, it must have been Vega. Where are we going now?"

The wind ruffled Javier's perfect hair. "To find out where he's got her."

"…and why. Have you figured that out yet?"

"I've been thinking about it. Maybe he thinks she knows where the book is. Maybe he wants to trade the book for her. I'm sure that Silvia's book is at the heart of this."

"Meredith doesn't know where I put it."

"Vega will try to find out. He'll cut her to pieces."

Nick had seen photos showing the corpses of cartel victims. God, he hoped they would find her in time.

"I SHOULD HAVE TAKEN A LOW-RENT CAR." Javier shoved his wallet into his trousers as they walked back to his car. "All my CIs expect big pay-outs because I'm driving a Porsche. They think I'm on the take."

Nick watched the scrawny man Javier had left at the curb. "Did he give you anything?" The informant sat under a tree, wiping his nose on the sleeve of his T-shirt.

"Yeah, but I need to verify it with one more source."

Nick nodded toward the man. "What? You don't trust him?"

Javier smirked. He slipped behind the wheel. "No, and his info is so fresh that I have to verify it."

"What did he say?" There was an insistence in his voice that betrayed his anxiety.

Javier glanced at him, his face expressionless. "He said a woman was brought in today. Apparently, she caused quite a fuss. I should be able to get more from another CI. Next, we go to PV." He flipped his phone open and punched a number. Javier spoke in familiar Mexican language, one of a superior speaking to a lesser. Nick listened, but not with a great effort. When Javier raised his voice, Nick couldn't help but hear. "Meet me by your truck in fifteen minutes. No excuses."

He griped about the Porsche, but Javier drove it with obvious appreciation. Nick's practiced eye noticed most of the cars in Mexico were older, dirtier, and more banged up than the average California car. Javier's sports car hugged the curves, and the engine screamed on the southbound straightaways of Highway 200. Had the circumstances been any different, Nick might have enjoyed the ride in a classic car.

They were in Puerto Vallarta in less than twenty minutes. South of the airport, Javier took a turn on Palma Real, then motored past the huge Corona bottling plant. He turned left across traffic and ducked into what appeared to be an employee parking lot. A balding man in a blue janitorial jumpsuit stood next to a dented brown Ford Ranger. The man leaned against the driver's door, a blue curl of cigarette smoke drifting above his head. He watched them as the Porsche approached.

"Simon." Javier nodded at the janitor. Nick stood behind and to the side of Javier, listening hard and trying not to look too eager.

Simon nodded back, not addressing Javier.

"I have information that I want you to verify. A simple yes or no will do."

Simon's glance took in the passing traffic.

"Does the big man in Sayulita have a house guest who is eager to come home?"

Simon's stubby fingers flicked his smoke on the asphalt. Grinding the butt with the ball of his shoe, he spoke like the words were being forced from his lips. "Yes, a young woman. The wife of the California policeman."

Nick stepped up to ask another question, but Javier's arm shot across his chest. Nick backed off. This was Javier's confidential informant, not his. Javier was cool as ice, not a bead of sweat on his brow. The agent's question came smoothly. "Simon, how do you know she is the wife of a California policeman?"

"It's what we were told. We don't ask questions, you know?"

"What room in the house is she in?"

"The cellar, I think. My wife has to make her food. Lupita—my wife—is afraid she will fall down the stairs because they are very old and in disrepair."

Javier nodded. "Does your woman know why she was taken?"

Simon reached into his shirt pocket for a pack of cigarettes. He shrugged, pulling one out. He lit it, then blew smoke over Javier's head. Simon's hand shook. "No, but word was out fast. This was different, even for Vega."

"One more question, then you can go." Javier's lips thinned. "Can your wife draw a picture of the house and grounds, with all the entrances and exits?"

"She won't do that. If Vega found out, he would kill her."

"He will never know, I guarantee it." Javier's voice lowered. "If you do this, all debts are paid between us." In a belated effort to seem friendly, Javier patted Simon on the shoulder.

"There's something else."

Javier waited, motionless, a cougar ready to pounce but holding back on instinct. In cases like this, there was always something else, wasn't there? And it was never good news.

"Two men have been coming around the house. Twins."

A corner of Javier's mouth twisted as he swore under his breath.

"Lupita says they are the brothers of la señora."

"Yes, I know who they are. I'll call you for the map at seven o'clock."

With a growing sense of doom, Nick glanced at his watch. It was after five now. Two hours. Not much time to plan an operation. Once they got the map, they needed to move.

Chapter Forty

EMILIO STEERED OSWALDO'S COUSIN'S TOYOTA CAMRY THROUGH thinning traffic down Highway 200. South of the airport, he turned left. Sticking to back roads as much as possible, he hoped to avoid any trouble. He was sure he wasn't being watched, but he kept his eyes on the mirrors, just in case. Even taking this circuitous route, he made good time. The modern neighborhood and well-paved roadway of Avenida Fluvial Vallarta gave way to older, cobblestoned streets. Every home featured an iron gate standing sentinel. Colorful stucco facades stood next to vacant, litter-strewn plots of scrubby weeds.

One-eighty-five Francia was on the left. A tan, two-story stucco building, it looked newer than its neighbors. Arched windows trimmed in heavy white iron matched a fence that ran across the front of the property. Potted plants lined the gated driveway. Emilio circled the block, his gaze scouring the neighborhood. He hadn't been followed. A dark Volkswagen van and a Ford station wagon sat across the street. Parking in the driveway, he noted a flat tire on the Ford. He smiled with the satisfaction that there would not be a threat from that vehicle, at least.

His eye caught movement from the patio. A curtain moved. Liliana.

His heart jumped as he waited at the gate. He missed his wife, his beloved. It had been two long days without her. Although he had savored the quiet moments, there was a hole in his heart that only she filled. More than that, he needed to protect her. With Rigo and Angela in San Vicente, and his wife in PV, his family was scattered. Better to have Liliana with him to keep her safe.

There she was, striding out the door, her straight gray hair billowing in the breeze, letting him through the gate, then into the house. Her sister, Rocio, was a paler version of Liliana. Rocio slammed the door behind them, then fell into Emilio's arms, sobbing.

Ah, the drama, he thought as he comforted her. Liliana stood near them, her hands fretting with her hair until Emilio peeled Rocio off his chest. His sister-in-law chattered—her voice rising, then dropping —in the way of people who used noise to cover their fear. Emilio embraced his wife, surprised and more than pleased that she wasn't hysterical. He pressed his fingertips into the small of her back, an intimate touch that pulled her closer. She hid her smile from her sister.

Rocio nattered on, suggesting preposterous situations and asking more questions than anyone had answers. When husband and wife separated, Rocio took a deep breath, struggling to calm herself.

"Did you find Rigo?" Liliana asked. "Is he safe? Or…"

"He is safe now and receiving medical attention."

"Medical?" Liliana searched her husband's face. "He is injured?"

"He will be fine. Bernardo is looking after him."

Rocio's voice rose. "But Bernardo is a veterinarian, not a doctor."

"He is in good hands." Rocio didn't know Oswaldo, so he omitted that information. Better anyway. He'd tell Liliana when they were alone.

"Are you sure you weren't followed?" Rocio's eyes darted to the door, then the front window. "I mean, I am here alone."

Suddenly tired of his sister-in-law's theatrics, Emilio scooped up his wife's suitcase and gave Rocio's cheek a light kiss. "You are safe." He turned for the door, knowing Liliana would follow.

Outside, Emilio took his wife's small hand. The walk across the driveway seemed to take forever. At the car, he threw her luggage in the back seat as Liliana slid into the passenger side. Emilio started the Camry, reminded his wife to fasten her seat belt, and they were off.

Deciding on a different route back to San Vicente, Emilio drove north, out of the residential area, then northwest toward Avenida Los Tules. More modern than Rocio's neighborhood, the road ran through a commercial area that had cars parked along the one-lane street. It could have been any suburban area in the world. Wide, smoothly paved streets wound around the business district. Then the neighborhood degraded to more depressing turf—litter-strewn lots, vacant and leveled for the next onslaught of civic development years ago, before the recession. In odd contrast, smartly landscaped medians separated the roads accented with bougainvillea, fully-grown trees, and a carpet of lawn.

It was easy for Emilio to spot the tail car. There wasn't much traffic, and most of that headed in the opposite direction. When he first noticed the silver Durango, it was far enough behind him that he wasn't concerned. Now, several miles later and in the middle of nowhere, he felt his pulse pounding. What he did in the next moments would change his life. He'd better make it good.

Emilio scanned the neighborhood, looking for a way out. There was nowhere here to hide. If he stayed on Los Tules, it would inter-sect with Highway 200. His hands sweated on the steering wheel. He pictured an action movie chase scene. He was sure his driving skills weren't up to the challenge. Glancing in his rear-view mirror, he noticed the silver SUV was closing the gap. Liliana asked him a question, but he ignored her, trying to concentrate. Approaching a sharp corner, he made a split-second decision. Jerking the sedan off the blacktop and onto the dirt shoulder, the car bounced over a rut and onto a dirt track. Tires broke traction on the loose surface, and the back end of the car swerved.

Emilio regained control. If he could hide his car behind the cottonwood trees, they might have a chance. He pressed his foot on the gas pedal, heading off the dirt road and aiming for the trees. If only he could get to the other side of the grove to hide.

Not far now, he thought. He saw the glint of the sun on something behind the clump of scraggly cottonwoods. Afraid to take his eyes off the dirt road, he aimed for the reflection. Twenty yards, ten yards— where did that creek bank come from? He felt a jolt, but it was already too late. His wife screamed into his ear. By reflex, Emilio jumped on the brakes. The Camry slid sideways into a 180-degree arc and then tipped. They came to a rest in a haze of dust.

Liliana looked up at him, her eyes wide with fear. Something was off. He looked down at her as she grabbed his arm. Her fingers dug into his skin, her mouth moved, but no sound came out. He felt dizzy, yet kept trying and rejecting possibilities in the split second.

The dust settled enough to see Avenida Los Tules off to his left. No sign of the silver Durango. Had he imagined it? No way.

Then he understood why he felt off balance. The Camry was tipped—passenger side wheels over the embankment and driver's hooked on the edge.

A harsh noise ground away underneath the car. Dust spewed around them again as his tires scraped the dirt and slanted down the bank. The din stopped. Tires on the passenger side thumped into the soft mud. Not daring to turn his head, Emilio stared straight ahead, over Liliana's shoulder. The reflection that had offered safety from the road was a creek swollen with last night's mountain rain. Turbid water streaked past in a race to get to the ocean. Below Liliana, the creek swirled in a deep eddy.

"Don't move," he whispered.

"Why? What is going on?" Liliana's voice rose in a wail. Her fingers reached to grasp his shirt. Her breathing was noisy and edged with panic.

His hand closed over her arm. He spoke with a fierceness he had never known. "Liliana. Do not move!"

She looked over her shoulder, to see what he was staring at. Her scream tore through the car, competing with a clamor now erupting from the underside. "Emilio!"

He grabbed her shoulders, trying to pull her close. "No, no, no," he chanted. He couldn't get a good grip on her. If they landed sideways in the creek, she would be underwater. He might make it, but she wouldn't. He pulled again, but the seat belt was secure, holding her prisoner. While he reached to undo it, the car tipped sideways, then plummeted into the creek, its side scraping against river rocks. Passenger windows shattered, and water surged into the gaping holes. The force of the flood bounced Liliana like a bobblehead. Emilio thought he saw blood in her hair, but everything happened so fast, he wasn't sure.

"Emilio!" Liliana's scream was cut short as creek water rose. She opened her mouth again as a wave crested over her. She coughed. Her arms shot out wildly, scrambling to pull herself above the water. Clutching at her husband, she bumped his arm but couldn't get a hold.

Emilio got his seatbelt free, took a breath, and plunged his body into the murky water. He let himself sink to Liliana while his fingers scrambled for her seat belt. He couldn't find it, but worse, her flailing limbs tangled the safety belt strap.

He needed air.

His head broke the surface. Emilio swallowed a desperate gulp of air. The Camry tilted slowly—passenger side down, about to go upside down. The water leveled out at the top of the steering wheel but still eddied through the car. Grabbing the dashboard, he dove into the turbulent water again and reached for Liliana. When he found her, her arms were still.

Emilio couldn't see. Shadowy swirls crowded out Liliana's face. The current caught the hazy water, whirling it away. Suddenly, he saw her. The sun pierced the water, her beautiful silver hair glimmering. Eyes wide open, mouth agape.

From above, outside the car, hands grabbed at him and pulled him up. He pushed them away, but he was exhausted. Another second, and this wouldn't have happened. Then, the regret was replaced by a deep ache. Part of his brain scrambled to come up with ways that he could still save her. A pocketknife was all he needed. A pocket knife, yes. He could cut the seat belt and free her. He could do CPR and bring her back.

On the creek bank, he groaned. "No, no, no. She's still down there." It was his fault; he shouldn't have driven so fast. He should have been more careful. If he'd just carried his knife.

A stranger came up with a pocketknife and the same idea. Emilio grabbed it and jumped to the car with new hope. He straddled the open window and dropped beneath the muddied water. Through the murkiness, he made out a shadow that must be Liliana. He descended to her. He sawed at the seatbelt. Then, his arm jerked in slow motion when the knife cut through. Emilio sidled up to her, wrapping his arm under hers. Seconds later, his head broke the surface, and he pushed her limp body to a pair of bystanders.

Two men laid her on her back. One of them bent over her, blowing into her mouth while Emilio helped with chest compressions. They continued until an ambulance arrived. Elbowing him aside, Emilio watched as Paramedics took her vitals, then covered her with a rough institutional blanket. When one of the medics told Emilio that she was dead, he dropped to her side and pulled the cloth off his wife's face. She looked so peaceful. He knew it wasn't so. She was a soul in torment, murdered by gangsters and his own failures.

Sobbing, he wrapped his fingers in her wet hair and laid his head on her still chest. Why didn't he die instead of her? He wanted to die, to be with her.

Oh, heart of Jesus, once in agony, have mercy on the dying.

Chapter Forty-One

THE SUNLIGHT HAD FADED ENOUGH THAT NICK HAD TO USE HIS flashlight to see the map. The CI's Ranger sped away, down a road where the dust settled in its sweet time. The Porsche engine tick-ticked as they bent over the hood, flattening out the paper. Indecisive pencil lines created a roughly drawn sketch. Windows and doors were outlined in faint, square print and been marked in the manner Javier had asked.

"Here." He pointed to a window. "It looks like we can get into the cellar from here."

"Did you find out about guards?"

"The info isn't that reliable. My CI's wife is a cook. She wasn't sure, but she said there are usually two armed men in the front and a third in the back." Javier stabbed the paper. "One of them is at the cellar window."

"Wait, what? Cellar window?"

Javier nodded. "It's a half window kind of thing, right at ground level."

"With bars?"

Javier nodded.

Nick forced himself to be more optimistic about their chances.

"Okay."

"I have some people I trust who can help us."

Nick held up a hand. "Let's plan something that takes just the two of us. The fewer, the better."

There was barely enough light to see. Javier squinted at him. "You don't trust any Mexicans, do you?"

Nick met Javier's gaze and held it.

Javier straightened. "You racist bastard. You won't even work with Mexicans unless you have to."

"No one but Emilio has given me any reason to want to." A warm breeze brushed Nick's arms when he went back to the map. "Let's go back to your office and figure this out."

MEREDITH SHIFTED IN THE CHAIR, trying to find a position where her ankles, wrists, and ribs wouldn't hurt. Left in the basement, she'd been gagged, her wrists and ankles duct taped together, then tied to a chair. She understood the reason they hadn't blindfolded her. She was a dead woman—sooner or later. Whenever Vega—she assumed he was El Jefe—figured out she didn't know where the book was, that would be the end of her. He was after Silvia's book. Her head still ached, but the soreness in her ribs was diminishing.

The room was twenty by forty feet, with stairs at one end. Small barred windows dotted the upper walls on two sides. A look around yielded nothing helpful. Straw baskets, empty cardboard boxes, and aluminum garbage cans. Tiny scraping noises came from the walls. She grimaced at the thought of competing with rodents for food.

The minutes crept on. Scenario after scenario played out in her mind, all ended with the same results. Terminal.

Then, she had a sign that she would be there for a while. They fed her. A gray-haired woman with a mole on her chin wobbled down the rickety stairs, her hands shaking so much that liquid sloshed from the pot. The guard ripped the duct tape off Meredith's mouth, then stood over while the woman spoon-fed Meredith a beef stew-like dish. She hadn't eaten in a long time. She should have been hungry, but she wasn't. Still, she choked down as much as possible.

Meredith watched the woman, her unsteady hands and slow movements. It was impossible to guess her age. Although she kept her head down, the wrinkles at her eyes hinted at years of squinting through cooking smoke or sunshine. Maybe both. What must her life be like that she had to feed a person who was nothing other than a prisoner? She must know something bad was going on here. Why did the idea of going to the authorities seem unreasonable? How fearful must she be of Vega, a man who would perpetrate a crime like kidnapping? He was capable of worse; that much was obvious. What indignities had she suffered to be so submissive?

Meredith shuddered. In Sonoma, she'd once accompanied the FBI in the execution of a federal search warrant for human trafficking. Twenty-six Hispanic women were kept in a tiny home, handcuffed, and tied to an iron rail. When the pimps freed them, it was to walk the streets, work the vineyards, and do other jobs at slave wages. The Feds told her that beatings were frequent and their captors used food and necessities as bargaining chips. Meredith would never forget the look of surrender in those women's eyes.

Few of them spoke English, but the message was clear. They were free now—to go where? Deported to Mexico or wherever they came from—for what? They already wore the unmistakable stain of defeat. There was no bettering yourself there. Their lives already were a study in betrayal and loss. She hadn't seen gratitude in their faces, nor celebration, just resignation.

Surprised at the memory, Meredith wondered how it fit the fabric of her own life. The recollection of those poor women wasn't what made her think—it was how she processed it. At the time, she'd viewed everything with professional detachment. The lack of response from the victims had tainted her view of the entire event.

Now, she felt closer to these people. Now, she was one of them. She was sorry she'd come to such a speedy and false judgment on those women. They were like this old woman feeding her. Meredith's survival mechanism got in the way of her compassion.

An odd warmth rippled through her. She felt for the first time in months. She'd been able to evaluate her responses to an earlier event and change her perspective. After her husband died, she'd put a lid on her emotions. The ensuing months had held nothing but sorrow, disillusionment, and pain. There came a time when, to get through the day, she had to put it all aside. Later, it was better to keep it there —just out of reach, in a place remote enough she'd have to work at getting there. She hadn't tried.

But she did today. Too bad it took a life-threatening incident to make it happen. Especially as the outcome of this adventure didn't look encouraging.

The guard called the old woman 'Lupita'. Meredith was glad to have a name to put to her forlorn face. She felt sorry for this woman who was afraid of everyone. After Lupita and the guard left, Meredith thought about her own life.

She'd never shown fear to anyone—particularly to her father. Her mother grew brittle and tired over the years with him, but Meredith hadn't caved in to his brutality—at least not outwardly. She found it hideously ironic that she chose the same career, despite earning her Bachelor of Science in Physical Education. He had shaped her, whether she admitted it or not. It dawned on her now that her relationship with her husband had grown to mimic the one she'd had with her father. Not that Richard was brutal—he was more of a manipulator. Had she feared him? Yes, she guessed so. Fear for his approval, his affection. She'd felt pressure to keep him appeased, but never let him see her afraid just as she had with her father growing up.

Maybe if she'd been different, Richard wouldn't have been killed on the way to his lover's home. No, that wasn't right. Giroud's hitman was told to find Richard and kill him. It was hard to get past the humiliation because Richard was having an affair—one the whole law enforcement community found out about because of the way he died.

Maybe…maybe she would live to see how meaningless it all was. How she had undervalued the good things in her life—David, her brother, now gone, too. They had always been close. Their bonds forged early in their childhood while hiding in the closet, as Daddy raged at their mother. She loved David and his big, irresponsible heart—that loved everyone. His wife, Christy, was her best friend. She stood by Meredith through all her problems, giving thoughtful, honest advice, and never demanding anything in return.

Then there was the job. Nick was right about that. When Superior Court Judge Stephen Giroud had pushed her limits, the Sheriff's Office administrators steadfastly refused to acknowledge his threats. She'd been left to resolve that problem herself. If Nick hadn't helped, she'd be dead. Maybe Nick, too, and everyone else close to her. In the end, the judge was killed as he tried to kill her. Afterward, the department protocol dictated the District Attorney's Office investigate the incident to avoid potential conflicts. The DA's lead investigator, LaRae Archibald, conducted a tough, insightful probe and recommended exoneration for both her and Nick.

After five weeks on administrative leave following the shooting, Meredith went back to work. She'd been working for eight months before leaving on this adventure in Mexico. She loved her job, but bitterness had become part of her attitude. Lieutenant Ferrua and the other brass abandoned her. They'd looked the other way because of the power the judge exerted. It wasn't right. They should have protected her—slapped him with a restraining order at the very least.

She didn't like the ugliness that was growing in her. Now, at this desperate hour, she regretted spending so much energy on it. She should have gone to Ferrua, talked it out, and gotten an understanding of the department's position.

Then there was Nick. Her best and closest friend, whom she'd kissed, and messed up their relationship. Maybe. If she got out of this, she'd make him listen to her apology. If she got out of this, she'd go back to work with a smile on her face, grateful to have a job she loved. If she got out of this, she'd sit down with Ferrua. Talk to him. Maybe she could make it easier for the next deputy who faced a crisis.

If she got out of this—which at the moment seemed highly unlikely.

Chapter Forty-Two

EMILIO MOANED INTO THE PHONE. "LILIANA IS DEAD."

"No. Jesus! What happened?" Nick's stomach turned. "Are you okay?" He sat on a chair at Javier's kitchen table.

"They were chasing us, and I drove off the road, trying to hide, but I didn't see the bank and..."

"Who was chasing you?"

"I don't know. An SUV. Gray, I think. A Durango."

"Have you seen that car before?"

"I don't know." Emilio wailed. "Everyone here drives an SUV."

"Okay, okay. Emilio, I'm so sorry. Where, exactly? Did the police show up?"

"Yes, because it was an accident." Emilio's voice cracked. "I told them I got distracted. I made sure they didn't know anything about being chased."

"Good thinking, Emilio." Nick leaned against the car while his fingers turned white holding the phone. "Where are you now?"

"At the hospital. I needed a few stitches. I called Bernardo to come pick me up. He should be here soon."

"You should go back to Bernardo's." Jesus, he didn't want to tell him his house had burned down. "It will be safer there."

Emilio took a deep breath. "Where else is there to go?"

"Emilio, I have to ask you something. Because you have lost so much—almost lost your son and now your wife, I feel I owe it to you to let you decide the fate of the book."

"It has cost me almost everything dear to me. I say burn it."

"Think about it, Emilio. If we give it to Javier, he will give it to the authorities to prosecute Vega." Nick wouldn't blow Javier's cover, even to Emilio. Javier's job had no bearing on Emilio's decision.

Emilio considered this. "I've seen how these cases are adjudicated. Judges and lawyers are bought off, witnesses murdered, and the guilty ones go free. That isn't justice."

"No, it isn't." Nick asked, "What do you have in mind?"

"Burn it."

"Then all this happened for nothing."

Twenty seconds of silence. "What are you thinking?"

"It needs to go where it will have the most impact."

"Do with it what you think is best. I trust you." Emilio made an impatient snort. "I can't think this through right now."

Nick swallowed. "I am so sorry, Emilio. This world is a poorer place for Liliana's passing."

Emilio said, "Yes." Then he hung up.

"What happened?" Even through the sunglasses, Nick read what Javier was thinking.

Nick re-told Emilio's story. "Liliana drowned while he was trying to free her from her seat belt."

Javier grabbed the map and threw it. "Goddam it!" He yelled, "She was one of the really decent people in this screwed-up world. Damn it to hell."

Nick felt a warmth flushing through his body. He didn't trust himself to open his mouth. The words that came to his mind shocked him. He clenched his jaw and kept them to himself.

Javier glared at Nick. "What if we catch Vega when we get your partner?"

"And do what with him? Kill him?" Nick rubbed his eyes. "That may be the way things are done here, but I'm not made that way.

And I don't think you want to do that either. Otherwise, what do we stand for? What separates us from them? Even if we can pull it off, if anybody finds out, your career is done." Nick shook a finger at Javier.

"That is, if we even make it out alive. Vega's got bodyguards all around him. You heard your CI's estimate, based on what the wife saw. We'd be outnumbered."

"I don't have enough evidence to arrest him." Javier's eyes narrowed. "Maybe it's time we get some help. There are people in my office who I trust."

"Too many things can go wrong." Nick shook his head. "If there's a leak, we're done for. If you or any of your guys get hurt, our asses get handed to us on a stick. And there is no due diligence on this crime. We don't have any evidence that we can take to a courtroom."

Javier took a step and closed in on Nick with clenched fists. "Well then, what do you suggest we do? You don't know these types. They'll kill everyone close to the book and their families."

"For revenge?"

Javier nodded. "And to throw fear at anyone close to them. A kind of warning, not to ever cross a cartel. They won't quit until the whole family is dead. That includes you, me, and Meredith."

The glimmering of an idea took shape in Nick's mind. "What about help from those we know we don't trust?"

Chapter Forty-Three

THE SLAP ECHOED THROUGH THE BASEMENT. MEREDITH BENT HER head to her shoulder, wishing her hand were free so she could rub the sting out of her cheek, then beat the crap out of Vega and his goon— a muscular soldier in BDUs with arms and neck tatted up in the worst way.

A freestanding lamp poured a bright fluorescent glow into a circle in the middle of the room. "Where is it?" Miguel Vega's voice, stuttering with fury, came from behind the light. Meredith saw the glint from the light on his oil-slicked hair. Vega's curls shook as he shouted. If the threat weren't so certain, he'd be tough to take seriously. In an obvious attempt to gather his composure, he lit a cigarette. Squinting over the flame, his features became clear in the light. Pudgy cheeks betrayed a dissolute character with flaring nostrils over full, red lips. A puke-green mono-grammed Polo shirt, khaki slacks pressed to a knife-edge, clothed the barbarous nature of a drug lord. The Wingtips were a nice touch, though.

She eyed him with disgust. She thought about spitting, but her lips still hurt from when they yanked the duct tape from her mouth. Still, she was sure it was Vega.

The tough guy lunged forward, slapping her other cheek. He hit hard, but she sensed he was holding back. Maybe they needed to keep her alive, or at least until she told them what they wanted. It was ironic that she didn't know where Nick had hidden the book. She guessed he'd hidden it in the tunnel when he went back to check for the guards following them. It was a long tunnel.

Vega nodded to his muscle, then flung his cigarette on the floor and ground it out with the toe of his shoe. Soldier Man drew something from his pants pocket and secreted it in his hand. His spine straightened as his eyes met Meredith's. What scared her was what wasn't there. It was like looking into the eyes of an animal—predatory, with no hint of humanity.

This is going to hurt.

Soldier Man gripped the object while squeezing his other hand around it. Even though Meredith was expecting it, the swing came from nowhere. The dull thud pounded through her jaw and vibrated into her brain. Shards of light shattered before her eyes. He hit her again, this time, on the other side. A third punch found the same place as the first. Her head snapped back with the blow. A punch by cement knuckles rocked against her jaw, and she felt the warmth of blood oozing down her chin.

Soldier Man stepped back, letting Vega take the forefront of Meredith's somewhat foggy view. An arm's-length away, he leaned toward her. "Angela, where is the book?"

Meredith's head shot up, anger and surprise clearing her vision.

"I'm not Angela, you idiot."

Vega's face twisted into a smirk. "You're lying."

"I can't give you whatever it is that you want from Angela. Turn me loose now, before Soldier Boy over here gets carried away and neither of you get what you want." Blood from the cut on her chin dripped on her shirt. "My name is Meredith Ryan, and I'm an American. I am not Angela."

Blistering Spanish erupted between the two men. Vega squared off with Meredith. "My men found you where the woman, Angela, has been staying. You are the same age and description. You haven't convinced me that you are not she."

"They didn't ask for my ID." Meredith shook her head. "Your gorillas grabbed me while I was naked, for God's sake."

He waved his hand, brushing aside her argument. "Alvino," Vega shouted to a guard standing outside the door. This time he used English.

"Tie her up until we can be sure she is Angela."

The guard bit out a response in Spanish and yanked Meredith's head back. He wrapped duct tape around her head, once again securing her mouth.

A reprieve, but not a stay of execution. Once Vega found out she wasn't Angela, he'd dispose of her. Pissed off at being caught, her ribs and head aching, and tired to the bone, she knew she was running out of time. Time to figure out how she was going to get away from here.

It wasn't all that promising.

Chapter Forty-Four

As the sun breached the Sierra Madre Mountains the next morning, the road to Puerto Vallarta was a traffic nightmare. Driving time was estimated at twenty minutes, and there wasn't a clear stretch anywhere on the road. Javier's knuckles whitened as he worked the Porsche's steering wheel. The car slipped sweetly into a turn, then straightened as it dropped into the valley. Javier accelerated up a small rise. The road ran through mango and banana trees, as well as palms. At the top of the hill, Nick hollered over the engine noise, "Off to the right, in that turn-out." They were almost at the Puerto Vallarta Airport. Javier downshifted and rolled to a dusty stop. He parked behind a silver Land Rover that sat under the shade of a scrawny palm tree. Two men dressed in ill-fitting suits stood by the hood. The men looked like refugees from a "Miami Vice" re-run.

A sudden doubt nipped at Nick. Maybe this was a mistake. No, we have to try. He breathed deeply as he got out of the car, forcing his racing adrenaline to slow. He took in everything about the men, to recall if needed. Both were in their mid-twenties, trim but muscular, and dressed for a business office. The shorter one wore mirrored aviator sunglasses. Both stood at a relaxed attention. From a distance, they looked respectable enough. As he and Javier drew nearer, Nick noted a bulge under the arms of both men, the narrowed eyes, and the ink creeping up the neck of the taller man.

The Aviator Glasses man sauntered toward them, then waved a hand. Javier raised his hands over his head, nodding for Nick to do the same. Javier told the short man he had a gun in his jacket pocket. The man pulled out Javier's 9mm and shoved it into his own waistband. The process was repeated with Nick, except the man smirked as he wrapped his fingers around the revolver.

Yeah, buddy. Laugh if you want, but it can kill you just as dead.

As Javier warned him, they were blindfolded, and their wrists duct-taped in front of them. Shoved into the back seat, and Nick wondered how this would all end. It had seemed like such a good idea, but now, as they were being transported to the dragon's lair, he wasn't so sure. He was encouraged that they used blindfolds. At least there was the prospect that they would be released to return to Javier's car. Had the guards not tried to conceal the location of the house, Nick and Javier would have known they were done for.

A short ride, no more than five minutes, on smooth asphalt. Then the men yanked him from the SUV. A man on each side of him, they jerked Nick along a flat concrete surface. He heard helicopter blades beating above and instinctively hunched over. Guided by his escorts, they pushed him inside the craft. A seatbelt snapped across his chest before they lifted off. He felt for Javier with his elbow and made contact with someone's ribs. He felt Javier grunt a protest—he couldn't hear him from the noise—then Nick settled in for the ride. All the precautions were reassuring, lending hope that Carlos Guzman Herrera would listen to them.

The helicopter lifted off, and Nick's stomach flipped with the motion. He'd been in a chopper before, a few years ago, during a rescue in the remote hills of Sonoma County. Then, as now, he suspected the stick jockey delighted in radical movement that scared his riders. It seemed to be a universal test, to see how much mettle the passenger had, or maybe both pilots had just been assholes.

Unable to anticipate the movement, Javier's body slammed

against him when tipped to one side. Showboating like this pissed Nick off. What did it take to make two blindfolded and bound men puke with fear? He should have expected this. He wouldn't puke for this clown—not for anything. The pilot eventually lost interest in aerobatics. The copter leveled out. Because he was blindfolded, Nick's other senses were hypervigilant. The very air vibrated with the motion of the blades. He heard occasional static from a radio and a muffled, tinny reply from the pilot. He expected there was another man up front, armed and watching them. He caught the odor of motor oil, filtered air, and someone's pungent aftershave.

It felt like a half hour to Nick before the craft began a descent. Gauging time and the motion of a helicopter would never lead him back here. His mind was just wired that way—to analyze and conclude from all the incoming information. Guessing this would be impossible

A soft thump announced their landing. As the engine powered down, Nick heard doors snap open. Hands forced him outside. Again, as before, there was a man on each side. They led Nick to a vehicle. He stretched to get in, so he figured it was another SUV. Funny how these drug lords lived a cliché. On the other hand, who was going to criticize them?

The road was bumpy as hell, intensified by the vehicle's short wheelbase. Nick and Javier jabbed elbows into each other while trying to stay upright. Soon, the SUV slowed to a crawl. If they lived through the next several hours, Nick would be leaving this place with bruised ribs.

Silly, what you think of during moments like this.

The road leveled, then the tires crunched on gravel for a time and eventually smoothed out—maybe asphalt. The vehicle jerked to a stop. Now someone pulled them out roughly onto a cobblestone surface. Landing on a hip, granite scraped across Nick's knuckles as he twisted for balance. Nick was righted, jerked up, and steered forward. He called out. "Javier?"

Javier's "yes" was cut short by a muffled thump and a scuffle. Nick didn't say anything more. Soon they were indoors. A guard positioned them side by side and told them in Spanish to stand quietly.

Nick estimated thirty minutes had passed; his back was getting tired. He hoped to see the boss soon, so they could figure out if this would work or not. He had to set the plan in motion. An internal "tick-tock" was clicking off the seconds until he got to Meredith. And if this gamble failed and they didn't make it...

Nick thought about kissing Meredith. Her lips soft and moist, yielding to him. The kiss told him that she was his, that they were more together than they pretended. He'd felt her shock, he thought— probably as much as his. She had fallen into him, promising...

Nick shook his head, as if to remove what popped up in his mind. Too many things could go wrong to think about them all.

The blindfold jerked from his eyes. It took a moment for his vision to clear. He tried to focus on the man bent in front of him, ripping the tape from his wrists. Nick heard the same noise next to him.

He and Javier were in a room lined with fully stocked book-shelves. A large view window stood to their right, but Nick had no angle to see outside. Before him was a traditional dark oak desk, where things lay in precise order. A door behind the desk opened. A big man in his seventies, with dyed Elvis hair, strode in. His posture showed that while barrel-chested once, he now just had a big belly. Taking his place behind the desk, he smoothed the placket of his blood-red Guayabera shirt. His creased, angular face showed nothing as he squared off with Nick and Javier. He might have been a teacher or a shopkeeper, but he wasn't. He was one of the most powerful men in central Mexico. Behind him, a taller version stepped into the room. A brother, practically a copy, this would be Fidelio. Javier's briefing had suggested he would meet Fidelio, the enforcer.

It's showtime.

"I am Carlos Guzman Herrera, father of Silvia Guzman Barajas." His jaw muscle flexed as he spoke. Fidelio stood behind Guzman, silent, with his arms folded across his ample chest.

Javier bowed respectfully. Once Nick had convinced him of the plan, Javier insisted he be the one to talk. Nick agreed. "I am Javier Davalos Aguilera, and this is Nicholas Reyes Gomez."

"I know who you are." Guzman nodded, looking at Nick. "You are a policeman, currently operating outside your jurisdiction. Your business has to do with my daughter, Silvia?"

"Señor Guzman, I am sorry to bear this news, but we think your daughter has been killed."

Surprise did not reach Guzman's dark eyes. Nick thought. Either he already knew Silvia was dead or didn't believe them. Then again, maybe he was just a cold-hearted son of a bitch.

"Why do you say this?" His demanding Spanish was formal, old school. Geography dictated isolation, enough distance from the styles of the day; his age suggested a preference for it. Nick thought Guzman might be holding back until he decided how he was going to deal with them. Starting with respect made a more facile transition downward to intimidation and threats.

"My partner, Rigoberto Borrego, had a conversation with someone with credibility who told him that Silvia would never return. Borrego took the inference that she was dead. This man did nothing to dissuade my partner from believing it."

Guzman climbed into his chair like a man who had aged three decades in as many seconds. "Go on." Fidelio held his silence, but his eyes wilted.

Nick nodded to Javier. He needed to tell the whole story.

"My partner and I operate a law practice in Bucerias, specializing in divorces. Silvia came in one day and retained Rigo for a dissolution action from Miguel Vega."

At this, Guzman picked up a pen. He rolled it over and over his fingers. The old man's eyes faded, as did his words. "I didn't know." Across the desk, Nick saw Guzman's face sag.

"Rigo and Silvia began a relationship. He says they fell for each other." Javier paused a moment as Guzman waved, brushing the idea away as impossible. Javier pushed on with his story. "At some point, she trusted him enough to ask him to hide the book."

"What kind of book?"

"It seemed like a diary. Small, but had names, dates, and money totals like a ledger."

Guzman nodded. A flicker of recognition shot across his face. Nick thought again that it wasn't news to the old man. How could he have known about the book?

"Go on."

Javier drew a deep breath. "Rigo was kidnapped last week. We thought it was for ransom, but only one call came, then nothing. Nick and his partner were able to rescue Rigo. The man who abducted him wanted money, now that threat has evaporated. We think there may have been a third party who took advantage of the situation. Vega's men searched Rigo's home—probably for the book. When they couldn't find it, they burned the house to the ground. Vega is still looking. He has kidnapped Nick's partner—an American police-woman. We presume he will try to ransom her for the book."

"Is he sure? Did your attorney friend see Silvia dead?"

"No, but the man's purpose was clear. He described Silvia as merely a bargaining chip that got in his way."

Guzman sighed. He sat back in his chair and rubbed the bridge of his nose. "Are you sure this man is Vega?"

At Javier's nod, Guzman continued. "Vega is a pig. It was Silvia's brothers who encouraged the marriage." Guzman glanced at his brother behind him. "We were right, hermano. He lied when he said she went to Paris."

Nick noticed Javier's reaction. This was a new wrinkle. An inti-mate family exchange from a drug lord? Nick kept on his work face, even though he was as surprised as Javier must have been.

"The twins told us it would be good for business," Guzman said, "the family business, you know?" When he glanced up, his gaze didn't take them in. "Vega wanted an alliance here on the coast between our families. I didn't like him. Too ingratiating. He was devious, and I told the boys that. Besides, he wasn't a proven entrepreneur. But they were greedy for the money he generated and the power. I know Silvia heard our discussions. She never wanted to marry him."

"And you think the book is Silvia's account of Vega's cheating on your investment?"

"Yes." Sighing, Guzman pushed his chair away from the desk. "She must have wanted to get away from Vega badly to have done this much work." Guzman's eyes betrayed a vulnerability that surprised Nick. In spite of the situation, Nick found himself with a glimmering of compassion for the old man. He knew how Guzman must feel to have lost his daughter.

Fidelio took a step. In a soft voice that belied the hardness of his face, he asked, "Do you know where she is…where her body is?"

Javier shook his head. "You'll have to ask Vega."

"Rest assured, I will." Guzman stood; any softness in him was gone. "And what brings you here to tell me such news? You want something."

Nick was pleased with the way the Mexican agent had played it so far. He still distrusted the man, but Javier knew how to engage these guys, he'd have to give him that.

"You recall I mentioned that Vega kidnapped Nick's partner?" Javier stood tall.

Guzman could have been a statute for his stillness. He didn't answer.

"We need help getting his partner out of Vega's house." Javier cleared his throat. "If we can lure Vega out, we will get her, while you will be positioned to ask him where your daughter is."

Guzman fixed his attention on the picture window, then swung to the man who stood behind him. Their communication was unspoken. The silence drew into minutes. Finally, Guzman spoke. "I have no interest in rescuing an American police officer."

Thick, protesting words churned in Nick's chest.

"Señor Guzman," Nick almost shouted over Javier. "I know what it is to lose a daughter. To never see her life fulfilled; never see your grandchildren or her smile—ever again." Nick had Guzman's attention. He spoke to him as a father, not a cop to a drug lord. "My daughter died of natural causes. If she had been murdered, and I had a chance to face her killer, I wouldn't hesitate over terms."

Guzman nodded, meeting Nick's eyes for the first time. "Yes, you are right. I will listen to your plan."

"Our maneuver will put you in a place of power over Vega, Senor." Javier had to be the icing on the cake.

"How are you going to make him vulnerable? And what do you want from me?" Guzman motioned for them to sit.

The tiniest smile crept onto Javier's lips. "We have the book, and a plan."

Chapter Forty-Five

MEREDITH HAD TO PEE.

There was no helping it. She thought about how books and movies always got it so wrong. Women had to pee at the most inconvenient times. During a stakeout, it was almost a rule.

There wasn't a guard in the basement, but she had heard the woman moving around upstairs during the day, the wood braces creaking. To get her attention, she first tried yelling through the duct tape. Nothing but a muffled grunt came out. She peered into the room's corners for something that would get the woman or guard's notice. There were baskets and bags, a box of old shoes, and dusty bicycle tires, but nothing that would make much noise. The duct tape tore at her hair as she looked over her shoulder. An aluminum garbage can. She couldn't reach it with her hands tied behind her back, so she went for broke. Rocking her chair back and forth, she pushed herself off balance and fell onto her back. An elbow caught her body weight as she slammed against the concrete. She waited a moment for the pain to subside, then, with her ankles still secured, she inched herself around, using her heels. She rolled onto her side and crawled toward the garbage can, the rough concrete grinding the skin off her elbows.

When she was close enough, she rolled to her back and smacked the can with her bare heels. The echo resounded through the basement as she banged with both feet at the same time. She kicked the garbage can until it rolled out of reach. Feeling with her toes, Meredith scooted towards the can. With all her strength, she slammed it with her feet. Again and again.

Above the noise of the clanging trashcan, she heard the raging voice of the man who stood at the top of the stairs. The door slammed into the wall. The guard Vega had called "Alvino" during yesterday's—was it yesterday or today?—pathetic interrogation yelled at her in Spanish. "Callate, perra."

Meredith's voice was stifled by the duct tape. She couldn't move her lips to articulate her problem, but she kept yelling into the tape, hoping the guard would come over.

He stood on the top stairs, watching her.

She began another tirade, shaking her head, insisting on attention.

He plodded down the stairs, cussing from the tone of it. He ripped the tape off her lips, by this time, he was shouting.

Ouch. "I have to pee." She yelled back.

"Mierda." She heard his heavy sigh behind her. She didn't have to see his face to know he was angry. A new fear filled her thoughts. He was a big guy. She could take him on, but without backup, she wasn't sure she would beat him. She'd thumped on big guys before, and save a few bruises and cuts, she'd prevailed. Then, help was always close by. Today, she was alone and unarmed. She was going to have to start something she wasn't sure she could finish.

Another man's voice called from inside the house on the first floor. He called Alvino's name, speaking terse words that Meredith didn't understand.

Alvino's hand was so big that it almost encircled Meredith's upper arm. With one hand, he jerked her to her feet. Jackass.

She shouted at his broad, flat face—like yelling was going to help him understand. "I have to pee."

"Okay." Alvino flipped open a silver-handled switchblade knife, turned her around, and cut the duct tape binding her wrists. A rude push toward a bucket in the corner sent her off balance and onto her knees. She rolled on her hip, growing angrier by the moment. This asshole was just a common bully—and she hated bullies. "C'mon, you stupid gorilla. Cut me loose so I can pee." She articulated each word with the maximum exasperation. She placed her ankles conveniently at his feet and took a chance on rolling to her back, ready for anything.

She studied Alvino. It was no big deal to him if she peed in her pants, but the man's boss had stopped the interrogation and kept her safe, if uncomfortably restrained. That inferred special attention. Meredith expected a burgeoning crime lord was used to flexing his muscles, not letting his minions make decisions. Alvino was in the unforgiving position of having to predict what his boss wanted. She couldn't guess what he would do. He might just pull out his pistol, shoot her, and be done with it.

"C'mon." Meredith yelled again to force his decision. To pee or not to pee.

Alvino dropped to a knee and, in a smooth movement, sliced through the tape. Meredith leaned back. With the blade swinging away from her freed feet, she punched her heels at his chest. A breath of surprise exploded from his mouth when he teetered off balance. The knife clattered across the floor as he tried to save himself from a fall. Tumbling onto his back, one hand reached for his sidearm.

Meredith burst to her feet, then dropped her knee across Alvino's neck. He twisted sideways and almost slipped away. She clamped her hands and body weight on his arms while pressing her knee down as hard as she could. Slivers of pain shot from a scraped-up elbow. She turned to shift some of her weight to his gun hand. The holster guard was unsnapped, but she ignored the pain and pinned his arm.

Alvino grunted with desperation as he began to lose consciousness. He wriggled his other arm loose and raised it, but when he hit her, it was a glancing blow. It fell without muscle—his energy was in the struggle to seize oxygen.

Bracing herself, Meredith shifted her hips and put all her weight into compressing Alvino's massive neck. Redness edged his tanned face, capillaries burst in his bulging eyes, and he gulped air like a fish tossed from its bowl. The horror of what she was doing crept around the edges of her consciousness, but she knew the man would kill her if she backed off.

She pushed harder.

Finally, Alvino's body failed. His arm dropped. Meredith heard the last whisper of air from his lungs. To be sure, she held her position for a long moment. She avoided looking into his protruding eyes as her finger touched a still carotid artery. Sweat trickled from her temple, stinging as it tracked into her eyes. She rolled off the body to lie staring at the rough timbers of the ceiling.

She'd killed a man—again.

Panting from the exertion, her entire body was soaked with perspiration. She clenched her eyelids shut, finding images of Alvino's struggle and Rusty Webber's death heavy on her mind. She turned her head, as if looking away would make the faces disappear. A vaporous detachment overwhelmed her. She saw herself from a distance, her chest heaving, her mind fighting to stay on track. Her pulse thundered in her ears as her brain jumped down disconnected avenues.

She bit her lower lip hard, until the pain forced her back to the basement in Mexico. She felt herself settling into the moment, even though it was one she hated to face. Her breathing slowed to normal, as did her pulse. When she got back home, she'd have to address this cloud of disengagement. It had happened twice now since she'd been in Mexico—once when the Federales drew down on Nick at El Rancho and now.

Meredith reached for the gun in the holster. A Beretta 9-millimeter—nice. Just like her own duty weapon. She unbuckled the rig, turning his body to pull it off him. When she let go, Alvino's dead weight thumped back to the floor. The movement made her shudder, and she stared for a moment, thinking he would wake up. She strapped the nylon belt and holster around her waist. Staggering to a corner, she rifled through the box of old shoes. Settling on a pair of worn huaraches, she tucked them into her back pockets and stayed barefoot. She crept up the stairs toward the way out.

She still had to pee. That would have to wait.

Chapter Forty-Six

THE CHOPPER DROPPED THEM OFF NEAR THE AIRPORT AT PUERTO Vallarta at the same spot where they'd left from. After picking up Javier's car, they were back at his office by eleven A.M. Two hours later, Javier came up with a private cell number for Miguel Vega. Guzman agreed to stay out of their part of the scheme. He had gone elsewhere with other logistics to manage.

Nick dialed his phone. A lot depended on whether he could get Vega to bite. He had to sound like he knew what he was talking about. He had to get him to the meeting place—four hours from now.

"Who is this?" A raspy voice answered in Spanish.

"My name is Nicholas Reyes Gomez. I am—" "How did you get this number?" Miguel Vega cut in.

"You're looking for something." It was a statement.

"Yes," Vega snapped. "You know that, or you wouldn't have called. Don't be coy."

"You are looking for something you need to find before your father-in-law sees what is inside."

A pause. "You seem to have private information." Vega's voice grew more interested.

"Yes, and I know where you can find the book." Nick let Vega consider this.

Vega asked, "How much?"

"The right question is 'Who do you want?'"

"Ah, the woman. Of course."

"I'm proposing a trade—the book for the woman."

A pause. "Tell me more, policeman."

"It's a simple trade: the book for Meredith Ryan. I know you have her. We agree on a place for the exchange in the next few hours."

"How do I know you have this particular item?"

"Because your wife wrote very specific businesses and amounts in it. I recall a balance owed of nine hundred thousand pesos to a uranium mining company, El Dolor in Jalisco, near Puerto Vallarta."

"So?" Nick strained to hear Vega's "tells", the poker term that represented giveaways to lies or discomfort. There was a breathless quality to the end of Vega's sentences. "And your point is?"

"There is no uranium mine operating anywhere near Puerto Vallarta. You're using the company to launder your drug money. The details are clear with dates, times, and locations."

Vega snorted. "You take a lot of liberties, policeman." No direct answer to Nick's accusation—a classic cue.

Nick sighed. "The woman for the book. It's that simple."

"All right." Vega sniffed, sounding like a man with all the cards but one. "Meet me at—"

"No, I decide where." Nick changed the phone to his other hand to flex his cramped fingers. "The Old Sotelo Mine off Mexico 200, halfway between Sayulita and Bucerias. Meet me there in four hours. Three P.M. Have the girl, and make sure she's healthy." He disconnected.

"You took a chance, talking to him like that." Javier's gaze bored into Nick. "You don't know what he'll do."

Nick crossed his arms. "I think Vega is predictable. He wants the book; he would expect to have to bargain to get it."

"You don't know what he'll do to Meredith."

"That's why they have to wait four hours. That will give us time to find her, I hope. And Vega won't have time to set up an ambush at the mine."

"Even without Meredith, Vega would show up. He can't miss the chance to get the book." Javier looked thoughtful. "How are we going to keep him busy? There are just two of us."

"You got some fireworks—something that goes boom?"

"Not handy, but I can get them fast."

"Then do it." Nick glanced at his watch. "Let's get moving."

THE TOP STEP SQUEAKED. Meredith stood below it, remembering when people had gone up and down the stairs. The top step squeaked every time someone stepped on it.

An earthy scent of beans simmering with frying onions drifted toward her. The door to the kitchen stood ajar. Meredith heard the muted, rhythmic sound of dough being kneaded. She hoped it was Lupita. Still on the second step, Meredith nudged the door all the way open and peered around the corner.

Lupita. There were no guarantees that the woman wouldn't call the alarm as soon as she saw Meredith, but she knew she couldn't get through the room without being seen. Lupita had fed her and, if she read her right, seemed to be concerned about her welfare.

Meredith put her bare foot on the top step. At the squeak, Lupita spun around, apron flaring. Their eyes met. Meredith pulled up to her full height, standing on the threshold. Her posture was a challenge to the woman.

Lupita's mouth drooped as resignation settled in. She stared back at Meredith. She must know if Meredith was in the kitchen, a body lay on the floor below. A long moment passed. Lupita reached a flour-covered hand into her apron, and drew out a silver ring with three keys on it. She glanced at the keys and stretched her hand out to Meredith.

In three short strides, Meredith closed her hand around the old woman's. She tipped her head in a thank you. Lupita took a corner of her apron and, with gentle fingers, wiped the drying trail of blood from Meredith's chin.

"Gracias," Meredith whispered.

The wrinkles around Lupita's eyes sagged with her sad smile. She turned and walked toward the far end of the kitchen. On the way, she stopped at a drawer long enough to grab a roll of electrical tape.

From the drawer in the corner, Lupita went to a door that Meredith hadn't noticed before. She followed Lupita to a larder—a ten-by-five-foot room lined with shelves full of bagged and canned food. A three-foot-tall ladder stood at a counter. Lupita stopped in the middle of the room and handed Meredith the tape.

Meredith knew what she had to do. She sat Lupita on the top rung of the ladder, then bound her arms and legs with the tape. Taking care to be sure the old woman could breathe, Meredith grabbed a linen napkin and stuffed it into Lupita's mouth. She ran the roll of tape around Lupita's head and across her napkin. She leaned into the old woman's ear and whispered one of the few Spanish words she knew. "¿Dolor?" Are you in pain?

Lupita shook her head.

Meredith locked the door behind her. Back in the kitchen, she glanced at the stove and counters, laden with corn tortillas and cheese, chile peppers in red, green, and yellow, and pork roast on a carving platter, in various stages of preparation. God, but she was hungry. Reaching over clay bowls of pungent spices, she grabbed a butcher knife with one hand. With the other, she peeled off a warm flour tortilla, then cut off a chunk of the pork roast and tucked it inside.

She was out the back door a second later, pausing to slip on the huaraches. They weren't as comfortable as her Keens, but they would have to do. Swallowing the last of the tortilla, she walked softly through a tile patio and out a gate. It led to a driveway and garage. She leaned against the garage and took inventory, worried about her stamina after the fight with Alvino. Abrasions on her elbows, but her chin had stopped bleeding, and her ribs felt okay. She recalled Lupita's gentle fingers mopping blood away. Reaching a cut, sharp jolts of pain throbbed in her elbow. Just a little discomfort, Meredith was sure she could make it out of this place.

She pulled out the guard's gun and flipped off the safety one-handedly. She gripped the knife handle in the other. She met no one in the backyard, but expected to see someone on the paved surface. This place must be Vega's headquarters. There had to be guards on the property. Feeling the gun on her hip helped her confidence. She had her advantage back.

She was ready.

The harsh smell of cigarette smoke caught her nose. She ducked behind a pyracantha bush. Two guards in dark BDUs ambled up the driveway that ran from the garage to the main house. With M-16s slung over their shoulders, they seemed in no particular hurry. She waited. Her pulse drummed in her ears. She heard a door close. A glance told her they were gone. Meredith sprinted in the other direction.

After a few yards, the road deteriorated from paved driveway to potholed gravel and dirt road. This was the way she'd come in—she'd felt every bump while rolling around naked on the floor of the SUV. Dense jungle bordered the road. She found the tiniest gap in the trees and melted into the vegetation. Standing for a minute to catch her breath, she took in the compound, noting that no one had sounded an alarm at her flight. She waited a few moments, then squatted in the bushes to relieve herself.

She set off, staying in the bush. The jungle pressed in on her. She wasn't normally claustrophobic, but the closeness bothered her. Late morning heat brought sweat to her forehead, armpits, and chest. The weight of the humidity slowed her pace. Trees, bushes, plants, and weird-looking bugs squeezed together in so little space. In places, she had trouble finding room for a foot, and often, she lost sight of the road. Her idea was to run parallel to it until it was safe enough to walk in the open. She expected switchbacks, the way the SUV had rocked back and forth. If they were anything like Sonoma County hairpin turns—sheer cliffs separated by a tenacious roadbed carved into the side of the rock face—she would soon be forced to venture from the cover of the jungle to the road. The plan was to get to the closest phone and call Nick's cell.

The way was torturous. Tree branches drooped at face level, and thorny bushes pulled at the gun belt and her clothes, scraping her skin. In the clearings, muck underfoot was so thick she had to jump over. The butcher knife was useless for hacking through the vegetation, but she held on to it.

After walking less than ten minutes, she stopped to shake off something from her pants—a centipede, millipede? Too many legs to count. Revulsion overwhelmed her, and a gasp exploded from her lips, the sound loud against the subdued but incessant noises of nature. Damn. If anyone was following her, she'd just telegraphed her position.

Meredith had to keep moving. She took a step, then nudged a sapling aside, taking care to be silent. Her elbow still throbbed every time she used it to pull brush aside.

A twig snapped to her right. She froze. Whatever—or whoever—had made the noise was also still. Bending, she slid the knife blade into a tuft of grass beside her foot, then tightened her fingers around the grip of the Beretta. With the muzzle pointed toward where the noise had come from, she waited. Her senses were razor sharp, powering through her fatigue. In the distance, she heard the high-pitched call of a bird. The leaves in the canopy riffled with the breeze, but the humming of the insects had stopped. Even a city girl like her knew that meant someone else was out here.

Danger. The message sparked through every cell in her body. Her heartbeat thundered. Her vision tunneled toward where the noise had come. A surreal fog edged her sight.

A vague silhouette of Rusty Webber formed in her mind's eye. Rusty had turned at the last minute and took her round square in the heart. She'd never forget the blossom of blood that spurted from his chest. He'd been dead before he hit the ground. Fighting the image, she shook her head. Rusty was still there. In the Quad at the Sonoma County Hall of Justice. She recalled the percussion of her Beretta, watching as the bullet blasted into Rusty's chest. She smelled the cordite and saw the smoke.

Meredith bit her lip, re-opening the scab on her chin. She bit down harder, trying to calm her breathing, splitting the inside of her lip. The pain brought her back to the jungle.

She held her breath, trying to think.

To her right, an outline of a man carrying a rifle appeared on a tree trunk. Then, from behind her, in Spanish, "¡Alto, manos arriba!"

Hands up. Crap.

A hand grasped her shoulder roughly, whirling her around. "What the hell?" It was Javier.

"Mere!"

Meredith stared wide-eyed at her partner. "Nick!" With an AR-15 at that.

His gun hand dropped to his side. "Are you okay?" He looked over her body, then reached out to her chin.

Meredith holstered the gun. She took a step towards him, thinking how much she wanted his arms around her right now. She hesitated, but Nick covered the few feet between them, shoving his arm through the rifle strap onto his shoulder. His huge arms surrounded her shoulders. As he tightened his embrace, he pressed her aching elbow, and she was conscious of the sweat on her body. She didn't care. His breath was hot on her ear. She couldn't hear what he was saying. It sounded like, "...lost you."

Confused, she fell back on the old status check. She let her partner know she was good to go. "I'm okay. Just bumps and bruises."

"Come on, you lovebirds," Javier said. "We don't have time for this." He pulled at her shoulder.

Nick jerked away, too. His dark eyes betrayed nothing, none of the confusion, ecstasy, or peril that poured out of her. Damn Nick and his cop face. She'd gotten so good at reading him—except when he wore his work face. Damn him.

Then he flipped his palm up for her to follow Javier.

"We're going that way." Javier pointed up the road, back toward Vega's compound—the wrong way.

She kept her voice low. "Hey, what's going on?"

"You just wait here. Rest until we get back." Nick's finger was a feather when he touched her chin. "You've been through a lot."

"Bullshit. I'm going with you."

Nick's frown silenced her questions. "All right. I don't have time to explain. Just follow along for now," he whispered. He'd fill her in soon enough. She hoped he would give her a satisfactory answer, because it made no sense to head back to Vega's compound. He had to know that she wouldn't take this without explanation for very long. She trusted him but was nosy enough to require the information.

Then she noticed the military-style rucksack on Javier's back. They're up to something. The idea pleased her, but it also made the hair on the back of her arms stand up. She fell in behind Nick.

They stayed on the road, trotting along its edge so they weren't in plain sight—a steady pace to make use of what stamina they had left. Javier went first, then Nick, with Meredith following. The black wrought-iron gate Meredith had bypassed while trekking in the jungle stood open. A quick survey revealed a camera lens mounted to the top of the gate. Javier sidestepped along the path to stay out of camera range. He used the butt of his HK to shatter the lens.

Nick took the lead and headed to the garage, a spot more sheltered from open views. The padlock on the back door was no challenge when Javier punched a hole in a wood panel. Nick pulled apart the splintered panel, then stepped inside and scanned the interior. Meredith followed. Three cars—all luxury sedans—were parked on one side of the garage. Meredith flipped open the deadbolt on another exterior door and peered out. This led to the driveway—a convenient exit if they needed one. Mechanic's tools lined the wall behind Javier, and to their left, there were racks of PVC irrigation pipe, boxes of fittings and heads, garden hoses, bags of fertilizer, and all manner of things used in a rural property.

Javier crouched his way through the door and shook off the backpack. Meredith walked back to watch him pull out the contents. Matches came out first, along with a bandana and a glass Jarritos soda bottle.

Meredith's voice was a whisper. "All you need is gasoline for a Molotov Cocktail."

Javier's eyes widened. "You're pretty quick for a woman."

She dismissed the indignant response that came to mind. She shook her head and turned away. There was no fighting this battle—not here. She didn't give a damn what he thought of her, anyway. She went to the busted-up door and glanced through the opening. "I'll watch for trouble."

"Nick, find me a hose, and get some gas in this bottle." Javier held up the Jarritos.

Nick swiped a utility knife from the tools on the wall and cut the coupling off a garden hose. He sliced off a five-foot length and walked to a platinum-colored Lexus sedan. "Mere, open the gas tank door from inside the car, will you?"

The gas door flipped open. Nick worked the hose in. He sputtered at first, then got a good siphon into the bottle. Meredith pulled a bandana from Javier's pack. She soaked it with gasoline, then took the bottle to Nick, who spat his mouth clean. He stuffed the bandana in the bottle, then drew out a corner to act as a wick.

They stood next to the Lexus, Javier holding the bottle. "Ready?"

"Wait," Meredith snapped. "What's the plan?"

"First, we light the bottle," Nick said, lighting the match. "Then, run like hell."

The bandana caught, and Javier tossed it into the Lexus' engine compartment. They were in motion when the glass hit the floor, shattering with a whoosh. The flame ignited, sucking the oxygen out of the room. Nick met Meredith at the door, flinging it open and inhaling a lungful of fresh air.

Meredith followed Nick outside with Javier on her heels. They ran across the driveway to the cover of the trees. They hunkered down. Anxious, Meredith asked, "What happened to 'run like hell'?"

Nick whispered. "Just wait."

Wait for what? Damn it, she hated surprises.

Seconds later, a muffled whump came from the garage. Then, orange flames slithered up the building's plywood siding. Dark smoke wafted from both open doors. The fire was a minute older when they heard shouts in Spanish. It didn't matter what they said, the purpose was clear.

They'd discovered the fire.

Chapter Forty-Seven

Nick watched the guards scrambling for garden hoses. A voice in Meredith's brain screamed, why the hell aren't we running? Three of the men reached the garage and stood gaping at the building, yelling at each other.

"Now," Nick said.

He grabbed Meredith's hand, yanking her out of the trees and back onto the road. He shouted, "Now, you run!" Javier fell in behind.

The shouts grew louder, then she heard a crack. A bullet ricocheted off a rock at her feet. With adrenaline surging through her body, Meredith's legs pumped like a machine. Her lungs struggled to take in enough oxygen to keep up. Nick dropped her hand, and she fought to keep her balance on the uneven gravel surface. The slick huaraches soles didn't provide any purchase on the rocks. The footing was dangerous, and she had to keep the oversized shoes on. Potholes and gullies made the way more hazardous, as if bullets weren't enough.

Track had never been her strong point, but she could move. Even in the huaraches, she pulled ahead of both men. Nick shouted to her. "At the next turn, drop into the ravine to your right." The men huffed behind her, trying to keep up. A cluster of wild shots thudded into the earth inches from their feet, spitting up geysers of dirt. She switched directions in a serpentine pattern.

The turn was ahead, to the right. She glanced at the shoulder of the road, slowing to find a break where she could see the ravine. There. Between the weeds, she saw a game trail heading down and out of sight. Skidding sideways on the rocks and almost losing a shoe, she took a quick survey of the path. It was steep and rocky, but she would use the vegetation to give her handholds.

Thick with waist-high bushes, the hillside sloped at a steep angle. She grabbed a sturdy-looking vine, looped it around her hand, and took a step. The huaraches skidded downward until her full weight jammed against the vine. Pain shot up from her elbow to her shoulder. She held on until her shoes found enough dirt to stand on. Her arm throbbed, a dull discomfort. Looking down, she saw more vegetation, although there was no vine to take hold of. Nick and Javier were close on her tail; she pushed herself harder. She slid five feet, then grabbed the base of a stubby bush. It looked like a coyote brush from back home. She dove downward, feet first.

Thorns pricked at her arms, hair, and face. Her T-shirt caught on something as she descended the path. Nearly flipping her, it yanked hard enough that the fabric ripped. She dared not stop or take her eyes off the path. She heard Nick and Javier breathing heavily above her, pressing on her to hurry.

The foliage opened enough to see her goal. A blue Porsche in a clearing. It had to be Javier's car.

Meredith slid the last ten feet down the hill on her butt. Then, at the car, waiting for the men, she brushed off dirt and leaves and tugged at the back of her shirt. As she thought, the shirt had shredded in several places.

Javier unlocked the doors from the base of the ravine and Meredith dove into the back. Two deep bucket seats lined with leather and carpeting made a hard landing. She righted herself, noticing the laceration on her elbow bled a little. A glance over her body showed she was a mess; dirty, bleeding, and clothes torn. Javier slid behind the wheel while Nick hopped into the passenger seat. The engine awakened with a roar, and Javier aimed the Porsche down the road.

She waited for her breathing to get back to normal. Meredith thought how tired she was of riding like a sack of potatoes in back seats over these shitty Mexican mountain roads.

She poked her head up and tried to turn in the cramped space, shifting the holstered Beretta on her hip out of her way. She had to know if they were being followed. Through the dust billowing behind the Porsche, she saw another dust cloud. "Now you've done it! They're after us."

Nick's tired smile flashed at her. "I certainly hope so!"

"Okay, what the hell is going on?" The car jerked to the left, and Meredith was thrown into a corner of the back seat. A bit late, Javier shouted, "Hang on."

As she struggled to push herself upright, she felt a familiar piece of cloth under her fingers. Her backpack. Warmth spread through her chest. Nick had brought the pack for her. He knew he'd find her alive. He came after her.

It wasn't the first time Nick had rescued her. He'd appeared when all hope was gone as she dangled over the chasm off the deck of her home in Forestville. Now he'd come again to save her as part of his quest to protect his family.

She sat up, braced herself, and wondered what the hell they were doing. In her you-better-tell-me voice, she said, "Nick? Fill me in. Tell me what's going on."

Nick struggled to stay upright, too, pushing against the dashboard with his hands. The road's twists and turns threw all of them against the leather interior as the car roared over the blacktop. Nick didn't wear a seatbelt. Javier did, and seemed hell-bent on a land speed record or a free fall over a cliff.

Finally, they turned onto a worn asphalt road that bisected the lush jungle. The elevation dropped several hundred feet over the course of a few minutes and dipped into a valley. Javier shifted up to fifth gear, and the car settled into its own momentum, careening through the jungle on the gray ribbon of road.

"Nick? Spill it."

He turned to her and raised his voice over the engine noise. "All right, but first, tell me how you got out of there."

She saw Alvino's milky eyes staring up at her. A ball of something—she couldn't identify it—blocked her throat. Revulsion, regret?

She couldn't speak. She had no words to convey what had happened. She waved her hand to sweep the ghastly image away and croaked, "Later."

Nick waited. She knew he wanted something from her, even if it was mere eye contact. She felt like he was inspecting her. In a way, she knew he was. He was attuned enough to know when something was bothering her. The softening of the lines around his mouth told her he understood. She would tell him in her own time—when no one else was around. Finally, he said, "We're going for the book. I hid it in the mine."

It didn't make sense. "But Vega's following you."

"Yeah. That's what we want." Nick continued. "We keep Vega and his men occupied for a while." Nick glanced at the grim smile on Javier's face. Meredith saw it, too. From her seat, she saw Javier's concentration on coaxing the most horsepower possible from the engine. Nick gave her an abbreviated version of what had been happening. When he got to Liliana's death, Meredith was shocked. "Who do you think was chasing them around? I mean, Vega didn't care where Liliana was. She had no value in this deal. What a waste."

"She would lead to Emilio, who would lead to Angela, who had the book."

"Are you sure there aren't some other players at work?" Meredith wasn't defending Vega, but her instinct told her that someone else was tracking the Borregos. "Who else has an interest in the book?"

Nick thought for a moment. "The twins, Silvia's brothers."

"Yeah, Guzman said the brothers pushed Silvia into the marriage. Maybe they had a deal with Vega to build up the business on the coast."

"Maybe the brothers were setting up to take over the Guzman business," Javier shouted. "The old man's in his seventies, you know.

They're vicious, and lately, there have been rumors about them falling out with someone else with power." He glanced at his watch. "We're right on schedule."

"Schedule?" Meredith thought she hadn't heard right over the roar of the engine. "Hey, I thought we want to keep the book away from Vega."

"Not today. We're going to give him the book, and he's going to meet his father-in-law."

"Oh. I'd like to be a fly on the wall for that."

"Mere, that's something you don't want to see. Take my word for it."

The implication was clear. Vega was going to pay for his poor judgment in killing Guzman's daughter. His end would be permanent, and none of them should be witness to it. As cops, they couldn't be part of a murder—even in a foreign country. While there was surely a specific law against it, the question was morale. How could they fulfill their duties of upholding the law if they witnessed and conspired to break it—a capital crime, no less? Javier's position would be in jeopardy, too. Meredith didn't know what Mexican law said about conspiring to commit homicide, but as a cop, his career would suffer. Even this setup was risky, depending on who made it out alive and who would testify in a court of law.

Cartels versus court? Not likely.

"Yeah, I guess you're right. But why did you set the place on fire?"

"We had to kill three hours while we got all our resources in place."

"You kept him busy." Meredith nodded.

"He knows we're going to the mine. Our deal was to meet there and trade you for the book."

"Go on." Meredith was impatient to have all the facts.

The road angled to the right again and Nick braced himself. The jungle fell away, giving in to the unforgiving desert landscape. Ahead, beyond another drop in altitude as the road pushed on, the desert nudged back to a higher elevation when the jungle resumed. There was little traffic.

"I couldn't assume Vega would keep you alive for the trade. Javier and I ran this little scheme…"

"And I thank you!" Meredith grinned brightly.

"We had to keep Vega busy so he wouldn't head to the mine and set up his own welcome party."

Meredith nodded with understanding. Straightening in the cramped seat, she stretched her back while glancing out the window. "Where are we anyway?"

Nick answered while Javier passed a chugging delivery truck. "Mexico 200, the main highway between Sayulita and Bucerias. We're almost at the turn-off."

Meredith looked out the back window. "They're still following."

"I want to keep enough distance that we're out of range if they start shooting." Reflected in the rear-view window, Mere saw the lines around Javier's mouth deepen. "We can't lose them."

THE CAR WAS SILENT. There was nothing to say. She ran down the possibilities. She wondered at the scope, the impossible magnitude of the game they played. People would die today. She couldn't help but compare this operation with her experience back home. The Sonoma County Sheriff's Office had rules. She didn't always like them, but she knew the merits of following them. She and her co-workers worked a time-tested structure forged by perceptions, mistakes, and good intentions. She realized how much she missed knowing the rules here. In Sonoma, even while being pursued by a maniacal stalker, she knew what to expect. Her lieutenant and the rest of the Administration might have let her down, but even so, her own course of action was always clear.

Here in Mexico, every card was wild. She was out of her element. Nick, too. Even though he spoke the language, he was in the dark about Mexican laws, local customs, and the damned cartels. Still, he acted when his family was threatened, even knowing how tenuous his position was. If he got caught, he could lose his job. Maybe worse. Maybe a lot worse.

Angela didn't know how lucky she was to be married to Nick. In the months without her, Nick hadn't varied from his commitment. He was a married man—the "till death do us part" kind. Even when Nick truly understood Angela didn't want to stay married, he honored his promise to her and her family. A man of his word.

Not like Richard, Meredith thought. Her husband had been killed on the way to see his lover. He'd given up on Meredith, left her to her career. Someday, she would take the time to sort through the shambles that had been her marriage. The betrayal hit her square between the eyes. A small ball of anger still roiled in her stomach. Maybe she was envious of Nick's loyalty to Angela.

She pushed it away. Not now, but she knew she'd have to face the failure and shame of her unsuccessful relationship. Someday… Those ghosts were nipping at her heels. She couldn't recall feeling—really feeling—grief over losing Richard. What was the matter with her?

Her time to grieve was pushing at her. She'd have to come to terms with Richard's betrayal and death. Too much had happened in the past year. She'd found comfort in the methodical actions of work. And she'd faked her way through the psychiatry, which might have helped. She'd been angry at the brass, but she still loved her job. The comfort work provided now seemed shallow. The real pain sat below the surface, like an iceberg.

Thank God Nick had been there—to break the news to her—and stay to console her.

Nick. It was always Nick. From her position in the back seat, she studied his profile, seeing lines around his mouth that she'd never seen before. Even in his grief over losing his wife, he was here defending her and her family. He could have walked away from this the moment when Angela made it clear they were through—but he didn't.

Then it hit her. A head-slap moment: the answer to the two things that worried her the most sat right in front of her. She'd been a fool to put so much value on what she considered her boss' "betrayal." While imperfect, Sonoma County Sheriff's Office system was predictable, governed by a set of rules universally acknowledged.

Her unique dilemma required an outside-the-box solution. Because the administration hadn't been equipped to handle an obsessive jurist, she and Nick had been forced to meet the challenge—knowing it might become violent. The important things were Nick and her career. If this operation didn't blow her employment out of the water, and if they made it out alive, she would go back to the Sonoma County Sheriff's Office with a new appreciation for the institution.

If they made it out alive, she'd still have a relationship with Nick. Partner, friend, or lover—it didn't matter. Now, she wanted more from him. She knew that now. Partner, friend, or lover? It was another thing she'd have to work on when she got home. Nick.

THE PORSCHE TURNED off the highway and onto yet another dirt road. Meredith shifted in the back seat, leaning away from the bulky holster. She felt like she'd stepped out of a spaghetti western, but she kept a protective hand on it. With no room, her position allowed no blood below her hips, and she tried to anticipate the impact from the largest of the potholes. She swore to herself she'd never drive off the pavement again. Every turn in the road forced her swollen elbow against unpadded walls, her jaw ached, and wrenched muscles and the week's accumulation of bruises begged for relief.

When she looked outside, the scenery was familiar. Trees thinned to scrubby branches, the earth turned to small bare patches of gray volcanic dust, a landscape of faded green bushes.

Soon, the scrubby jungle pushed into the dead-end road. At one time, the road continued up the hill, but a gravel berm had been shoveled to block it. They were close to the back end of the mine. Slowing to negotiate between potholes, the Porsche rumbled up to the escarpment below the exit. This was the road Nick and Meredith had walked with Rigo.

Javier downshifted, shouting above the engine. "I can't tell if Vega is in the car behind us." The Porsche came to a stop at the berm. Dust billowed in the shape of cumulus clouds, obscuring their view. From here, the only way to the mine was to hike to it.

"We'll have to chance it." Nick craned his head around like he had special powers to see through the dust. It didn't matter. Vega's men could find this place from the dust cloud alone.

Javier shut off the engine and yanked on the parking brake. He grabbed two flashlights from the glove box, handing one to Nick. They scrambled from the car, and everyone searched for a way up the hill. Meredith slipped an arm through a strap of her backpack while flexing her leg muscles to get blood flowing.

She studied the overgrown remnants of the road. A thin wildlife trail ran up one side. As long as the animals didn't slither, or crawl on more than four legs, she figured she was okay. She studied the shadows of the overhanging tree branches for snakes. Nothing. She pointed to the road.

Javier took off first. Nick handed the flashlight to Meredith and then waved her on. She held it like a weapon, ready to light up a path or knock out a bad guy. Javier signaled for them to follow. Meredith brushed aside a swinging branch, and it smacked Nick in the face as he fell in behind her.

Chapter Forty-Eight

THE HEAT MADE MEREDITH WISH FOR A SWIMMING POOL AND A BEER. Or at least a pair of shorts. Her jeans were soaked through with sweat, now in the hottest part of the day. She missed the cooling fog that rolled in through the Petaluma Gap, chilling the miles of warm earth beneath it. She missed more than just the fog, she thought, as another drop of sweat coursed down her temple. Beneath her backpack, her shredded T-shirt was drenched, too. She also wished she had a bra. While she'd never considered herself well-endowed, a little support would have been nice.

Hell, she just wanted to be home, asleep in her own bed.

Leaves as large as elephant ears, scabby brush, and spindly vines all conspired to slow their pace. Nick stopped to step over a low tree branch that extended across the path at waist height. As he examined the ground, Meredith walked back and peered over his shoulder. A scaly green iguana perched on the branch, inspecting them with a gray face and one beady eye. The reptile skittered down the branch and back into the anonymity of the jungle. Apparently, they weren't interesting enough to hang around. A screeching howl from the canopy jerked her attention upwards. A parrot, a monkey? Were there monkeys in Mexico? She didn't know, and hoped she didn't find out firsthand. It sounded more like a bird anyway. She hoped.

Single-file, they walked into deeper underbrush, the path narrowing. The trail headed steadily uphill. Meredith kept Javier in sight above her. She was grateful for his forethought in bringing flashlights, but how did he know where to go? She'd been to the mine once before, but this trail wasn't familiar.

What if the whole set-up was a trap? What if Javier worked for Vega? Or worse, Guzman's sons? What if they were lost? She felt for the Beretta.

Lost in the jungle? Holy crap! "Javier, do you know where you're going?"

Javier scrambled up to a boulder the size of a dump truck. "If we keep going up, we come out at the mine," he panted.

"Are you sure?" Meredith pushed a tree branch aside and clambered up the boulder to catch up with Javier. "I mean, in vegetation this thick, we could walk right by and never see it."

"We'll find it. We're not far now."

"Can you tell if Vega and his men are behind us? I can't see or hear anything."

Javier stopped on a rocky outcropping and towered several feet above her. He met her gaze. "Trust me." His voice held a finality that silenced her. "Vega will find the mine." He turned, marching upward. Ever the skeptic, she thought, yes, but will we?

As good as his word, Javier broke through the last thicket and onto a small rise. It looked down on the meadow and the mine entrance. Relief flooded through Meredith. They had overcome a huge obstacle—finding the mine opening. With more to come, she spent no time savoring the victory.

Now, to meet with Vega. There would be no negotiating. Vega couldn't trade her for the book, and she was certain the cartel leader wouldn't leave without it. He would try to kill them, and Nick would have factored that into his strategy.

She followed Nick and Javier, her senses on higher alert than they had been in the jungle. She was intrigued about how their plan would play out. Here in the meadow, the potential for ambush was huge. The trees that edged the bowl-shaped ground provided concealment for hostiles. Even without an ambush, the land itself was treacherous—low-growing shrubs, not large enough to hide a man but with thorns or sharp blades that would cut a leg and fill it with infection. Around mining operations, there was always the matériel left behind, rusted iron scrap, broken glass, and God knew what else. Javier had told them to be watchful. With guns drawn and mindful sorting through the scene, they picked their way across the meadow safely.

At the top of the wide shale track, the mine opening was a maw of shattered boards. Yesterday, Vega's guards must have smashed through to get in. They looked like jagged teeth in the mouth of a giant dragon. Meredith shivered but followed Nick. Javier pulled her back as Nick disappeared inside. They stood outside the entrance but close enough to take cover behind a boulder. "He'll be right out." He glanced around the meadow and the hills above it. "I need another pair of eyes."

Surprised that he would trust her enough to ask for help, she stood, then turned her gaze to scan the perimeter.

Meredith nudged Javier, pointing her chin toward the path they'd used to the meadow. Trees and brush came alive with hushed voices and movement. The sound of a violent slash suggested a bush or small tree had been hacked by a machete. Meredith's attention was on the noise. Ready for a fight, she slipped into her warrior mindset.

Her body became a solid piece of iron, sharp and pointed.

A machete-wielding fighter hacked through the last thicket, doubling the width of the path. A stocky soldier in olive drab fatigues and crisscrossed bandoliers lunged into the clearing. He sheathed his machete, then swung an AR-15 into position before him. Another followed a twin in uniform and arms. Both men arced their rifles 180 degrees to aim at Javier and Meredith. A terse command came from behind the soldiers, and they separated like griffins guarding a portal.

From the trail, Vega emerged into the clearing, preening like a bird, his greasy ringlets shining in the dappled sunshine.

Chapter Forty-Nine

JAVIER GRIPPED HIS HK PARALLEL TO HIS LEG. MEREDITH PULLED the Beretta from the holster, slipping the safety off. She hoped Nick would be out soon. She had no desire to face a drug lord and his gang with just two guns, but here she was. Was this, too, part of the plan?

In khakis and a roomy Hawaiian shirt, Vega might have been attending a backyard barbeque for his demeanor. He climbed the short, beaten incline to the meadow. Eyeing Javier and Meredith, he walked the flat part of the grassy bowl. Watching his arrogant saunter, Meredith thought of the horror this man had caused. Liliana's needless death, Silvia, Alvino, Rigo's torture. And more to come.

A dozen of his soldiers followed, then fanned out in a semi-circle behind him.

Vega stopped, his eyes narrowing. How many others were in the brush covering her with guns, Meredith wondered. She backed toward the mine entrance, and Javier did the same. Where was Nick? Still inside?

From the jungle behind Vega and his men, leaves rustled, a twig snapped. A man's voice, a terse cry. Then, another, ten feet to the left. A louder scream came from behind. Then, the brush rustled to the right of the thicket. Five soldiers neutralized. Disabled? Dead.

Whose army did they belong to?

Vega turned in time to hear the last mortal groan of one of his men—and see ten soldiers materialize from the brush. These weren't his troops, obvious by their dress and demeanor. They weren't undisciplined gangsters. They were well-equipped, battle-hardened men, dressed for guerilla fighting in the jungle. Some had blood on them.

Vega's men twisted around, their eyes narrowing as they studied the camouflaged fighters. Some shifted from foot to foot, others used their forearms to brush sweat from their faces as they waited for their leader's command.

"Vega!" The voice came from the opposite side of the meadow. Beside the mine entrance, a large boulder rested from a long-ago slide. Carlos Guzman stood on top, like a lion on a perch studying his prey. He stood alone, taller than life, dressed formally as in the old times in a white tropical suit which defied the humidity of the jungle

"Carlos," Vega's voice held a false pleasure, grating on Meredith's ears. His attempt to sound familiar fought with her last image of him—standing beside the bastard who beat her. She suddenly wanted to be part of his end or at least to witness it. She was sure that he would meet it here today.

A subtle wave to Vega's men held them in place—for the moment.

"You have taken something from me." Guzman's simple statement encompassed the death of his child and the theft from his empire.

"No, Carlos." Vega's gaze skittered to Javier and Meredith. "These policía want you to believe that so we will fight amongst ourselves, weaken our organization."

Guzman shrugged. "This will happen, anyway."

He waved an arm. Two men stepped from the bush below his position. A mere ten feet away, each man aimed an AR-15 at Vega's chest. Vega stopped, looking at Guzman as if he had been betrayed. "Carlos?" His jaw dropped in shock and his spine stiffened.

"Where is Silvia?" Even from this distance, Meredith saw the deep lines on Guzman's face. He already knew the answer.

"She is in Paris," Vega's voice unleashed his indignity at the question. "It is as I told you last week."

"Enough!" Guzman's hand snapped up to stop the lie. "Tell me where she is. Where have you put her?" It was ironic that a crime lord could suffer the same pain he so casually inflicted on others. His head tilted away from Vega, the thin-lipped frown and his stiff posture told the story: he was convinced his daughter was dead. He wanted to find her body to put her to rest. Then deal with Vega.

Vega shook his head. "Carlos, don't fall into this trap—"

"Where is she?" Guzman ground out the words. Did Vega see how risky his position was?

"Paris, as I said." Vega's attention swept the meadow. He seemed to reassess his chances of survival, to find them wanting. Taking a tack he had tried before, he pointed to Javier and Meredith. "How can you believe what these policemen tell you? Americans." He spat. "And a traitor to Mexico."

"Americans, yes. And yet, they have provided me with the closest thing to the truth that I've seen from Bucerias and Sayulita. Your turf, Miguel." The air was thick with a cloud of doubt cast between the two crime lords. "They will provide to me a book, written in my own daughter's hand. A book that proves your betrayal."

"Lies!" Vega collected himself, his shoulders squared. "You are a fool to believe these policía corrupto over me."

Deceits hung between them. Guzman raised his hand toward the opening of the cave. "Hermano."

All eyes went to the mine opening. Fidelio stepped out, his face solemn as a gravestone. "I am here." Nick stood behind Fidelio.

"Do you have the book?" Guzman spoke to his brother but kept his attention on Vega.

"Yes." Nick raised the book over his head, so all could see.

"Is it in Silvia's hand?"

Fidelio answered, "Yes, Carlos."

"What message from her nameless grave does she have for me?"

"This is a clear account of how Miguel Vega has cheated you for over two years. In pesos, the amount is about two million."

Vega's chest puffed up. "Lies perpetrated by these gatecrashers," he shouted. "They want a piece of the pie, so they are cutting me out."

"Enough." Guzman raised his hand. "Where is my daughter?"

"Paris," Vega began.

"Miguel Vega. I have never liked you, even as my son-in-law. I should never have let others talk me into this alliance. My instinct tells me you are a fraud, and you know where Silvia is."

"Carlos," Vega whined, looking around. His eyes narrowed. Meredith saw desperation creep into his face as he recognized all his plans were crumbling around him.

"¡Bastante! I am tired of your treachery. Your time is over." Guzman's gaze cut through the distance between the two cartel kings.

Vega puffed out his chest, giving his father-in-law a coy smile. "I have assets you don't know about."

Guzman's face gave nothing away, not fear nor dread nor anger. "If you tell me where she is, I will see that you die as a man befitting your position."

Two slender men in tropical suits stepped from the brush behind Vega. Twins, if Meredith trusted her eyes. Twins who looked just like their old man. Guzman's gaze drilled his sons across the meadow. His mouth twisted like he'd just drank a cyanide cocktail.

Vega's lips curled with menace. "You know, Carlos. Maybe I don't need the book after all. I mean, if I kill you, your whore daughter's ledgers won't mean anything, will they?" He drew a small Ruger 9-millimeter pistol from his pocket, took aim, and squeezed off a shot.

Fidelio was ready. Before they heard the report, a La Familia bullet slammed into Vega's chest. His own shot went wild as he crumpled to the ground. The meadow erupted with gunfire between the two armies. Vega was down, a man who an hour ago had the world in his hands now met his end.

From the top of the boulder, Guzman's body jerked sideways,

and blood soaked his white jacket. He looked at the blossoming bloodstain on his hip with wide eyes, his mouth slack. Two body-guards pressed against him, pushing him away toward cover. Fidelio sprinted toward his brother while he fired at Vega's men.

Javier's hand found Meredith's forearm. "This isn't our fight." He waved for her to follow him.

It was against her training not to take action. Still, Javier was right. These monsters had to settle this themselves. They tucked themselves in an alcove to the side of the opening where Nick waited. Javier found a space for the barrel of his HK between two time-shrunken timbers. He pointed it outside. Meredith shifted to the other side with Alvino's Beretta pointed toward the meadow.

Vega's men now took orders from the twins. Both of Guzman's sons jumped for cover behind low boulders—one of them shouting a terse order. Their soldiers inched around the perimeter of the meadow, angling toward the wounded Guzman, shooting at the rock. Automatic gunfire blasted so loud and so long that it seemed one tone.

Guzman's army cut Vega's to shreds. Men dropped with the awkwardness of mortal injury. It didn't appear that many of his soldiers wore protective vests. They paid the ultimate price for that machismo stupidity.

From between his guards, Guzman materialized, his shoulders slumped and his hair falling into his eyes. He waved the 'hold' signal to the six men still standing, then glanced up at the mine opening. She wondered why he would stop the assault to protect his deceitful sons. He had no concern for the safety of Nick, Javier, and her. Yet he nodded to Javier with a concern that said, "Go with God."

Meredith's attention shifted to Nick. His face was smooth with professional detachment—his work face. He'd been expecting this.

Javier and Nick were on the move, away from the cave. As he ran past her, Nick grabbed Meredith's hand. While they rushed down the shale path toward the meadow, she dared a glance at Guzman. He was still on the boulder, unsteady on his feet but still a proud and angry father. No—more than that. Before she looked away, she glimpsed the set of vengeance around his eyes. Then she understood what was going to happen.

She hesitated, but Nick yanked her arm to keep up. They picked their way around rusted iron scrap, rocks, and bodies. Gun smoke hung in the humid air with the promise of more to come. They had to get out of there before Guzman did what she expected. She didn't have to be told twice. Tightening her fingers around her pistol grip, she glanced around the meadow.

The split second of inattention had its price. Her foot caught the bootsole of a dead man. She stumbled and slowed enough to take in what her mind hadn't allowed her to see before.

Bodies. Oh, God.

How many? It didn't matter. Blood, brains, and tissue blown into places that should never see them. She had to get out of here. She heard a groan.

Vega.

He sat up, dazed, pulling at his shirt, ripping it off. What she saw chilled her to the core. She knew they were in trouble. He wore a Kevlar vest with a dent in the chest. His eyes were glossy with shock, but he fought it, shaking his head.

If they kept running, they'd go right past him. He still had his Ruger, now sitting in his lap. Could they disarm him? Kill him —again?

Javier veered away from Vega. Nick turned to follow, but the drug lord recovered fast—fast enough to grab Nick's ankle. Nick slammed to the ground, his Smith bouncing into a bush. Vega was on his feet, yanking Nick to his. Vega dug the Ruger into Nick's throat. "This is all your doing." He spat the words out. Meredith stood, frozen, her gun still in her hand. She should shoot Vega, but she couldn't move.

Nick's fist slammed into Vega's groin. Vega bent, his breath whooshing from his lungs as Nick twisted away, grabbing at the Ruger.

Vega, elbowing Nick away, grunted while frantically shielding his privates. Nick was back on him, chest to chest, bending the hand holding the gun, twisting, then slamming his wrist into his own knee.

Meredith heard a pop in the man's hand, then a howl as the gun fell in the dirt. Nick stepped backward, panting, as he scanned the dirt for the guns.

Behind them, someone shouted in Spanish. Meredith only heard the urgency and knew this was going from bad to worse.

Before she knew it, she'd launched herself at Nick in a perfect linebacker tackle. Her shoulder caught the back of his knees. He grunted as he went down, her body on top, shielding him. They stayed down.

The gun blasts deafened her. She felt the breeze from the rounds whizzing by her and worried that one—or more—would find her. She choked on the smoke and swore she felt gunpowder on her skin.

Vega's body thumped to the dirt beside them. Meredith turned her head away once she saw his lifeless gaze. He had so many holes in him that she wouldn't have been able to recognize him if she hadn't seen him two seconds ago.

Someone called a halt to the shooting. Nick and Meredith scrambled to their feet. Nick grabbed both guns. They found Javier twenty yards away on another path that led downhill. He waved for them to hurry. After the short detour, it joined up to the main trail.

In the meadow, men yelled at each other. As they reached the brush, the voices faded. Javier, Meredith, and Nick crouched through single file, each scanning the brush beside them for threats. In the lead, Javier slowed enough to negotiate the rough trail. Nick pushed Meredith in front of him and they kept running. The hush of the jungle was unnatural, as if the parrots and monkeys were watching this violent circus played out by humans before their eyes.

The stub of a blown-off hand peeked out from under a huge leaf. Meredith ran past it knowing the fate of the first wave of Vega's soldiers.

A scream punctuated the din. It was the cry of a man whose life was cut short. Another scream trailed away to silence.

They ran downhill, twisting and turning through the jungle. The path seemed longer in this direction. Meredith stumbled in the huaraches, grabbing a thorny vine for support. Stickers punctured her hand. She whispered a mild curse, righted herself, and caught up with Javier.

In ten minutes, they were at the car, pulling huge breaths of air into their lungs. Meredith again lunged into the back seat. Javier stuck the key into the ignition. Two huge explosions thundered from the mountainside. One from over the ridge, the other from the meadow.

Clipping on his seatbelt, Nick turned his head toward her. "Both ends of the mine are sealed up now."

"Guzman?"

"Yes." Javier fired up the engine.

"What about the brothers? And Silvia's grave?"

"I don't know who will make it out alive. Guzman looked pretty bad off."

Meredith glanced from Javier to Nick. "I can't believe the brothers would work with Vega knowing he killed their sister. Then, ambush their father and uncle. How could they do this?"

Javier must've given this some thought. "Greed for power." He shifted into reverse and backed the car. "Money is nothing in Mexico without power. What we just witnessed was a power grab between family members who have no allegiance except to themselves."

"If the brothers make it, how could they trust each other after this?"

"They won't make it." Javier shrugged. "My money is on Fidelio. He has the army. He'll have to take them out to insure his own position."

Meredith considered all this as she fidgeted to find a comfortable position.

The Porsche jumped forward, racing back to Bucerias.

Chapter Fifty

MEREDITH FELT DAMN GOOD. SHE'D HAD A SHOWER, PUT ON CLEAN clothes, and the remains of a fine meal sat on the table before her. She sat back, stretching her feet to a nearby chair and wrapping her fingers around a thick wineglass. The bruises on her ankles from being bound turned to deep purple, finger marks plainly visible. The swelling in her elbow would soon go down when the aspirin kicked in. She felt the soreness in both sides of her jaw where Vega's soldier had hit her with brass knuckles, the bruising covered her jaw and most of her cheeks. The ragged cut on her chin had scabbed over but promised to leave a scar. All in all, a damn sight better than it might have been.

Swirling the ruby pinot noir, she sighed, and a small smile crept to her face in spite of a chewed-up lower lip. She turned her head to see Javier in a robe, just out of the bathroom and toweling dry his thick hair.

"Your food is in the microwave." Nick pushed away his plate.

Leaning back, he patted his full belly contentedly. "We couldn't wait."

Javier nodded, threw the towel over a chair, and went to the microwave. It hummed while his meal heated.

"How did you get Guzman to go along with your plan?" Meredith sipped her wine while she waited for someone to answer her. "It was a crappy plan, by the way. Too much to go wrong."

Javier's voice rose over the noise in the kitchen. "It was Nick's idea. Turns out he knows more about Mexicans than I gave him credit for." The oven beeped. "Nick knew that even as a drug kingpin, Guzman considered himself a good Catholic. It's part of our culture to have the dead buried in sanctified ground."

"More than that," Nick picked up the story thread. "I knew Guzman would want to know what happened to his daughter and bury her. His remorse over forcing her to marry Vega was the only normal human quality we could count on. That was our bargaining chip. His revenge was a bonus."

"What happened to the book?" Meredith sipped the wine.

"Fidelio has it. Guzman wanted it. It was against his empire, too. He will destroy it. His daughter gave her life to get that information to him. As for the accounts, he already has someone tracing Vega's books, so he'll soon get a full accounting of the discrepancies."

"Not that we are concerned with his financial losses or Guzman, who didn't even know what he was missing. It's all crime money, no matter how you cut it." She took a sip of wine. "Did Emilio want the book to go to Silvia's family?" She didn't think this sounded like Emilio. The man didn't have a vengeful nature.

Nick's eyes lost focus for a moment. He was somewhere else. "He just wanted justice. It was our idea to give the book to Guzman, well, Fidelio. Guzman isn't doing well. His brother is taking over for now."

Satisfied that Emilio's justice was served, Meredith emptied her glass. "Have you heard anything about Silvia's brothers?"

Nick filled Javier's wine goblet. "Guzman or maybe Fidelio has dealt with them. Fidelio confirmed they were in the Durango that ran the Borregos off the road. It's a guess, but we think they believed Emilio and Liliana would lead them to the book. They won't be chasing anyone around. As for Vega, now there's one less drug lord." With a smile, he lifted his glass in a toast. "To a small dent in the cartel crime of Mexico."

Nick refilled Meredith's glass. "To an equitable solution to Rigo's kidnapping."

They drank.

Meredith considered what her toast would be. "To inter-agency cooperation, although you took long enough to show your cards." She tipped her glass to Javier.

After they drank, Javier frowned. "You know this never happened, officially."

"Even better." Nick raised his glass again.

Meredith was confident that news of their adventure would never reach the Sheriff's Office, a bonus they hadn't expected twenty-four hours ago. With all of their careers intact, she thought of one other conflict that needed to be settled.

Angela.

Chapter Fifty-One

TWO DAYS LATER, THEY BURIED LILIANA. A WAKE WAS HELD AT HER sister Rocio's home, then a standing-room-only Mass was said. At the gravesite, the tearful family tossed handfuls of dirt on her coffin. Nick watched the family and friends crying, saying goodbye, and in some cases wailing their loss. He found it difficult to reconcile his own stoic nature with Latin emotionalism. Granted he'd worked at suppressing his feelings. In an insightful moment, he decided that wasn't all due to his job. Watching Emilio's strength during the previous days led him to believe that one didn't have to be emotional to be passionate. And he was passionate. He couldn't deny that any longer.

After the funeral, Nick and Meredith, the Borregos, and Rocio returned to Bernardo's in San Vicente. From the patio, Nick watched Meredith and Emilio as they walked the dusty path outside the horse paddock. Persistent clumps of dandelion edged the space under the fence. A bee buzzed from one cluster of blooms to the next in the stillness of the afternoon sun. Red highlights glistened in Meredith's coffee-brown hair. Her head was bent as she listened to Emilio talk. Every now and then, she'd stop and put a hand on his forearm. Nick almost heard her words of encouragement. They walked on.

"Papa will need me now." Angela's sentence trickled away, refusing to articulate the words as if saying her mother was dead would make it so.

"Have you talked with him about what he will do?"

"No. I don't believe that he would discuss his future with me."

Nick thought that might be right. Emilio was first, last, and always Angela's father. Not her friend or confidante. He wasn't sure he would talk to anyone about his plans—or lack of them. "There's no need to rush him. Bernardo said he can stay with him for now."

Nick didn't ask about Angela's plans. She wouldn't be Angela without something up her sleeve. Whatever she had in mind, he couldn't be witness to her happiness. He figured she'd marry Javier and have the family she wanted so desperately. Javier seemed to care for her. She could do worse. Javier had a bright future ahead of him.

Then again, a lot of Mexican cops ended up dead.

He knew he would find out about her plans soon enough. Maybe if it were far enough in the future, it wouldn't hurt as much. Not likely.

"He loves you like a son." Standing beside Nick, Angela's voice was soft. "Mama suggested I call you for help with Rigo. Papa jumped at the idea. He was so sure that you were the answer to our troubles. I think he believed if you were down here that we would reconcile."

Nick nodded, turning to the bay Thoroughbred nosing his elbow. "I'm closer to him than I was to my own father." Nick's fingers stroked the velvety softness of the horse's nose.

"I'd hate for you to lose him, too."

Nick's throat closed as the reality settled into him. He nodded. "We're done, Nick. You know that, don't you?"

He nodded again, waiting until he trusted his own voice. "I knew it after the baby. Maybe even before that, I knew you weren't happy with me." I just didn't know how to quit, he thought.

Angela studied her fingernails. "You withdrew from me. I never knew what you were thinking."

Nick raised his hand to stop her.

"No, listen." Her voice rose. "It wasn't just Mia. Even before that…happened, you pulled away from me. I know some of it was because of your job, but there's a place inside you that you always keep to yourself. I needed more than you would give."

Nick's mind cataloged all the times he tried. "I gave you all I could. Everything."

Anger glinted in Angela's eyes. Was there a faint snarl on her lips? "No, you didn't. You hid from me at work. You gave more to your job than you ever did to me." From the corner of his eye, he watched Angela rub her empty ring finger.

Wait, Nick thought. He'd taken time off after Mia was born. He changed her diapers, bottle-fed, and burped her, walked miles in the middle of the night when she was colicky. Confused, Nick wondered aloud. "What are you saying?"

"You never loved me the way you love that job." Angela turned her face rock hard. "Or maybe it was your partner."

Disgust spurted through his mind. Then, it was gone as fast as that. He was too good at dealing with people at their worst to rise to the bait. Meredith? He took a deep breath as he found the right words. "There was never anything more than friendship and respect between us. You are wrong."

She shrugged, holding it a second. The same gesture as Javier. "You can say what you want, but I believe you two were having a cheap affair."

How could she believe that? He was a married man and wouldn't have considered an affair—with anyone. Even after Angela left, he never even looked at another woman. A wad of defensiveness almost closed his throat. How could she accuse him of that? He thought she knew him and his standards of loyalty and faithfulness.

His voice was firm when he found it. "You're wrong." Then, he recalled the moment he kissed Meredith on the Mary Elisabeth. While it wasn't the time frame that Angela was referring to, he was still married then. Even though it was merely on paper.

She faced him. "I don't believe you." Her eyes drew into a menacing V. She was more than angry; she was spoiling for a fight. Her full lips thinned with malice.

Nick felt like he was being allowed to glimpse her nastiness through a curtain of pretense. Had she always been this thoughtless and self-absorbed? She couldn't have fooled him that completely, could she?

It didn't matter. She was gone and never coming back. Her outburst made it that much easier to sever the relationship. Right now, he was too worn out to get into a fight.

"Angela, don't do this. It's your mother's funeral. This isn't the time to talk about our divorce."

"Really?" Her voice rose.

Rocio glanced over at them. Enough. Nick turned and walked toward the house, letting Angela yell as he walked away.

Chapter Fifty-Two

MEREDITH WATCHED EMILIO AS HE WITNESSED ANGELA AND NICK'S argument. She wanted to say something to take the sting out of Angela's attack but couldn't think of anything genuine to offer.

Meredith had been talking with Emilio—about the funeral, the relatives, Bernardo. Their conversation was general, but the substance seemed truly important to Emilio. She felt he was talking through some problems, using her as a sounding board. Maybe even coming to decisions. Meredith liked Emilio—very much. His loyalty to family reminded her of Nick. Also, like his son-in-law, he was deep and passionate but kept his feet firmly planted on the ground. It was clear to her that Emilio had accepted his wife's death. It would have been unreasonable to deny it. He was devastated, but the knowledge that he would join her someday in heaven was a comfort. She liked that he had such faith in God. That would carry him through.

Angela was a fool to take a wonderful father for granted. Meredith would have given anything to have a moral, loving father like Emilio.

"Emilio, you should think about coming up to visit Nick in Sonoma County. It might do you good to get away from here."

Emilio smiled, and he blinked away sadness. "I will consider it someday. I have just found out that I have no pension, so I must go back to work. Also, I have a grandchild coming. I don't know what living arrangements Rigo and Angela will make. They will need their father to help with their plans for a while. I must also find something for myself."

He looked away, and she saw the track of a tear on his cheek.

MANEUVERING AROUND HER SWOLLEN ELBOW, Meredith snapped the seat belt into place. She stretched back against the upholstery. She carried a rolled-up copy of the LA Times. She waited while Nick settled in, then leaned toward his ear. "Did Javier tell you? He found Rigo's cell phone in Oswaldo's apartment. Vega's personal phone number was on the 'recent calls' list right after the Borrego house phone."

Nick fingered the armrest. "Yeah. We thought he might have made the ransom call, then abandoned the idea when he figured out the family didn't have money."

"I thought he might have done it for the money or to redeem himself from his failure with his cousin." She searched Nick's silhouette against the light from the oval window. "Would you have gone home, except for Oswaldo's meddling?"

"Because we had no leads?" He was silent for a second. "Not a chance."

She eyed him, wanting an explanation.

He shifted in his seat and looked into her eyes. "No one tells me to walk away from my family."

She had to say it. "Nick, they aren't going to be your family for much longer." She knew what he was thinking. The Borregos would always be his family. That wouldn't change by a mere signature in a civil courtroom. Now he understood Angela would no longer be his wife.

Meredith shook her head at the irony. "You are so loyal." The very order that was supposed to scare him off did exactly the opposite. He saw it as a threat to his family's safety, for which he was responsible.

"It was the same thing when Judge Giroud kept after you." His eyes narrowed. "When it was obvious Admin wasn't going to back you, I had to." He glanced away. "It's the way I'm built, for better or for worse."

What an odd turn of a phrase, for better or for worse. What would make him use that? She thought of the kiss on the boat. Then afterward, how he'd called it a mistake. Was it?

She just didn't know.

He turned in his seat and leaned in to her. "I have a question for you."

Her nerves started jangling. His jaw muscle flexed. This was important.

She looked past his shoulder and out the window. "Okay, shoot."

"How did you escape from Vega's basement?"

Oh, God. She'd buried that with Rusty Webber memories. Jesus.

"Later." It came out a mumble.

His voice was a caress, a lover's stroke to make her feel better.

"Mere, it is later." Only, it didn't make her feel better.

But this was Nick, and Nick was about as safe as safe could get.

Her voice was a whisper. "I killed a guy."

"Jesus Christ, Mere." She felt him studying her face. "I'm sure you had to."

She looked away, sighing. "Yes, but…"

"One of Vega's guards?"

She searched his face for his reaction.

He stuck out his chin in a stubborn gesture that said he understood her motives. "You hesitated when Vega had his gun on me."

"I didn't want to shoot him, but I had to do something."

His gaze searched hers. "I'm glad you did. Getting us out of the way and letting everyone else shoot the bastard—that was a stroke of brilliance."

She couldn't take any credit for her actions.

"Mere, you need to talk to someone about this. You also hesitated at El Rancho when the Federales took us into custody." She thought he hadn't noticed. She sighed again.

"Listen, when we get back, you tell Leahy you need some stress counseling. He'll set it up."

"For PTSD? No, thank you, I hate shrinks. Besides, Leahy will use it against me."

He shook his head. "Leahy is a means to an end. He won't capitalize on your needs. Trust me."

Meredith considered this. At some point, she felt she needed to start trusting the system again. Hard to do when you've been burnt once so badly. And Leahy was such a jerk. However, what could save her were the protocols for an employee to get help with this kind of thing. They called it Post Traumatic Stress Disorder. She didn't buy the label but knew she needed guidance. It was beyond Leahy. Thank God the Sheriff's Office had anticipated the need and had procedures already in place.

"Everyone hates counseling, but you need someone to help you through this." Nick went on. "You're a cop, Meredith. A shoot situation will come up again. You can't afford to let this slow you down. It might cost someone his life, and your career, if you can't put it firmly behind you."

"I don't want to go." She blew out a breath of exasperation, her fear winning the moment. "I hate counseling."

"I know." He took her hand. "Counseling is a Band-Aid for the healing to get started and help you over the rough spots. The real fix comes from you. A counselor will help you start, that's all."

Her heart thumped in her chest. She felt very small and vulnerable. Much like she did as a kid hiding from her father in the closet.

"Will you help me?"

He smiled. "Yes." He squeezed her hand.

Acknowledgments

My books would not be complete without a nod to an early supporter, John Ungersma. His encouragement bridged many doubts. Chris Lynch and Alan Jacob for marine information—boat types, seas, travel-time-estimates. Your help was invaluable. My incredible critique group: Billie Payton-Settles, Julie Winrich, Andy Gloege, and Frederick Jonas Weisel challenged me to reach places I didn't think I could go. Karen Barrett Henley took such good care of Casey, freeing me to keep my butt in the chair—to you, a thousand thanks for what you do every day! My family and built-in fan club, Pat, Katie, Kevin and Tim Miller, and sister Nancy Mulcahy, the Andersons, especially Chere Berman and Sandie Tillery—thanks for never having doubts that I would accomplish my writing goals. And the support of my two dearest friends kept me striving to meet their expectations: Lori Ference-Smith and Jan Cotter.

A Look At Book Three:
With Malice Aforethought

Detective Meredith Ryan is tagging along with newly promoted Sergeant Nick Reyes on a homicide investigation in the remote Sonoma County hills when they unsuspectingly stumble into an army of white nationalists.

Fighting to survive against the militia—and a voracious wildfire—they uncover a plot to release a dangerous pathogen into the local water supply that could devastate local law enforcement agencies.

Making their way to safety, Meredith and Nick vow to stop this terrorist plot before it's too late. But as they fight to keep their heads above water and race against the clock to get information, it becomes increasingly clear that they may not make it out alive.

With Malice Aforethought is a police procedural thriller about a brave, young deputy who identifies and faces her enemies—both within herself and the real world.

AVAILABLE MAY 2023

About the Author

Thonie Hevron is a retired 35-year veteran police Community Service Officer, Records Supervisor and 911 dispatcher who grew up in Mill Valley, California. She now lives in Petaluma, California with her husband, Danny, two rescue dogs and a cat. For ten years, she lived in the High Desert town of Bishop, California, working as a dispatcher and writing monthly columns for the *Inyo Register*. Returning to the Bay Area in 2004, she worked for a local law enforcement agency and wrote a regular column for the *Tri-Valley Times* and the *North Valley Times*.

Thonie's writing includes four award-winning mystery novels and short stories. She is a member of the California Writers Association/Redwood Writers Chapter, SistersinCrime/NorCal Chapter and the Public Safety Writers Association.

Her work has appeared in the *Beyond Borders: 2014 Redwood Writers Anthology* and the *Felons, Flames and Ambulance Rides: Public Safety Writers 2013 Anthology*—along with recently releasing in *Cops Writing Crime Fiction: To Serve, Protect and Write*. She is the author of four award-winning mystery thriller novels, re-edited and published by Rough Edges Press. Her website, www.thoniehevron.com, includes a blog with law enforcement guests as well as a writers' column.

When not writing, Thonie rides horses, actively participates in her parish church community and enjoys traveling.